"I Want to Talk to You, Nina."

"Is there anything more to be said between us?" she asked wearily.

"A great deal, I'd say. Yesterday you and I threw some pretty nasty remarks at one another; you can't deny it. So why don't we call it quits? Come with me somewhere quiet, where we can talk."

"No!" she cried, a warning flashing in her brain. "It's not possible."

"Anything is possible, Nina," Dexter said, his voice soft with meaning, "if you want it enough."

NANCY JOHN
is an unashamed romantic, deeply in love with her husband of over thirty years. She lives in Sussex, England, where long walks through the countryside provide the inspiration for the novels that have brought her a worldwide following.

Dear Reader,

Silhouette Special Editions are an exciting new line of contemporary romances from Silhouette Books. Special Editions are written specifically for our readers who want a story with heightened romantic tension.

Special Editions have all the elements you've enjoyed in Silhouette Romances and *more*. These stories concentrate on romance in a longer, more realistic and sophisticated way, and they feature greater sensual detail.

I hope you enjoy this book and all the wonderful romances from Silhouette. We welcome any suggestions or comments and invite you to write to us at the address below.

Karen Solem
Editor-in-Chief
Silhouette Books
P.O. Box 769
New York, N. Y. 10019

NANCY JOHN
Summer Rhapsody

Silhouette Special Edition
Published by Silhouette Books New York
America's Publisher of Contemporary Romance

SILHOUETTE BOOKS, a Simon & Schuster Division of
GULF & WESTERN CORPORATION
1230 Avenue of the Americas, New York, N.Y. 10020

ISBN: 0-671-53575-7

First Silhouette Books printing February, 1983

10 9 8 7 6 5 4 3 2 1

Map by Ray Lundgren

SILHOUETTE, SILHOUETTE SPECIAL EDITION
and colophon are trademarks of Simon & Schuster.

America's Publisher of Contemporary Romance

Printed in the U.S.A.

Summer
Rhapsody

Chapter One

$\mathscr{P}$oised high on her points, Nina Selby held a graceful *arabesque*, taking the imaginary applause and then gratefully relaxed.

"Right, that's fine, Nina," said Boyd Maxwell, the Assistant Director, with a nod of approval. "Now exit left, then come on and take your bow." Glancing away, he addressed her male partner. "Robin, you'll have to restrain those enthusiastic *grands jetés* of yours, or you'll be leaping right through the window and ending up among the rose bushes on the terrace. Now, let's go through the entrances and exits just once more. Having that door center left poses a bit of a problem."

Members of the Regency Ballet Company were running through a quick rehearsal for the evening Charity Gala performance, working out the changes needed in the absence of their usual stage facilities. The great Painted Gallery of Haslemere Hall was noisy with workmen bringing in the two hundred folding chairs and placing them in rows, and from another part of the house came sounds of the caterers' staff setting up tables for the grand buffet.

"For heaven's sake, boys and girls, smile and get some life into it tonight," Boyd exhorted loudly. "It may be an extra performance to you, but don't forget that the audience will have paid a small fortune for their tickets. So we want to give them their money's worth, don't we?"

At long last Boyd clapped his hands and nodded at the pianists, Charles and Keith, indicating that they could pack up their music. "Okay everyone, that'll do." He glanced at his wristwatch. "Now, you all have two hours and ten minutes to do whatever you like before you need to be in your dressing rooms. Don't be late." As the dancers broke up and wandered off with sighs of relief, he came over to Nina and said ruefully, "Sorry, darling, I thought we'd manage some time together this afternoon, but I'm afraid it's impossible. I've got a hundred and one things to see to."

"Not to worry, Boyd," she assured him, smiling. "I'll be happy having a quiet look around this place. Isn't it absolutely gorgeous?"

"The country life isn't quite my style," he said, making a face, "and it must cost Dexter Rolfe a bundle to keep this vast estate going. Still, he's filthy rich, so if it's what he fancies, why not? See you later, love." Boyd gave her a quick, distracted kiss on the cheek, and hurried off to shout instructions to someone bringing in lighting equipment.

Nina caught up with her friend Cheryl Wyatt on the gilt-balustered staircase, and they went together to the spacious guest bedroom which had been allocated to them. Decorated in green and ivory it contained some gems of period furniture, and the two long windows gave a lovely view of the extensive grounds, with a magnificent cedar of Lebanon and other fine parkland trees. A long vista led the eye to the glint of water, which Nina knew must be the River Thames.

Cheryl dropped onto a velvet boudoir couch, kicked off her pumps, and released a pleasurable sigh. "What sheer luxury after our poky little flat. I could easily laze here like this with my feet up for the whole of our free time. How about you, Nina?"

"I think I'll wander around the grounds. They look heavenly."

"You can count me out of that. Walking isn't my favorite pastime, as you well know. Anyway, I want to write a letter to Jeremy."

"A letter?" queried Nina. "But you were talking to him on the phone for ages this morning before we set out."

Cheryl smiled fondly, as she always did when speaking of her five-year-old son. "Mother says that now that Jeremy can read he loves getting letters from me that he can take with him to show at school." She sighed. "I wish my parents didn't live so far away and I could see more of him. If it wasn't for this charity gala I'd have been able to get home this weekend, but I'm dancing again on Monday night, so there won't be time."

"Well, don't forget to give Jeremy my love," said Nina, as she peeled off her rehearsal leotard and tights, and slipped into jeans and a fawn-colored sweatshirt, pushing up the sleeves to just below her elbows.

Descending to the ground floor again, Nina received admiring glances from the army of men who were scurrying about getting everything ready for this evening. As befitted a ballet dancer, her figure was slender and graceful, the legs long and shapely, with slim ankles, and every movement of her body had a relaxed delicacy. Her shining dark hair was now tied up in a careless bunch with a yellow ribbon, revealing the full length of her ivory neck. There was a warm friendliness in her lustrous, amber gold eyes, and her mouth was softly curved toward a smile. It was rare to find such beauty combined with a natural, unassuming charm.

Nina viewed herself, however, as no more than ordinarily good-looking, with a modest degree of talent. But she had a fierce, burning ambition to rise to the ultimate heights of her chosen profession. She cherished the hope that if she persevered and pushed herself to the very limit, she would one day achieve the exalted position of prima ballerina with the Regency company. At twenty-five years old, though, she still had some way to go before reaching the full maturity of her artistic skill and interpretive ability. It had once been said by a famous Italian ballet master that there could be no true ballerina under the age of twenty-eight. Besides which, the great Sonia Lamartine was far from ready to step down from her high pedestal. Lamartine hadn't come to Haslemere Hall as she was performing tonight at the theater in London, and Nina accepted with quiet confidence that much of the responsibility for the gala's success rested on her own slender shoulders.

Leaving the house, Nina lightly ran down a flight of shallow stone steps, flanked by two marble urns containing primroses and trailing ivy, that opened out onto a lower terrace. The April sunshine held a delicious warmth, and the gardens stretching before her looked green and sparklingly fresh. She descended further to smooth emerald lawns studded with flower beds which glowed with spring bulbs and richly scented, ruby red wallflowers. There was a large circular pool containing a fountain, the water jets spouting high into the air from the mouths of sculpted nymphs and tritons. For a few minutes Nina sat on the curving stone rim, trailing her fingertips in the limpid water. She was strangely affected by the tranquil beauty of these surroundings. In her busy life she'd had so little time to savor the joys of country living, to hear the soft twitter of birdsong all around her, and smell the freshness of pure, unpolluted air.

She rose to her feet again and wandered along the flagstone path. Passing through an archway in a tall, clipped yew hedge, she came to a long meadow that sloped down to the river far below, its glistening silver surface snaking through beech woods. Nina gasped aloud in delighted astonishment; never in her life had she seen so many daffodils growing all together, bright and shining against the lush green grass.

As she stood entranced, a little girl wearing a red jump suit ran out from a grove of young oak trees some fifty yards away and laughingly bent to pluck a flower. Behind her came a man, tall and lean and husky, who snatched the child up in his arms and held her poised high in the air above his head. The child shrieked in pretended fear, then teasingly brushed the man's nose with the trumpet-shaped blossom.

"Hey, you'll make me sneeze," he laughed. Then he suddenly noticed Nina, and called, "Hello. I didn't see you standing there."

"I'm sorry," she faltered, embarrassed at having been caught staring. "I was just strolling around."

As he came striding toward her, still carrying the child and followed in great lolloping bounds by a young yellow labrador that had just emerged from the oak grove, Nina knew for certain what she had at first suspected. This man was Dexter Rolfe, the owner of Haslemere Hall, chairman and chief executive of the giant precision instrument manufacturers, Rolfe Industries. And most important from her own point of view, the sponsor of the Regency Ballet Company, which would be hard pressed to survive without his financial support.

When it suited him, Nina guessed, Dexter Rolfe could look stern and autocratic, every inch a captain of industry. But right now he was smiling and friendly, so that her sense of embarrassment melted away. She caught herself wondering if perhaps it was the secret of his spectacular success at the early age of thirty-four, that he was able to put people completely at ease just as effortlessly as he could intimidate them. She knew instinctively, with a little inward shudder, that it wouldn't be an enjoyable experience to find oneself at the receiving end of this man's displeasure.

Up close, he was alarmingly tall. Six feet two at least, she judged, mentally measuring him against Boyd's five feet eleven. He wore a short-sleeved shirt that revealed bronzed forearms, and his long legs were encased in thigh-hugging brown slacks. His wind-ruffled hair, which was a dark teak brown, glinted with coppery lights in the slanting sunlight. There was an uneven ruggedness about his lean features which somehow added to his sensual attraction. The tawny-colored eyes, under straight dark brows, were deep set and vividly intent.

"I take it you're with the Regency Ballet," he went on as he drew near. "I'm sure that I've seen you on the stage."

"That's right. I'm Nina Selby," she told him, responding to the dog's enthusiastic greeting by patting its beautiful golden coat.

"Of course. You're one of their principal dancers, aren't you? I should have recognized you, Miss Selby, but I'm afraid I'm not able to see the company perform as often as I'd like to, with so many other commitments. And you do look rather different offstage."

Nina smiled. "You don't need to apologize, Mr. Rolfe. It's enough that you support us financially. I don't know where we'd be without your generous backing."

He gave a dismissive shrug. "I think it's important for industry to do what it can to support the arts." Setting the child down on her feet, he added, "This is my daughter Mandy, by the way. And our four-footed friend is Bojo, who joined the family three months ago on Mandy's sixth birthday. Say hello to Miss Selby, darling."

"Hello, Miss Selby. Daddy is going to let me stay up late tonight so that I can watch the ballet."

"How nice. I hope that you enjoy it, Mandy."

"Oh, I know I shall. I love dancing, and I want to be a ballerina when I grow up." She wasn't in the least shy, neither was she precocious; just pleasantly in between, Nina decided. And a very pretty little girl, too, with a cloud of finespun chestnut hair and eyes as blue as summer forget-me-nots.

"That's a very good ambition to have," Nina said with a smile. Then, awkwardly, "I do hope, Mr. Rolfe, that you don't mind me wandering around your grounds. They're so lovely that I couldn't resist coming out to explore."

"Feel free. I'm only too grateful that you Regency people have come here to give your services in aid of the home for handicapped children."

"It's the least we could do," Nina murmured, "considering what you do for us."

15

Quite naturally, it seemed, they began to stroll on together, and after a moment Mandy and the dog ran off on some secret game of their own.

"What a delightful little girl she is," Nina said. "You must be very proud of your daughter, Mr. Rolfe."

"I am," he acknowledged simply. "Mandy is the joy of my life. You may have heard, perhaps, that she has no mother?"

"Er . . . yes, I believe I did," Nina said warily. It was well known to the whole ballet company that their sponsor had lost his wife some eighteen months before, but Nina didn't wish to give him the impression that he was avidly gossiped about. "It must be difficult for a man to bring up a small girl," she added sympathetically.

"I'm lucky to have my sister-in-law as a surrogate mother for Mandy. Mrs. Hooper is divorced, you see, and she has made her home with us at Haslemere Hall."

No one in the Regency Ballet could avoid knowing about Phyllida Hooper. A dazzling redhead of about thirty, she had an unwelcome habit of appearing at the rehearsal rooms in an old church hall near Elephant and Castle, and behaving generally as if it were she who footed the bills rather than her brother-in-law. Mrs. Hooper fancied herself as an artist, and thought nothing of expecting a tired dancer to pose for her while she sketched.

Not paying sufficient attention to where she was stepping, Nina stumbled and her foot caught on a tree root. Dexter quickly shot out a large brown hand to steady her.

"We mustn't have you twisting your ankle," he said with a warm smile that lit up his leanly handsome face.

Shaken by her lack of care—unforgivable in a ballet dancer—Nina drew herself away from his clasp. But the touch of his long fingers still burned on her bare forearm, and she tried to conceal her confusion with a laughing shrug. "Goodness, no! I don't know which would be worse . . . not being able to dance tonight, or the terrible trouble I'd be in with Boyd."

"You mean Boyd Maxwell, I presume?"

Nina nodded. "I can just picture the long lecture I'd get about jeopardizing my whole career by a moment's carelessness."

"I seem to recall that before he became Assistant Director to Sir Hugo Quest, he was the dancer with whom you were most frequently partnered."

"Yes, that's right." She felt pleased that Dexter Rolfe should have remembered. "Boyd decided that he'd have a better future going into the administrative side," she explained. "He rarely appears on stage these days except in roles that require more miming than dancing."

"I imagine," Dexter went on, turning his head to give her a speculative glance, "that two people who dance together regularly must develop quite a strong rapport?"

"You certainly need to feel in tune with one another," Nina agreed.

"But the same need doesn't exist between a ballerina and the Assistant Director?"

He was clearly fishing, and Nina didn't intend to explain the precise nature of her relationship with Boyd. Dexter Rolfe's easy charm had made her forget for a moment that this man was renowned as a womanizer. So far, he'd never taken up with any of the girls in the ballet company, though she'd more than once heard a dancer make a half-joking, half-wistful remark to the effect that they wouldn't yell for help if he cast a lustful glance in their direction.

"Boyd and I have a good relationship," she told him

evasively. "In fact, all of us in the Regency Ballet get on well together. It's a remarkably harmonious company." She pointedly glanced at her wristwatch. "Heavens, look at the time. I'd better be getting back."

"I'll walk with you," he offered, and called to Mandy and the dog to come along. For some reason Nina felt unnerved by this meeting with Dexter Rolfe. There was a dynamic aura of virility about him which she found curiously disturbing, and she was acutely aware of the nearness of his leanly muscular body as they strolled together toward the house. He questioned her about herself and her background in a friendly way to which Nina couldn't possibly take exception. She explained that her mother had died when she was still a baby and that she had been brought up by her father until he too had died eight years ago, when she was seventeen and still at ballet school.

"It shows that it *can* work," Dexter commented thoughtfully.

"I'm sorry, I don't quite follow."

"Just like me, your father raised his daughter on his own, without a wife. That encourages me." He smiled at her warmly. "If Mandy turns out to be as determined and capable a young woman as you obviously are, I won't have any complaints."

Nina felt hot color flooding her face and glanced away quickly. She was relieved to see a bunch of Regency people on the terrace, relaxing at little white tables or perched on the stone balustrade, drinking tea.

"If you'll excuse me now, Mr. Rolfe," she said, "I'd better go and have some tea, or I might not get another chance."

For a moment, as he hesitated, Nina feared he was going to say he would come and join them. But then, with another warm smile that crinkled the corners of his tawny eyes, he wished her luck for the performance.

"We shall be watching you especially, won't we, Mandymouse?"

"You bet!"

The thought wasn't the least bit comforting to Nina. The knowledge that this child—and, even worse, her adoring father—would be observing her with especially close attention tonight was more likely to cause her to stumble or make some other stupid mistake.

"Any tea left?" she called to her colleagues a moment later.

"Sure," said Robin Wayne, who was Nina's principal partner these days. "You'll find it on a table inside the door of that conservatory there. Just help yourself."

"There are masses of sandwiches and all sorts of lovely gooey pastries for anyone who dares," added his girl friend Jilly Francis, a pretty, fair-haired dancer in the *corps de ballet.* "Say, Nina, how'd you manage to talk to Superman Rolfe? You clever thing you!"

"Oh . . . we just happened to bump into one another."

"Why don't things like that ever happen to me?" sighed Lisbet Paton, who was a principal soloist like Nina. "It's a good thing Boyd isn't around, or he'd blow his top. But don't worry, we won't breathe a word to him."

Nina ducked into the conservatory so that her high color wouldn't be noticed. It was ridiculous, she chided herself furiously, to allow her friend's kidding to get under her skin.

The gala program that evening was a tremendous success, despite the difficulties of performing without a proper stage, no curtains and portable lighting equipment.

The smart-set, county-type people who made up the

audience were not for the most part balletomanes. Rather, they had come because it was the thing to do. Even so, the subtle magic of dance reached them and the applause was warmly appreciative. For Nina, after a flawless execution of the difficult thirty-two continuous turns in the Black Swan *pas de deux* from Act Three of *Swan Lake,* there was even louder applause, and cries of "Bravo!" Taking her bow, she caught the eyes of the excited little girl sitting in the front row, and gave Mandy a special bright smile. Then, to her dismay, Nina found herself meeting the dark gaze of the man seated beside the child, and she quickly glanced away in confusion. As a result, her exit was somewhat clumsy, earning her a sharp rebuke from Boyd.

"What the dickens is the matter with you, Nina?" he snapped. "Why did you have to spoil a brilliant performance by coming off like a timid first-year student?"

"I'm sorry," she muttered. "I was a bit thrown."

"Thrown? By what? It's a marvelous audience."

How could she admit to her boy friend that her professional poise had been momentarily destroyed by an admiring glance from Dexter Rolfe? "Oh . . . nothing special," she evaded. "Just the . . . the applause, and everything. Look, I'd better get changed for *Les Sylphides.*"

At the conclusion of the gala performance, each of the girls was presented with a magnificent bouquet, donated by their host—even the members of the *corps de ballet,* which thrilled them to bits. Afterward, as soon as the dancers had changed and removed their makeup, they were free to mix with the guests and help themselves from the lavish buffet supper which was spread out on a long table in the green and gold dining salon. Nina received enthusiastic congratulations from all sides, until she felt dazed by such adulation.

"May I rescue you?" a deeply resonant voice murmured in her ear.

Startled, she spun around and found herself face-to-face with Dexter Rolfe. Towering above her in his black tuxedo, he looked even more dynamically handsome than he had when she'd met him this afternoon on the grounds.

"People have been falling over themselves to tell you how wonderfully you danced tonight," he said with a smile that set her pulse thudding, "so I'll just tell you instead how very attractive you look. That coppery shade is exactly right for your coloring, and the dress fits you to perfection."

What a line he was shooting, Nina thought wryly, but all the same she couldn't help feeling pleased. She covered up her pleasure with an offhand shrug. "We all like to dress up a bit whenever we get the chance. So much of a dancer's time is spent in costume or rehearsal clothes, and otherwise we normally wear jeans."

"And very nice too, judging by this afternoon," he commented, his tawny gaze giving her slender body a lingering appraisal. "Nina, I want to ask a favor. Mandy went up to bed right after the performance, but I know she'd love to tell you how much she enjoyed your dancing. D'you think you could restrain your appetite and slip upstairs for five minutes, to say good night? It would be a real thrill for her."

Nina looked up at him uncertainly. "Well, I suppose . . ."

"You won't get lost," he assured her. "I'll be there to show you the way." His eyes sweeping over her again, he added, "And tempting as it would be to kidnap you and carry you off to my bedroom, I promise to bring you straight back downstairs afterward."

Nina felt her cheeks grow warm at this blatant reference to her physical attractions. "Okay then, why not?" she said lightly. "I'll be glad to come up and see your daughter, if you think it would make her happy."

"Furthermore, it would make me happy, too," he observed, and put a hand under her elbow to steer her through the crush of people.

Together they mounted the great staircase to the gilt-railed gallery, and proceeded along a wide corridor lined with glass-fronted cabinets containing pieces of fine porcelain, valuable Meissen and Sèvres and Crown Derby, Nina guessed, to judge from the look of them.

"My father was the china enthusiast," Dexter explained, "but my own collecting enthusiasm is more for paintings. You must come and see my latest acquisition sometime, one of Degas' delightful ballet pictures. It's in my London apartment, though, not here."

Nina made no comment, not knowing quite what to make of that remark. They halted by one of the doors just as a plump young woman in a blue sweater emerged.

"I've just tucked Mandy in for the night, Mr. Rolfe," she said, nodding shyly at Dexter.

"That's all right, Lucy. Miss Selby and I won't keep her awake for long. Just a few minutes . . . okay?"

"Of course, Mr. Rolfe," the girl mumbled, and went on her way.

Dexter opened the door and put his head around, turning on the light as he did so. "Hi, Mandymouse. I've brought a visitor to see you."

"Who is it, Daddy?" demanded an excited little voice.

Slipping an arm across Nina's shoulders, he drew her inside triumphantly. "Your heroine of the evening, darling. I've been telling Nina how much you enjoyed her dancing."

It was a charming room, decorated in bright colors,

with an attractive fairy-tale wallpaper. It looked very homely with dolls and other toys arranged on the shelves. But Nina's keenest awareness was of Dexter's fingertips on the bare skin of her upper arm, sending tingling pulses through her veins. So she quickly broke free and hurried forward to the bed, perching herself on the edge. The little girl was sitting up under the pink coverlet, her blue eyes wide and shining with excitement. Tucked in beside her was a large teddy bear, obviously a much loved companion.

"I'm glad you liked the ballet," Nina said, smiling at her.

"Oh, I did! And you looked *so* beautiful."

Embarrassed, Nina said dismissively, "I have my costume and the stage makeup to thank for that, Mandy."

"But you're beautiful now, as well. Nina *is* beautiful, isn't she, Daddy?"

"Very beautiful," he agreed gravely.

Nina sought around hastily for a change of subject. "Have you seen any ballet before, Mandy? In the theater, I mean."

"No, only on TV. But tonight . . . oh, it was wonderful. I'm going to ask Daddy to take me to the ballet often, now."

"I doubt if she'll have much difficulty persuading me," said Dexter, his tawny eyes meeting Nina's across the bed in a meaningful look. She felt a spark of anger against him. He was making use of the child to flirt with her, and Nina wanted no part of it.

"I'd better be going now," she said, rising to her feet.

"Will you come and see me again soon?" Mandy asked eagerly. "Please!"

Nina gazed down at the child uncertainly, not knowing quite what to say, and Dexter answered for her.

"You can count on that, Mandymouse. Say good night now."

"Good night, Nina," she said obediently, and held her face up expectantly. Bending to kiss her, Nina found it curiously moving to feel the little girl's warm arms clinging around her neck, almost as if the mother-less child was seeking the sort of loving that she had missed out on. Which was nonsense, Nina told herself sharply. Hadn't Dexter explained that his divorced sister-in-law had taken up the role of surrogate mother to his daughter?

As if on cue, the door behind them opened and Nina glanced around to meet the unfriendly green eyes of the woman in her thoughts—the dazzlingly attractive red-head, Mrs. Phyllida Hooper.

"Well, well!" she said in a lazy drawl of amusement, the slender eyebrows arching high on her smooth forehead. "And what is this touching little scene all about, might I inquire?"

"Miss Selby kindly popped up to say good night so that Mandy could tell her how much she enjoyed the performance," Dexter explained. "You know Mrs. Hooper, I expect, Nina?"

She nodded, putting on a pleasant smile. "Yes, we've met once or twice backstage at the theater."

"You danced very well tonight," Phyllida Hooper observed, in a tone of queenly condescension. "But I think this is neither the time nor the place to discuss your artistic merits. Mandy has already been kept up quite late enough, and at this rate she'll be fit for nothing tomorrow."

As if, Nina thought angrily, I'm expected to make a humble apology for keeping the child from her sleep. But I was *asked* to come up and see Mandy by her father, for goodness' sake.

Dexter, though, seemed ready to placate his sister-in-law. "We're just on the point of leaving, Phyllida."

"I'm relieved to hear it. Now then, Mandy, lie down at once and get off to sleep." There was no gentleness behind the brisk order, and Nina felt instantly sorry for the little girl. She gave Mandy a quick warm smile before crossing to the door.

As the three adults made their way to the staircase past the display cases of porcelain, Phyllida observed crossly to Dexter, "You really should know better than to get the child excited like that at bedtime."

"But this is a very special night for Mandy," he returned equably. "She was so thrilled with Nina's dancing, and I knew how delighted she'd be to see her."

Phyllida tossed her elegant shoulders, which were bare under the halter-neck black taffeta dress. "Children get these ridiculous short-lived crazes. They want to be a ballet dancer this week, a tennis star or showjumper or whatever next week. I don't believe in pandering to Mandy's whims, Dexter. And neither would you, if you had the day-to-day responsibility for her."

It really was the limit, Nina thought bitterly, that she was coming in for all this implied criticism through no fault of her own. Darn the pair of them! The moment they reached the dining salon, she excused herself and went to the buffet table. But before she could reach it she spotted Boyd beckoning her from where he was chatting to a group of admiring women.

"Hi, Nina," he greeted her, and slipped an arm carelessly around her slim waist, to the obvious envy of his female admirers. Though Boyd Maxwell rarely performed nowadays, he still possessed the lithe physique of a dancer; and this, added to his dark Latin good looks, made him very attractive to the opposite sex. A fact, Nina often found herself thinking, of which Boyd was only too plainly aware.

Their special relationship had been developing from the time, some five years or so ago, when Nina had first been picked out for soloist roles and they had been paired to dance together by Sir Hugo. Boyd, seven years older than she, had already been with the company for some time. From the very start it had been one of those wonderful partnerships that audiences love to watch, and critics pick out for special mention. Their movements seemed to blend so fluently, and they were so much on the same wavelength in musicality and role interpretation that they danced together almost as a single fluid entity. It was only natural that they should have grown close on a personal level, too, and they could overlook the fact that they didn't always agree about other aspects of life. For them both, dancing was the one really vital thing.

Like all male dancers, Boyd was conscious of the fact that the professional life of a *danseur noble,* with the extreme demands of strength needed in lifting a ballerina, is comparatively short. Consequently, he had seized the chance of becoming Assistant Director to the elderly and much revered Sir Hugo Quest when the opportunity presented itself at the beginning of the previous season. This had also given Boyd scope to develop as a choreographer, and he had become even more single-mindedly dedicated to success. It was his intention, he told Nina, to create new roles specially suited to her unique combination of virtuoso technique and delicate lyricism, and he believed that he could build her to a point when she became the unchallenged successor to Sonia Lamartine. Boyd undoubtedly had a talent for bringing out a dancer's best qualities, and already Nina knew she was being formed as the company's prima ballerina by almost everyone, from Sir Hugo himself down to the youngest member of the *corps de ballet.*

"I'm dying for something to eat, Boyd," she told him now.

He turned to look at her sharply. "What on earth have you been up to, darling, not to have helped yourself yet?"

"I . . . I was held up," she said evasively.

"Too bad. You'll have missed your chance at the smoked salmon and caviar, but there's still plenty of other food left. I'll come and join you. I wouldn't mind another slice of that York ham." He led the way to the long buffet table, and waved his hand at the lavish display of food on silver platters. "Quite a spread, isn't it? They're saying that this affair has made a real bundle for the handicapped children's home. Way over any other benefit that they've sponsored, what with the ticket takings and the auction of a pair of Lamartine's ballet shoes, etcetera. And, more to the point, it'll get us a lot of useful publicity."

"I hardly think that publicity for the Regency Ballet was the main object of the exercise," Nina remarked dryly.

"Don't be so sanctimonious, love," he rebuked her. "Us getting a spin-off in publicity won't take a penny away from what's raised for the kids in the home."

Something made Nina glance around at that moment, and she found Dexter Rolfe's tawny eyes fixed on her from across the room. She had the oddest sensation that he knew what she and Boyd were saying, and that he endorsed her attitude. But that was ridiculous. If he could overhear—which he couldn't possibly—he would be sure to endorse Boyd's approach. Captains of industry didn't carve their worldly success out of wishy-washy sentimentality. His support for the handicapped children's home and his sponsorship of the Regency Ballet, were probably calculated to bring maximum advantage to himself and his firm, plus some deductible benefits taxwise, no doubt.

"I suppose you're right," she told Boyd. "Are there any reporters here?"

"Sure there are," he grinned. "You don't think our estimable host's PR agency would miss out on an obvious trick like that?"

Later, when they'd finished eating, Boyd suggested a stroll outside in the moonlit grounds. But Nina felt oddly tense and on edge this evening, and not at all in the mood for Boyd's kisses. So, pleading tiredness, she went up to bed quite early.

The ballet company left Haslemere Hall soon after breakfast, Sunday being the one day of the week they could visit family and friends. The bus was brought around to the front entrance and Dexter Rolfe, with Mandy at his side, stood at the head of the wide fantail of steps to see them off.

Sir Hugo, a distinguished bearded figure in long cape and black velour trilby, whose Rolls-Royce awaited him, made a little speech of thanks on behalf of the dancers and musicians for the warm hospitality they had received.

"The pleasure has been entirely mine," Dexter said disarmingly. "Mine and my guests'. I am extremely grateful to each and every one of you for your help." While speaking his glance swept around the assembled company and it seemed to Nina that it rested on her for an extralong moment. Irrationally, she felt a little glow of pleasure. Mandy gave her a wave, to which Nina responded smilingly. Phyllida Hooper, coming out to stand beside her brother-in-law, caught the movement and treated Nina to a coldly hostile glare.

Aboard the bus, as it spun along lanes banked with golden buttercups, everyone was in high spirits, laughing and joking.

"What are we going to do this evening?" Nina asked Boyd, who was in the seat beside her. "I noticed that there is rather a good concert at the Barbican Center."

Boyd shook his head. "I'll pass tonight, if you don't mind. I want to do some work on my new ballet."

"Okay," Nina agreed, finding that she wasn't as disappointed as she might have expected. "How's *Summer Rhapsody* coming along, Boyd?"

"Great! I see no reason why it shouldn't be ready to go into the repertoire by the autumn. You're going to love it, Nina. I'm choreographing some marvelous virtuoso solos and *pas de deux* for the ballerina. Apart from Sonia Lamartine, there's nobody in the company except you who'll be capable of doing the role justice. It's exactly the sort of thing you need at this stage of your career, darling, to give you that extra prominence. Very soon now I want you to work with me and try out some of the steps."

"Who are you planning to have partnering me?" she asked. "Robin, or Barry?"

"It had better be Robin," he said, frowning. "There are some very sensuous sequences in the wedding night scene, and I don't want Barry to start getting ideas about my girl friend."

"For heaven's sake," Nina protested. "When you're dancing a *pas de deux* with someone, it's all just part of the job. You don't think about being in an intimate situation with them."

"Maybe *you* wouldn't," he said darkly. "But I don't trust Barry. I've seen the way he looks at you sometimes."

"Oh, Boyd, I'm sure you're imagining it."

"If I am, so much the better," he grunted. "In any event, I'd prefer you to be dancing with Robin, who only has eyes for Jilly. Barry can partner Lisbet, or perhaps Elli, as one of the understudy pairs, and Alan and Cheryl can be the other."

Nina sighed. When Boyd got a bee in his bonnet, there was no arguing with him. But as it happened, of the two male dancers she preferred to be partnered with Robin. Barry could be moody and temperamental sometimes, whereas Robin was always good-natured and easy to work with.

When the bus reached London, Nina and Cheryl got off at Knightsbridge and took a taxi to the furnished flat they shared in Battersea. After lunch they spent the afternoon in the way they spent so much of their precious free time, washing their hair and repairing their leotards and tights in readiness for the following week. And, of course, going through their usual day-off routine of exercises to avoid the risk of finding themselves stiff and lacking in suppleness for the next day's class.

By mid-evening, Nina felt almost glad that she hadn't made arrangements to see Boyd. It was sheer bliss to relax completely and watch TV with Cheryl. They both groaned when the phone rang, then Cheryl said with a grin, "I reckon it's my turn," and got up to answer it. "Hello! Yes, she is. Just a moment." She made frantic gestures at Nina, her face a picture of astonishment.

"Who is it?" Nina asked.

Cheryl clamped her hand over the mouthpiece. "That deep, sexy voice could only belong to one person—Dexter Rolfe. What have you been up to, Nina?"

"But it can't be him," she protested. "I mean, why should he be calling me?"

"There's one way to find out, sweetie. Talk to the man."

Her heart fluttering in the oddest way, Nina took the phone from Cheryl. "Hello, who is this?" she asked cautiously.

"Hello, Nina. Dexter here. I just wanted to fix the details of when we meet."

"When we meet?" she echoed bewilderedly.

"You remember, you're coming to see my Degas painting. As it turns out, tomorrow evening would be very convenient for me, and I happen to know that you're not dancing then. So how about it?"

"But . . . but I . . ." Nina hadn't seriously expected that he would follow up on his suggestion. Alarm bells were jangling in her brain, and, but for the fact that Dexter Rolfe was so indispensable financially to the Regency Ballet, she'd have given him a curt answer. As things were, she'd better make her refusal diplomatic. "I'm sorry, Mr. Rolfe, but I'm afraid it isn't possible."

"Pity! Never mind, we'll fix another evening. When will you be free?"

"No . . . I mean, I can't. Not at all."

"But you promised. And Mandy will be terribly disappointed. She was chattering about you all this afternoon."

"Mandy! Would she be there?"

"She has a couple of days' holiday from school," he explained. "I'm taking time off tomorrow so we can visit the zoo, with a cream tea to follow."

"Oh, I see!" Nina said, her resolve weakening.

"We'll drop around to pick you up," Dexter clipped, briskly finalizing the arrangement. "Would six o'clock be too early for you? Mandy had better not have another late night or I'll be in my sister-in-law's bad books."

"Er . . . yes, that's okay by me."

"Fine! I already have your address, from the phone book. See you!"

There was a click on the line. Nina stood staring dazedly at the dead phone. Cheryl burst out in a voice of intrigued astonishment, "Did I hear that right? You've got a date with Dexter Rolfe?"

"It's not what you'd call a real date," she mumbled. "Mr. Rolfe was telling me that he'd recently bought a Degas ballet painting, and he thought I'd be interested to see it . . . I mean, just because I'm a dancer myself," she finished lamely.

"Heavens above!" laughed Cheryl. "He might just as well come straight out with it and invite you around to see his etchings."

"No, it's not like that," Nina demurred earnestly, as much to convince herself as Cheryl. "His daughter will be there, too."

"That's what *he* says."

"They're both calling here to pick me up tomorrow. If Mandy *isn't* with him, if he's alone, then I won't go."

"I advise you not to go at all," stated Cheryl. "Honestly, Nina, you're just begging for trouble. You know perfectly well that Dexter Rolfe goes through women like we go through ballet shoes."

"But I can't very well put him off now," Nina said miserably. "I've promised to go."

"You can always tell him that you're not feeling well. He'll get the message." When Nina shook her head, Cheryl became serious, her voice pleading and urgent. "For heaven's sake be careful, Nina. Remember what happened to me. Okay, I was only nineteen then and I didn't know any better. Nowadays, that smooth-talking guy who got me pregnant with Jeremy wouldn't fool me for a single moment. They're all out for what they can get, these stage-door admirers. And Dexter Rolfe is just another one, in his different way. He backs the Regency company with big money, and I suppose he thinks that it gives him a perfect right to take his pick from among the ballet girls."

"You're seeing danger where none exists," Nina protested uneasily. "Okay, I know that offering to show me his Degas painting is just a pretext to get me around to his apartment. But it's not for the reason you think. Don't forget that he's a man with a six-year-old daughter who's lost her mother, and all the money in the world can't buy his wife back. So when Mandy gets excited about something, like she did about seeing us dance, he wants to do everything he can to please her. Dexter Rolfe is guilty of spoiling his daughter a bit, if you like, but that's all."

"I bet you're wrong," said Cheryl scornfully. "I think he's just wheeling in the child as a way of putting more pressure on you."

"So if I find I am wrong," Nina retorted with a shrug, "I'll get out. I can look after myself."

"Can you, though? Dexter Rolfe is a terribly attractive man, and he's had a great deal of practice in seducing women."

"Seducing! You must think I'm feeble, Cheryl, if you imagine I'd let myself be seduced."

"It happened to me," she pointed out darkly.

"But that was different. I mean . . . well, like you said yourself, you were very young at the time."

"Some people," Cheryl remarked in a warning tone, "never seem to grow up. I wish to heaven you'd listen to me, Nina."

"Honestly, you sound like an old aunt. I'm going to make some more coffee. Want some?"

"Yes, please," Cheryl said, and added, "You're being stupid, know that?"

Nina did know it. And she was also learning to her humiliating discomfort that sometimes it's quite impossible to stop oneself from behaving stupidly.

Chapter Two

*I*t's very cozy in here," Dexter Rolfe commented, glancing around the living room of the flat. "I like the theatrical posters on the walls. They add the right dramatic touch."

Nina had made little attempt to clean and tidy in preparation for his visit, determining grimly that Dexter would have to take the flat as he found it. She had spent her usual busy, strenuous day at the rehearsal studios. At ten-thirty there had been the routine daily class at which the entire company went through the time-honored series of exercises for limbering up and strengthening the body. After a short break for coffee, she'd had costume fittings, and the entire afternoon had been taken up in rehearsing *Giselle,* which was being brought back into the repertoire the following week, with Nina dancing the name part and Robin partnering her. After riding home on a rush-hour bus, she'd just scurried around with the vacuum cleaner and thrown the worst of the mess into a closet.

Mandy was bouncing up and down excitably on a huge bean bag on the floor. "It's ever so comfy, Daddy," she exclaimed. "Can I have one like it?"

Nina laughed apologetically. "It would hardly fit in with the rest of the decor at Haslemere Hall."

"A home is meant to be lived in," said Dexter with a grin. "It's not a museum. We'll see about getting you a bean bag, Mandymouse."

Nina felt ridiculously nervous. She half-wished that Cheryl was here to give her moral support and was half-glad that her friend was dancing this evening. She wondered whether to suggest making a cup of coffee; the only alcohol they had was the remains of a bottle of cheap wine opened several days ago. Fortunately, Dexter obviated the need for offering anything, by saying, "If you're ready, Nina, we'll get going, shall we?"

"Yes, fine."

They clattered down the two flights of uncarpeted stairs and out into the street, where a gleaming metallic blue Bentley was drawn up at the curb. They all got in, Mandy sitting between Nina and Dexter on the leather-upholstered seat.

For the same obscure reason that she'd not done much about tidying up the flat, Nina had decided to wear nothing more dressy than blue jeans and a simple blouse. She felt relieved that Dexter was just as casually dressed, in navy slacks and a white turtleneck sweater.

"I had a ride on an elephant at the zoo," Mandy confided to Nina as they drove off.

"How exciting! That's something I've never done."

Dexter glanced across at her and grinned. "Now

there's a gap in your education. We'll have to put it right sometime, won't we, Mandymouse?"

"You bet!" she agreed, with what seemed a favorite expression of hers. "When, Daddy?"

"How come the pet name—Mandymouse?" Nina asked quickly, in an attempt to sidetrack the conversation.

Dexter flicked a glance at his daughter, and winked. "Because she's always such a quiet, timid little thing, just like a mouse," he explained, with a deadpan face.

They crossed the Thames by Chelsea Bridge, and in scarcely more than ten minutes they were cocooned in the luxurious hush of Dexter's apartment in Mayfair. It was split level; a spacious living room with enormous windows overlooked Hyde Park, subtly decorated in mushroom and blue, and furnished with discreet comfort. The bedrooms and so on led off from doors in the square entrance lobby.

Nina took it all in admiringly, and glanced around at the many paintings on the walls. They were mostly of the Impressionist period and later, and some were obviously very valuable. But there was no ballet painting that she could see.

"Where is your Degas?" she asked Dexter.

His tawny eyes flickered with amusement. "In my bedroom."

Nina's heart sank. And yet, surely this couldn't be a seduction setup, not with his daughter on the scene? At that moment a door to one side opened and out came a middle-aged woman, neatly dressed in a dark skirt and sweater.

"Good evening to you, Mr. Rolfe," she said in a lilting Scots voice. "Is there anything I can get for you?"

"Nothing, thanks, Mrs. MacDonald." He introduced

her to Nina as his London housekeeper. "Miss Selby and I will be leaving again very soon," he went on, "and then perhaps you'll give Mandy her supper."

"Aye, of course. By the way, Mrs. Hooper telephoned this afternoon to say that she'll be here to collect Mandy tomorrow morning on her way back to Haslemere Hall."

"Fine!" When the housekeeper had withdrawn, he explained to Nina, "Phyllida is making a duty visit to an elderly aunt who lives in Brighton. She would have taken Mandy along, but I wanted her to spend the day with me."

To provide him, Nina wondered fleetingly, with an excuse to invite her around to his apartment? Then she dismissed the thought. It would be crediting herself with altogether too high a rating in Dexter's eyes, considering his record of success with women. In a happier frame of mind she followed him to his bedroom, Mandy tagging along, too.

It was luxurious, like the rest of the apartment, though with a touch of masculine austerity. The wide bed had a wickerwork headboard, and was covered with a Spanish patterned spread in tones of blue and green. Nina felt a curiously erratic beat to her pulse, as if the mere act of crossing the threshold of this room had taken her several steps toward a more intimate relationship with Dexter. Unwillingly, she found herself imagining what it would feel like to be made love to by him, to have those strong, sensitive hands of his caressing her body. With an effort she jerked herself together, straightening her back and lifting her chin.

The Degas painting occupied a prominent position above the carved white alabaster mantel, a single splash of vibrant color against the neutral tone of the wall. Like other Degas originals which Nina had seen at the Louvre when the Regency Ballet did a short season in Paris two years ago, it was a superb piece of work, deceptively casual yet shining with inner truth. Against a background glimpse of a *corps de ballet* on a stage, a ballerina waiting in the wings was seizing the chance for a final moment's practice. The fluid, sculptured line of her extended arms and leg, with her head slightly tilted back, was breathtakingly beautiful.

"It's really lovely," Nina said in sincere admiration.

Dexter smiled. "I'm glad you think so, too."

"You must have great interest in the ballet," she went on thoughtfully, "to support the Regency company as you do. And buy this Degas."

"I *am* interested," he agreed. "I admire the ballet for its unique combination of the visual arts with fine music. But the reason I bought this Degas was rather different."

"Oh?"

Several moments passed before Dexter replied, a slight frown marring his brow. "The subject reminded me of someone."

Nina's curiosity was roused, but she felt it unwise to ask him who. They discussed the painting in greater detail, Nina explaining, in answer to Mandy's question, that the dancer's pose was *en attitude,* a frequently used position in ballet originally derived from the famous statue of Mercury.

"Now I want to show Nina *my* bedroom, Daddy," the little girl said presently.

"Right, Mandymouse. You go ahead and I'll join you in a minute, when I've had a word with Mrs. MacDonald."

It was a pretty, sunny room with a doll's house in one corner, and lots of toys. But as Nina began to admire it she found that Mandy had another, more pressing reason for bringing her here away from her father.

"That painting, Nina," she began solemnly. "The lady in it reminds Daddy of my mummy."

"I see! But your mother wasn't a ballet dancer, was she, Mandy?"

"Oh no, it's just her face." The child frowned, seeming puzzled and even a little awed at something she couldn't entirely grasp. "It's only a tiny bit like the way I remember Mummy, but Daddy says it's *exactly* like she was when they fell in love and got married."

Nina found herself wanting to ask Mandy more about her mother, but she felt it would be sneaky somehow, behind Dexter's back. A couple of minutes later, while they were glancing at one of Mandy's storybooks, the door opened and he looked in.

"Can a mere man interrupt your female powwow? If you've seen everything, Nina, we'll have a drink and then I think it's time we were on our way."

Back in the main living area, Nina refused an alcoholic drink and joined Mandy in having some fruit juice. Dexter himself drank a malt whisky. The conversation was relaxed and easy with Mandy there. She was a very intelligent child and appeared to be knowledgeable for her six years. Questioned by Nina, she chattered happily about school and her young friends. She seemed to be keenly interested in a number of things—swimming, riding her pony, which was named Starlight, as well as dancing.

"It's just a free expression dancing class she goes to," Dexter explained. "There's no attempt at formal teaching."

Mandy pulled a face. "Miss Pardoe won't let us do any of the ballet steps," she grumbled. "And she gets cross with us if we try to stand on our points."

"I should think so, too," Nina said forcefully. "You're far too young, Mandy."

"But it's not fair. I can get right up onto my toes and

stay there. Look!" In a trice she was demonstrating, holding her arms high above her head in a typical ballerina pose.

"No, Mandy, *no!*" Nina protested in horror, and the little girl came down at once, looking shocked and startled at the sharp reprimand. "You could do the most dreadful damage to your feet like that," Nina went on in an altogether gentler tone. "Honestly, you *must* believe what I say. It's very important that you do, otherwise you'll never have any chance of becoming a professional dancer when you grow up. When you're as young as you are now, your toes are too soft and tender to bear your weight standing on point. You have to be at least ten years old before they're strong enough for that, and even then you have to be very careful."

"There, you see, Mandy," put in Dexter. "Your Miss Pardoe isn't as unreasonable as you think. Nina agrees with her, and you can believe that a real ballerina knows what she's talking about."

Mandy was looking deeply thoughtful, and still a bit shaken. Nina smiled at her. "Don't worry, Mandy, I was just the same at your age. So will you promise me not to try and dance on your points for a few years yet?"

"You bet!" she said, with a quick smile that lit up her face. Then she gave a deep sigh. "But I don't know how I'm going to wait till I'm ten."

Dexter laughed. "Don't worry, Mandymouse, it'll come soon enough." He stood up, and glanced at Nina. "Shall we be off, then?"

They all three walked to the front door, and Nina turned to kiss Mandy good-bye. "It's been lovely coming to see your London home," she said, smiling.

"Will you come and see us again, Nina?" There was a note of pleading in her voice.

Dexter answered before she could think of the best reply to make. "Yes, Mandymouse, I promise that you'll be seeing more of Nina. Lots more."

To save an awkward silence in the lift going down, Nina chattered about how much she'd liked the apartment. Dexter said little, just smiling and watching her face with his tawny dark eyes. She couldn't tell what he was thinking behind those handsome features. In the car he surprised her by saying, "We can hardly go anywhere like the Ritz, dressed as we are. How about having dinner at the National Theater restaurant, overlooking the river?"

"But I don't . . ."

"The food's not bad there," he interrupted.

Nina suddenly felt annoyed; it looked as if Cheryl's dire predictions were about to be proved right. She said with firm dignity, "I'm sorry, but I certainly can't have dinner with you, Mr. Rolfe."

"Dexter," he corrected. "What's stopping you, Nina? Don't tell me that you have a dinner date already?"

It would be so much easier, she thought forlornly, if she could have lied and said an emphatic "yes." But she knew from past experience that she always gave herself away by coloring up the instant a lie left her lips. "No," she admitted, "I don't actually have a date."

"Well, then?"

Nina swung around and faced him, her chin up. "I only went to your apartment because you said that Mandy would be disappointed if I didn't."

"Which was quite true."

"I'm not suggesting it wasn't. But having dinner with you would be quite another thing. I don't know what Boyd would say."

"Boyd?" he queried, one eyebrow raised. "How does he come into it?"

"Boyd happens to be my boy friend," she stated pointedly.

"I see! You're engaged to him, are you?"

"Not exactly," she said coolly. "But . . ."

"In that case," Dexter cut across her, "he doesn't have an exclusive claim on your company." Reaching forward he pressed the starter and the car sprang to purring life. "I'm only suggesting that we have dinner together, you know, Nina. Afterward, I'll drive you straight home to your flat and we'll say good night on the doorstep."

Nina was beginning to feel distinctly foolish, knowing that she was behaving like a nervous teenager. Okay, so maybe Dexter had planned this evening in the expectation that she'd prove an easy conquest. If so, he would soon discover that he'd badly miscalculated. The episode would be a salutary lesson for him. And for herself? If only she could accept his invitation in a lighthearted way, as just a pleasant outing in the company of an interesting, cultured man. An occasion which would linger pleasantly in her memory. But some instinct warned Nina that after an evening spent with Dexter Rolfe, nothing would ever be quite the same for her again.

As the car sped away into the traffic, she realized to her dismay that Dexter was taking her agreement for granted. She had an impulse to tell him to drop her off at Piccadilly Circus, so she could make her own way home by bus. But he would only laugh, accusing her of overreacting. With a sigh she sank back in the cushioned seat of the Bentley and let the big car sweep her luxuriously through the busy west-end streets.

It was a lovely balmy evening for April. After leaving the National Theater restaurant, she and Dexter, by unspoken consent, strolled along the riverside promenade of South Bank. The tide was high and the dark, choppy waters danced with reflections of floodlit buildings on the opposite bank. Upriver, the light glowed above the Big Ben clock tower, indicating that Parliament was in late session.

Nina had only taken a single glass of white wine with her meal, yet she felt herself floating featherlight, as if she'd imbibed half a bottle of champagne. There was magic in the soft spring air, the sort of dream-filled, fairy-tale magic which she herself helped create night after night in the theater. A spellbinding magic which held the mundane world at bay. When Dexter laid an arm lightly across her shoulders, Nina shivered with a delicious sensation of tingling warmth.

"Happy?" he asked softly.

She smiled a dreamy smile. "Oh yes!"

"You're a naturally happy person, aren't you? It shines out of you like starglow. That's what makes you so very special to watch on stage, Nina . . . why the audiences appreciate you so much. Doesn't it give you a wonderful sense of satisfaction to receive the kind of enthusiastic ovation you were given on Saturday?"

"I'm only a small part of the total ballet experience," she said, with an embarrassed little shrug.

"But one day, Nina," he said seriously, "you'll be prima ballerina of the Regency Company."

"Maybe, if I have a lot of luck."

"Play your cards right, and nothing can stop you getting there."

Like all dancers, Nina was sometimes full of self-doubt, and Dexter's words registered in her mind as a gratifying vote of confidence. Glancing up at his chiseled profile, she murmured, "It's nice of you to say so."

Dexter halted his steps and drew her around to face him. Nina found herself trembling, feeling torn in two by conflicting emotions. She knew that he meant to kiss her, and she didn't want him to . . . yet she did, she did! Her indecision was her undoing. Dexter drew her closer, until she found herself weakly capitulating and melting against him. His lips brushed the silken mane of her hair, then slid across her cheek and claimed her mouth, holding her in sweet slavery to his will. Nina was acutely aware of the firm contours of his lean, hard-muscled body, headily conscious of his male warmth and the subtle musky tang of him, and she felt herself drowning in his potent aura of blood-stirring masculinity. This was not just another kiss, such as she had often received from Boyd, and one or two earlier boy friends. This was something altogether different— something on a totally different plane of experience. It felt as if her soul had lain in wait for this moment from the very beginning of time.

But after a few brief seconds Nina was forcefully pushing him away. The common sense which had temporarily deserted her came rushing back, and with it a blazing anger. She burst out furiously, "You gave me your solemn word that you wouldn't act like this, and . . ."

"I gave you my word that I wouldn't kiss you?" he cut across her in an astonished voice. "What in heaven's name are you talking about, Nina? I did nothing of the kind."

"You . . . you said you were just taking me for a meal," she stammered wretchedly. "And you promised to take me straight home to my flat and say good-bye on the doorstep. You can't deny it."

"I don't deny it," he clipped. "I'll take you home now, this minute, if you like. But aren't you making a big deal out of a simple, friendly kiss?"

"It was a lot more than that," she protested, backing away from him. "I . . . I knew it was stupid of me to agree to see you this evening, and now I've been proved right."

For a few moments Dexter stood looking down at her with a dark frown on his lean face. Then he said abruptly, "Come on then, let's find the car and I'll drive you back to Battersea. You'll be safely tucked in bed—alone—in a half hour or so."

He didn't speak again until they were spinning along the Albert Embankment beside the curving river. Nina, feeling a lump in her throat, wished perversely that London didn't look so romantically beautiful on this lovely spring evening.

"I've got to spend a few days in Stockholm," Dexter announced abruptly. "But I'll be returning on Friday morning. So shall we meet that evening?"

"No!" The refusal burst out of her emphatically.

"Why not? Are you already fixed up with a date for Friday?"

"You seem to forget," Nina said sarcastically, "that I work in the theater. I'm dancing every night for the rest of this week . . . including Friday."

"I knew that. I was thinking of some supper afterward. Okay?"

"No, it isn't okay, Mr. Rolfe. Will you please understand that I regard this evening as a big mistake. A mistake I have no intention of repeating."

"That's how you feel at the moment," he remarked calmly, as he pulled out to overtake a red double-decker bus. "So let's just leave it for now, and I'll phone you when I get back."

"You'll be wasting your time," Nina retorted. "Anyway, I won't be home."

"I'll find you," he said confidently, "wherever you are. Now let's see . . . if I make a left turn here, that'll be about right for your place, won't it?"

"Yes," she said in a tight voice.

The instant his Bentley drew up at the curb, Nina jerked open the door and jumped out. Calling a brief good night over her shoulder, she ran up to the front door and let herself in with the key that she had ready in her hand. But in the hallway she stood still, flushed and embarrassed. Hadn't she acted like an idiot, scurrying away as if from some deadly danger? Dexter Rolfe must be laughing his head off.

And yet, as she continued slowly upstairs, Nina knew that she had truly been in danger. If Dexter had kissed her again just now, she might well not have found the willpower to push away from him a second time. A vivid memory of that kiss was still with her. Unaware of what she was doing, she pressed the back of her hand to her mouth as if retaining the sensuous imprint of his lips on hers.

Cheryl looked up from the ironing board as she entered the flat. "Hi, you're back earlier than I expected." She gave Nina an interested glance. "How did it go?"

"The object of the exercise was achieved. I saw the Degas painting, and I saw his daughter."

"That didn't take all of four hours," Cheryl pointed out logically.

"Oh well . . . we dropped in for dinner at the National Theater on the way back."

"I see!" Cheryl pressed her lips together disapprovingly. "You're not getting yourself hooked on the man, are you, Nina?"

"Don't be absurd!" She went out to the little kitchen, and noisily filled the kettle. Cheryl came to stand in the doorway.

"Are you seeing him again?" she queried.

"No."

"Didn't he ask you?"

"He did, and I refused. Satisfied? Now, how about a cup of coffee?"

Perhaps it was the coffee which kept Nina awake long after Cheryl, in the other bed, was fast asleep. The events of the evening churned in her mind . . . his luxurious apartment, his delightful young daughter, their meal together. Dexter Rolfe, astonishingly for a hard-headed businessman, was a very easy person to get on with, and interesting to talk to. Added to which, he had to be rated the most excitingly attractive man she'd ever encountered. Nina tried her best to stifle that thought, but it kept recurring . . . as did the disturbing memory of his kiss and the turbulent feelings it had evoked in her.

And then another recollection suddenly flashed in her brain. Strolling with her on the riverside promenade, he'd been speaking of her career as a dancer. If she played her cards right, he'd said, nothing could stop her from becoming prima ballerina of the Regency Ballet Company.

Play her cards right! With *him*, he'd meant. Nina felt sick to the stomach, horrified by this new interpretation of his words. Why on earth hadn't she realized at the time what was so blatantly obvious to her now? Dexter Rolfe, as the ballet company's chief financial sponsor, could obviously wield tremendous influence. His expressed wishes would be difficult for Sir Hugo and the board of management to resist, whatever other ideas they might have about their future prima ballerina. As much as Nina longed to achieve the exalted, much coveted position, she wanted to make it on sheer merit alone.

She felt a sense of rage and bitter hatred against Dexter Rolfe. He was playing fast and loose with her emotions, caring nothing about the effect he had on her.

Next morning, because Nina couldn't help feeling a sneaking sense of guilt about Boyd, she sought him out the moment she arrived with Cheryl for morning class at the rehearsal studios at Elephant and Castle.

"How are you fixed this week?" she asked him pointedly.

"I told you, darling, I'm up to my eyes. Why?"

Nina shrugged, feeling a bit embarrassed. "It's just . . . we seem to be seeing so little of each other lately, Boyd."

"Well, you know how it is. And I thought we'd agreed, love, that work commitments must come first with us both."

"I know. What about Friday, after the performance?"

"Why Friday, especially?" he asked curiously.

She felt herself coloring. "Oh, no reason. Just, it would be nice, that's all."

"Sorry, but it's impossible. Sir Hugo wants me to look at a couple of Northern theaters we're considering adding to our touring circuit, to check up on their facilities, and I'm driving up overnight."

Nina had to hurry and get into her practice gear. Going through the daily class routine of *barre* and center exercises, she felt gripped by a kind of desperation. Boyd was her boy friend, the man she expected to marry, but it seemed that fate was being malicious and trying to push her into another man's arms. Dexter Rolfe possessed a dynamic, magnetic attractiveness that she felt helpless to resist. The way he'd kissed her last night had made her feel more excited, more vitally alive, than ever before in all her life. It was just a temporary fit of madness, she told herself sternly, something she must strenuously resist. It would be the height of folly to jeopardize her whole future with Boyd for the sake of a few cheap sensual thrills. If only Boyd would be more demonstrative and show his feelings for her more lovingly, she thought with a sigh, then this problem with Dexter would surely never have arisen.

Queuing up behind Cheryl at coffee break, she asked her friend if she had anything planned for Friday night.

"Yes, I'm grabbing the chance to go home and see Jeremy and my parents," said Cheryl, turning a happy face to her. "I was going to tell you, Nina, I've just this minute heard that I won't be needed on Saturday. I should have been dancing *Coppélia* at the matinée, but Sir Hugo wants to try out Elli Kyle in the Swanhilda role. So if I get away right after Friday's performance, I can catch a late train. I'm so excited. It's been six weeks now since I've seen Jeremy."

Nina had to try and look pleased for Cheryl. But it seemed like one more confirmation that fate was working against her.

It was a typical hardworking, strenuous week. Nina was scheduled to dance the principal role in a full-length *Swan Lake* on Tuesday night, and again at the Thursday matinée, with less exacting roles at other performances. But then on Wednesday she had to stand in for Sonia Lamartine, who'd slightly strained her knee during rehearsal, and dance *Sleeping Beauty*. Each day she reasserted her determination to be firm in her refusal when Dexter contacted her. Yet when on Friday she was summoned to the secretary's office to take a phone call, she felt a sense of panic. Trying to mask her nervousness, she put on a bright and breezy voice. "Oh, hello. How was Stockholm?"

"Fine. I did some useful business—the Swedes recognize a good product when they see one. Nina . . . about this evening . . ."

"Listen, I can't . . ."

"We've been invited to a party," he continued smoothly, as if she hadn't spoken. "I explained about you dancing tonight, and that we'd be late arriving. Marjorie said not to worry."

"Who's Marjorie?" she queried, trapped into showing interest.

"Wife of Patrick Farr, who's the publicity director for Rolfe Industries. You'll like the Farrs, Nina."

"But I haven't said that I'll . . ."

"I checked that the performance ends at ten-ten. Give you time to change, and I'll collect you at ten-thirty. Okay?"

"But . . ."

"I can't stop and chat now, Nina. My secretary's making urgent faces at me. See you."

There was a click, and the dial tone began. Nina stood holding the phone, staring at it stupidly. If Dexter thought he could hustle her into going out with him like that, he could think again!

For the remainder of the day Nina was preoccupied, twice earning herself a sharp rebuke from Boyd during the afternoon rehearsal of *Giselle* because she seemed incapable of mastering her solo in the first act. It was crazy, she hadn't the slightest intention of going out with Dexter that evening. But . . . just in case she decided to change her mind at the last minute, she'd brought a dress in red and gold sari silk and some high-heeled sandals. Now, she was in a dither of indecision.

Chapter Three

$\mathcal{I}$t was with a sense of inevitability that Nina found herself driving to Islington that evening with Dexter.

The Farrs lived in a terrace of smart town houses, each with brass carriage lanterns beside the brightly painted front door. As they went inside, she felt relieved that she'd chosen the sari silk dress. Besides being the easiest to pack, it also happened to be the most glamorous outfit she possessed. She knew that the subtle red and gold were ideal with her dark hair and ivory complexion, and altogether the dress gave a much needed boost to her confidence. The house was crowded with elegant, sophisticated people. The women clearly didn't have to bother about calculating every penny they spent on clothes, the way Nina and all her dancing friends did, and their groomed good looks and assured self-confidence filled her with envy.

Their hostess bore down on them, a tall woman of

about thirty-five in a slinky black dress, wearing a jangling collection of bangles and colored beads.

"Dexter!" she exclaimed, greeting him with a kiss on the cheek. "So this is your new girl friend. You didn't exaggerate about her one tiny bit on the phone, my friend. She's absolutely lovely. Nina, you're very welcome."

Nina warmed at once to Marjorie Farr, sensing in some obscure way that this gauntly attractive woman was on her side. But it wasn't so with some of the other women she was introduced to, who seemed to regard her as an interloper. It didn't help that Dexter kept his arm about her waist possessively all the while they were chatting with other people. One of the women, a dazzling honey blonde named Esther, took the chance of Dexter's absence fetching fresh drinks to murmur in Nina's ear, "I hope you don't imagine that you'll hold onto him for long."

"I don't understand what you mean."

"Oh, you understand all right! I'll give you six weeks, two months at the very outside. That's the most that anyone can expect from Dexter before he ditches them and moves on to seek fresh pastures."

"Are you speaking from firsthand knowledge?" Nina inquired maliciously, with a sugar sweet smile.

She received a venomous look in reply. But then Dexter was back with the glass of white wine she'd asked for. "You don't look too happy," he observed. "Is something the matter?"

"I just wish I hadn't come," Nina told him.

"Why d'you say that?" When she didn't answer, he studied her face with shrewd eyes, then hazarded, "Was Esther getting at you?"

"Something like that," she shrugged.

Dexter grinned cheerfully. "Surely you've learned

not to be bothered by a few catty remarks? After all, it's only to be expected."

Because Nina felt so tense and on edge, she let her anger at him flare. "That's typical of the male chauvinist attitude. All women are gossips, all women are bad drivers, all women are catty to each other over men. None of it's true, of course, but I suppose it pleases the male ego to think so—it makes them feel nice and superior."

"Have you quite finished?" Dexter asked calmly, his lips curving in an amused smile.

"There's a lot more I could say," she hissed, "but that'll do for starters."

"Good. So now I'll finish what *I* was going to say. When someone possesses your sort of unconscious beauty and grace, as well as being highly acclaimed in her chosen career, it's bound to make other women green with envy. Therefore, some of them try to take you down a peg or two. Perfectly understandable behavior under the circumstances—and not specifically feminine."

"You needn't try to flatter me," she flung at him crossly.

"You don't like me being honest?" he inquired, quirking one eyebrow. "Of course you are beautiful, Nina, with a magnificently sensual body, and every movement you make is sheer joy for a man to watch. You wouldn't be where you are today unless you possessed all the physical qualities that go into making a leading ballerina."

"Wherever I've got," she retorted with quiet fury, "has been on my own dancing ability. And that's the way it's always going to be."

"An attitude I highly applaud," Dexter said. "But I wonder why you're making the point in such a belligerent way."

"I think you know why," she countered, her nostrils flaring.

"But I don't. I'm not in the habit of asking questions to which I already know the answer."

Nina regarded him stonily. "Play your cards right . . . that's what you told me the other night. You made it clear that I could expect favors careerwise if I was . . . cooperative."

Dexter's eyes went cold as steel and his voice was tight with anger. "I've never stooped to making that sort of bargain, Nina, and I don't intend to start now. Furthermore, it would hardly be possible in your case. Do you seriously imagine that an independent character like Sir Hugo Quest would tolerate interference in the artistic direction of Regency Ballet, from me or anyone else? He'd tell me to get lost in no uncertain terms—and to hell with my sponsorship. Quite right, too."

Nina flushed. "I . . . I'm sorry, I shouldn't have said that. I . . . I wasn't thinking straight."

Dexter flashed one of his quick, charming smiles—but it wasn't meant for her. Nina turned to see Marjorie Farr coming toward them.

"Now then, you two," she jollied them reproachfully, "this is meant to be a party, not a cozy *tête-à-tête*." She slipped her arm through Nina's. "There's someone over there who's just recognized who you are, and I've promised to take you over to meet her."

It was close to two A.M. when they finally left the Farrs' house. As Dexter started the car and drove off, he said in a critical tone, "You didn't seem to enjoy yourself very much, Nina."

"What did you expect?" she flared, and added, "I should never have come."

"Taking you to a party could have been a mistake,"

he conceded. "Next time, I'll make it just the two of us."

"There isn't going to be a next time," she retorted.

Dexter didn't respond to that. As they continued to drive through the night quiet streets of central London, Nina found herself sneaking glances at him. From behind her lashes, she observed the clean, firm lines of his profile, watched his hands on the steering wheel, his long fingers lightly gripping its leather-covered rim. She could see his left leg, the dark fabric of his trousers stretched taut across the muscled hardness of his thigh. Nina was well accustomed to the sight of magnificent male bodies; in the ballet world they were common-place, with no one having any time or inclination to bother about mock modesty. Yet never before had any man had this intensely disturbing effect on her, this magnetizing of all her senses. A shiver ran through her that was part excitement, part fear, and she drew her white mohair coat more closely about her shoulders.

It was a relief to her when they eventually pulled up outside the house in Battersea. Refusing to permit herself the same indecorous flight from him as on Monday evening, Nina remained seated for a few moments, then said lightly, "Well, this is it. Good-bye, Dexter."

He turned, and in the darkness she caught the glitter of his eyes. "I'll be driving down to Haslemere Hall in the morning, Nina."

"Have a nice time, then. And give my love to Mandy."

"It's too bad you're dancing tomorrow and can't come with me," he went on smoothly. "Mandy would be over the moon if you did. However, I'll be returning to town on Sunday morning. I have a lunch meeting with an American buyer . . . it's the only day he could manage. But I should be free about two P.M. onward. D'you like sailing?"

"I've never done any."

"Then it's high time you did. I have a boat I keep at Chichester Harbor. The weather is supposed to be fine on Sunday."

"No, I . . . I couldn't possibly come."

Dexter laughed softly. "Little Miss Obstinate!"

"Don't patronize me," she snapped.

His fingers closed around her upper arm and it was like an electric contact, the current seeming to surge through from him to her. Nina felt transfixed, powerless to move. Dexter leaned forward until his leanly rugged face was only a few inches from her own. "Patronizing you is the very last thing I want to do, Nina," he murmured. "Believe me, I have the greatest respect and admiration for you. So please . . . say you'll come sailing with me on Sunday."

"What's the point?" she asked despairingly.

"The point is that it would give a lot of pleasure to me, and I don't think you yourself would feel the day was entirely wasted. It should be glorious out on the water in this mild weather, and you'll learn something about sailing."

Nina was tempted almost beyond bearing. "Please," Dexter added in a husky whisper. He touched his lips to the petal soft skin of her cheek just below her right eye, drawing back at once, but even though his kiss was so fleeting it filled her with an indescribable yearning, and she longed to sink into the bliss of his embrace.

Dexter was waiting for her answer. Nina heaved a deep, shuddering sigh of resignation, and said chokily, "If . . . if I did come, it wouldn't mean . . ."

"No, that's understood." He kissed her a second time, as fleetingly as before, then released her reluctantly. "I'd better let you go in now to get your beauty sleep," he said, leaning across to open the door on her side. He waited, watching, while she went to the front door and inserted her key. Then, with a final wave, he drove off.

She was a fool, an utter fool, Nina chided herself as she wearily mounted the stairs. And yet . . . if that little scene were reenacted, she knew to her shame that the outcome would be exactly the same. It wasn't the mere fact that she'd weakly agreed to another date with Dexter that made her feel so disloyal to Boyd. It was because she wanted to be with Dexter so desperately. The thought of going sailing with him on Sunday was making her pulse race in eager anticipation.

She spent a miserable, restless night, struggling with her conscience. She must put a stop to this madness at once, she warned herself, she mustn't let this dangerous situation go any farther. In the morning she would call Dexter at his Mayfair apartment and tell him that the Sunday date was off. But when morning came she did nothing. Her longing to see Dexter was too strong to resist.

They took the main Portsmouth road out of London, then turned off into quiet Sussex lanes, bathed in a golden glow of April sunshine. Trees were uncurling their tender new leaves, and several times Nina saw pale yellow primroses nestled coyly in the hedgerow banks. Appreciatively, she breathed deep of the soft, fragrant air that wafted in through the Bentley's open windows. Somehow, from the word go, the atmosphere between them was completely different from Friday evening and she felt happy today, happy to be with Dexter.

"Apart from coming to Hàslemere Hall last weekend, I haven't been in the country since last autumn," she told him. "We did our usual winter tour, of course, but that's all to big cities."

He grinned. "Then this little outing isn't a moment too soon." They passed through a picture postcard village nestled at the foot of the South Downs, its attractive little houses faced with flint chips under thatched roofs. A sparkling stream skirted two sides of the triangular village green, where white-clad cricketers were playing. "You'll love it in the South of France," he said after a moment. "Have you ever been there before?"

Nina turned to him eagerly. "Is it true, then? There've been various rumors about the company doing a short season in Nice, but nothing definite so far."

Dexter made a wry face. "It looks as if I've been talking out of turn, so perhaps you'd better say nothing until you hear it officially. But it *is* true, Nina. And I've rented a villa at Cap Ferrat where all of you will be staying, as your headquarters. It was built in the thirties by a millionaire banker, and it's now used mainly for conferences. There's a large ballroom that can be fitted up as a rehearsal studio."

"How marvelous!" she exclaimed, then asked artlessly, "Will you be staying there too, Dexter?"

"Part of the time. I shall come whenever I can, but I mustn't let myself get lazy and neglect Rolfe Industries."

The tall, graceful spire of Chichester's ancient cathedral pointed them on to the harbor, a vast network of sheltered creeks and inlets which comprised one of the finest yachting centers in the South of England. Now, at high tide, the extensive sheet of water glinted in the bright afternoon sunlight, dotted with craft of all shapes and sizes, some at rest, some with their sails unfurled, skimming before the frisky breeze. Dexter parked the Bentley at the quayside, and they sat for a few moments admiring the scene.

"What a very beautiful spot," she breathed.

"And it's a perfect natural harbor that's been used over the centuries—right back to Roman times, and probably even before that."

"Really?"

"Yes, this harbor has seen lots of history. There's one quaint legend I rather like about a marauding party of Danes. Apparently they seized one of the bells from a monastery at a village just across the water from here, and carried it off with them. The monks were naturally very distressed, but when they next began to ring a hymn the missing note came singing out across the water from the Danish ship. The bell itself promptly fell through the ship's planks to the bottom of the harbor, and it's still supposed to be there—waiting, so the legend goes, for a team of white heifers to turn up and haul it out."

Nina smiled. "You're a surprising man, Dexter. Business tycoon, keen on sailing, supporter of the ballet, collector of paintings—and of charming old legends. What else do you like doing?"

"Shall I demonstrate?" he asked, a meaningful look in his tawny eyes.

"Be serious."

"I was being serious," he grinned. "Alternative pastimes I enjoy are golf and squash. Then I go gliding sometimes, and I like skin diving."

"Diving, eh? So you could check out that sunken bell," Nina suggested with a laugh.

"No thanks, the bottom here is far too muddy. I prefer the Mediterranean or the Caribbean for skin diving. Come on, let's get to the boat."

They rowed out in a squat little dinghy to where his yacht rode at her mooring. It had a graceful pale blue hull, and twin masts—a ketch, Dexter explained in response to Nina's query. "She's a vessel I can handle on my own, without a crew," he added, as they clambered aboard.

"I hardly think of you as a loner," she commented.

"I'm not, usually. But sometimes, out on the water— out of sight of land, even—it feels good to be completely alone. It helps you to get things in perspective."

Nina had noticed the name painted on the bows. "What made you call your boat *Judith?*" she asked.

"It was my wife's name," he informed her in a cool, clipped voice.

"Oh, I see."

She felt embarrassed, bitterly regretting that she'd ever raised the subject, which certainly seemed to have put a damper on Dexter's spirits. From a hanging locker in the cabin he found an extra sweater each, bright yellow waterproof slickers and lifejackets. When Nina inquired if there was anything she could do to help, he shook his head. In silence, he hoisted the sails and cast off. The wind flapped the canvas, then caught with a slap, and *Judith* slid smoothly from her mooring. Nina felt she might not have existed for all the notice Dexter took of her, and she guessed that he was thinking of the woman who had died—his wife and Mandy's mother. Had he loved her very deeply, so deeply that even eighteen months or more after her death, the casual mention of her name by his current female companion made him feel somehow disloyal to her memory? But surely Dexter wasn't the type to brood? Sooner or later, there had to be room for a new woman who was important in his life.

Nina felt her cheeks grow warm, realizing that she was picturing herself in that role. And then, tumbling into her mind like a cold shower, came memories of all the gossip she'd heard about Dexter Rolfe and the numerous women he had dated. Not one of whom, apparently, had meant a thing to him. In most ways, Dexter was an intelligent, sensitive, highly cultured man, but where women were concerned, he was utterly shallow. Ruthless, even. She began to wish that she hadn't come sailing with him this afternoon. It had been a foolish mistake, just like going with him to the party the other night, giving Dexter the impression that she would eventually be ready to go along with the plans he had for her . . . plans that were designed to end, sooner rather than later, with them in bed together.

"Does Mandy like sailing?" she burst out, to break the silence that was jangling her nerves.

Dexter roused himself from his reverie and smiled at her. "She loves it. In fact, when she heard this was what we planned to do this afternoon, she was quite cross about not being allowed to come along."

"So why didn't you bring her?"

"I don't like to interfere with Phyllida's routine too often. Having had Mandy with me for the day last Monday, I thought I'd better not suggest it."

"From which, do I gather that your sister-in-law doesn't like sailing?"

"Right!" He laughed, and added teasingly, "Besides . . ."

"Besides what?"

"We wouldn't have wanted a crowd, would we?" He caught and held her eyes in the capture of his dark gaze.

At least, Nina reflected with an inward sigh, as she made herself glance away, Dexter's somber mood was broken. She consoled herself with the thought that he would be fully occupied navigating the boat in the busy harbor, so there could be no danger of him making a pass at her.

As they proceeded Dexter taught her some of the

rudiments of navigation and seamanship. They were out of the harbor now in the open waters of the Solent, the dark shape of the Isle of Wight's cliffs looming against the westering sun. The sea was choppier, with curling white wavelets dancing on the surface, and Nina felt her cheeks glowing from the exhilarating sting of salt spray. She forgot her fears and regrets, and began to enjoy herself unreservedly. The scudding shadow of their three tall sails upon the water grew longer as, very gradually, the daylight of the spring day began to fade.

"We'd better be getting back," Dexter announced, pulling around the tiller, and it seemed all too soon to her.

Behind them now, the sun went down in a glorious glow of crimson and orange that stained the dark-veined blue of the sea, filling Nina with a strange, wistful happiness. By the time they reached *Judith's* mooring and stowed away the equipment, twilight shadows were stealing across the water. They rowed to the quayside, but left the car where it was and strolled to a charming old pub with an upstairs oaken gallery from which the harbor could be observed. Its name, painted on a swinging sign, was apt—*The Mariner's Compass*.

While Dexter ordered their drinks, he was greeted on all sides in the friendliest fashion. It was obvious that he made no play of his wealth and status, being just another amateur sailor among the many here. He introduced Nina to a number of people, who viewed her with speculative interest. They stayed on to eat a simple dinner, a succulent mixed grill, which they enjoyed at a small round table in the gallery. From here Nina could look out across the dark harbor and see the navigation lights of those vessels coming in late, and the various marker beacons flashing red and green and white signals. She felt more relaxed and at ease with

Dexter than ever before, and she didn't want this lovely day to end. But soon after nine they began the drive back to London.

It was a dark, moonless night, the Bentley's powerful headlights cutting a great swath of light which fleetingly illuminated the ghostly shapes of wayside trees and the occasional isolated country cottage. At one quiet stretch of road, where it ran between pinewoods of pencil-straight trunks, Dexter stopped the car and cut the lights and engine. For several long moments they sat in silence, though Nina's heart was thudding so loudly that she felt sure Dexter must be able to hear it.

"I don't know when I've enjoyed a day so much," he said eventually, a husky note to his voice.

Nina didn't comment, scared to give him any encouragement. She sat rigidly still in the leather seat, staring through the windshield at the stars that spangled the dark, velvety sky.

"Didn't you enjoy it, too?" he asked softly.

Faced with the direct question, Nina could not lie to him. "Yes, it was wonderful. I . . . I'm very grateful, Dexter."

"I'm the one who's grateful." With a catch of breath he reached out and drew her toward him. The touch of his hands was like a catalyst, setting free Nina's locked-in emotions, and she let herself melt against him with a shivering sigh of pleasure. Whispering endearments, Dexter pressed his lips to the silken softness of her hair, while his hands roamed her slender body, exploring the supple curves and coaxing her to a state of sensual arousal in which the last remnants of her determination to resist him withered away and died.

"You're so lovely," he said hoarsely, from deep in his throat. "I want you, Nina."

Held close against the solid, muscular wall of his chest, she could feel the rapid beating of his heart mingling with her own. Involuntarily, her hands slid upward, clutching at his broad shoulders, then moving on to clasp around his neck, her fingers digging into the crispness of his hair. She felt herself floating in a sweet daze of pleasure as he trailed tiny butterfly kisses across the satin smooth skin of her brow and temples, her lids fluttering closed as he gently touched each eye in turn. Then, as his mouth claimed hers in a long, drugging kiss she was seized by a great surging wave of erotic excitement. His lips were persuasively demanding, making glorious promises, forcing her own lips apart to allow access to his questing tongue.

"I want you, Nina!" he whispered a second time, as he momentarily drew back. "I want you so much." Then again he was kissing her, with deepening passion, until she was swamped by her need of him, by the feverish longing which swept aside all caution and common sense. She responded with a breath-catching moan as his hand slid up beneath her sweater to cup one breast, his fingertips caressing its soft warm outline, then finding the nipple and teasing it to a peak of tingling hardness. She wanted this sweet agony of excitement and desire to continue forever. She felt that she could willingly die in this state of ecstatic bliss.

On the quiet road a car flashed by, its headlights briefly flickering over them. The sight and sound of it snapped Nina back to her senses. She felt a surge of revulsion, against Dexter, but mostly against herself, for indulging in this meaningless sexual titillation. With a sudden desperate strength, she put her two palms to his chest and forced herself back from his grasp.

"What the devil?" he jerked out in astonishment.

"Let me go!" she cried.

He half-obeyed, but still retained a loose grip on her shoulders. Nina dragged herself away from him, and hastily pulled her clothes straight.

"That was unforgivable," she said furiously.

"Why? I did nothing, Nina, that you weren't ready and eager to receive. Can you deny it?"

"I don't want to talk about it. Please drive me home."

"Not yet. First we're going to get this straightened out. What have I done that's so terrible?"

Nina was quickly regaining a measure of self-control. She said coldly, "I suppose, to a man like you, it's just the normal routine. You take a girl out, buy her dinner a couple of times, treat her to an afternoon's sailing or whatever, and then expect the payoff. You certainly want to get your pleasures cheap, don't you?"

"Do I take it," he asked in a voice laced with sarcasm, "that you come more expensive, Nina?"

She gasped aloud, dismayed that he could speak to her so coarsely. "How dare you!"

"Okay, I'll take it back," he said placatingly. "But it's no use your standing on your dignity and pretending that you didn't invite what happened. You made no protest when I stopped the car, and you didn't offer the slightest resistance when I started to kiss you. Far from it. The way you responded, it was obvious that you wanted me every bit as much as I wanted you."

Nina took a deep, shuddering breath. "You're being horribly unfair. I made it absolutely clear before I ever accepted your invitation to go sailing today that I wasn't prepared to . . . to . . ."

"And I didn't *expect* you to, at the time I asked you. But we've moved on from there, haven't we? If two people find themselves attracted to one another and have an urge to make love, why shouldn't they?"

"Make love!" she cried protestingly. "You may be an expert in sex, Mr. Dexter Rolfe, but you don't begin to understand the meaning of the word love."

"You think not? But then you know so little about me, Nina."

"I've heard things, though."

"So that's it! I'm the subject of gossip. Haven't you ballet girls got something better to talk about?"

"What do you expect," she returned, "when our sponsor carries on like you do? You're absolutely notorious."

"In which case," he challenged, "I'm surprised that you agreed to come out with me, Nina. Weren't you asking for trouble?"

"I was stupid enough," she said vehemently, "to believe that, against all hearsay, you were a gentleman."

"Well, now you know that I'm not. Nor do I want to be a so-called gentleman. No one ever got to build a commercial empire by using kid-glove methods, Nina."

"And that goes for your relationships with women, too, I suppose?"

Dexter was silent for a long, tense minute, and she knew that she'd scored a telling point. Then he said stiffly, "I think we both made a mistake, don't you? So let's call it quits. Now I'll drive you home, and that'll be that."

"Suits me fine!"

For the remainder of the journey back to London Dexter scarcely uttered a word, driving at high speed once they reached the motorway. He dropped Nina off outside the house in Battersea with a brief good night, and made no suggestion of seeing her again.

Entering the flat, Nina found to her relief that Cheryl wasn't home yet. With a leaden feeling in her limbs she prepared for bed, then stood at the window gazing out at the star-studded night sky. She was ready to leap into bed and feign sleep the moment she heard Cheryl arrive home, because she couldn't face talking to her friend tonight.

Dexter really was hateful and vile to play her along with smooth reassurances, when all the time it was his fixed intention to seduce her. He was utterly ruthless in business dealings, and in his private life too, uncaring about the feelings and susceptibilities of other people. Everything was secondary to his own selfish needs. And yet, piercing through these bitter thoughts came the recollection of a different sort of man. A cultured man who collected fine works of art, who gave unstinting financial support to her own ballet company. A tenderhearted man who, as she had witnessed with her own eyes, showed the deepest kind of love and devotion to his six-year-old daughter.

Dexter Rolfe was truly an enigma, and she didn't know where she stood with him . . . didn't know what she wanted from him. And what about Boyd? she asked herself despairingly. What had happened to her sense of loyalty, that she could let herself become so emotionally involved with Dexter? She was supposed to be in love with Boyd, yet he had never stirred her physically the way Dexter did by just the slightest touch of his fingers, by just the way he looked at her. It was all so horribly confusing.

Chapter Four

At the end of class on Wednesday morning, Sir Hugo Quest announced to the assembled company that the Regency Ballet would be performing a four-week season in Nice during the month of August. He went on to explain about the villa at Cap Ferrat that Mr. Dexter Rolfe had rented for them, and said that they would all be staying there for the preceding three weeks while they rehearsed and prepared for their forthcoming autumn season in London.

"I've asked Boyd not to work you *too* hard," he went on, stroking his Vandyke beard and smiling benignly, "so I trust that you will all enjoy your time on the French Riviera. Nice holds a very special place in my heart, for it was there that I became engaged to my late wife, the great Janina Silkova. Silkova and I had only recently been partnered, and in learning to dance together, we fell in love."

Queuing up for lunch in the cafeteria, everyone was

excitedly discussing the trip to the South of France. Nina tried her best to join in the chatter and not reveal the fact that she'd already been given the news by Dexter. Would he still be coming himself, she wondered anxiously, considering how things stood between them? If so, it was going to be a wretched time for her.

Standing behind her and Cheryl were Boyd and Alan Kent, the dancer with whom Cheryl was most often partnered. "It's great of Mr. Rolfe to take that villa for us, isn't it?" Alan said. "We'll get a taste of the good life in the Mediterranean sunshine."

Barry Nolan, who was just ahead in the line with Elli Kyle and Lisbet Paton, turned his head and grinned. "You don't have to go to the South of France for a taste of the good life. Eh girls?" He slipped an arm around each of their shoulders. "Come rain come shine, I'm always available, ready and willing."

"Shut up, Barry," the two girls chorused good-naturedly, and fell to talking about the clothes they'd need to buy.

Nina chose a portion of Quiche Lorraine and a green salad. Then, carrying her tray, she glanced around for a suitable table. Boyd nudged her from behind. "Over there in the corner."

"But that's only a twosome table," she pointed out. "What about Cheryl and Alan?"

"We don't need them tagging along," he said impatiently.

Nina hesitated. Cheryl wouldn't thank her for being left alone with Alan. But Alan would! So, glancing back in a sort of half-apology to her friend, she followed Boyd.

"I do wish Cheryl would see sense about Alan," she sighed, as they sat down. "He's such a nice chap, and he's really devoted to her. But she always keeps him at arm's length. It seems such a terrible waste."

"If she doesn't fancy him, she doesn't fancy him," Boyd said dismissively. "I wanted to talk to you alone, Nina. I've got some good news."

"Oh?"

He grinned at her triumphantly. "Sir Hugo has agreed that *Summer Rhapsody* will have its premiere at Nice. What d'you think of that?"

If only she could feel more enthusiastic about going to Nice, like the rest of the company. But she couldn't dismiss her feeling of apprehension concerning Dexter, and what might possibly develop if they should meet there.

Boyd frowned in reproach. "You might look a bit pleased, Nina. I really worked hard on Sir Hugo to get you this big chance. With Lamartine out of the way guest-starring at the New York Met, it means that you will get all the attention for the first performances. There'll be nobody to outshine you in Nice."

Nina pulled herself together, not wanting to seem ungrateful. "It's really great, Boyd. The only pity is that you won't be partnering me, like Sir Hugo did with Silkova for all those years. These days we don't seem to see nearly as much of each other, now that we're not dancing together."

Boyd shrugged that aside. "I can do a darn sight more to build your career this way than I ever could as a dancer. I'm telling you, Nina, just put yourself entirely in my hands, and you'll end up as great a ballerina as Silkova ever was."

"Let's hope so," she laughed awkwardly. She still found it difficult to believe that such a dizzy future was actually within her grasp—as people seemed to think. If only, she thought wistfully, the forthcoming season at Nice could set the seal on her romance with Boyd. Nina tried to imagine the setting . . . ideally in the gardens of the big villa where they were going to stay, by

71

moonlight, and with the quiet waters of the Mediterranean lapping softly in the background. Boyd would propose to her, and she would joyfully say yes.

But somehow the image wouldn't gel in her mind. Suddenly, with shattering clarity, Nina realized that she could never marry Boyd Maxwell. For a long time past, even though their relationship had never been very passionate, she had believed herself in love with him. But she realized now that it wasn't so. The specialness of her feelings for Boyd had been due to their working so intimately close, and the fact that—as far as ballet was concerned—their minds were tuned to the same wavelength. That wasn't the same as being in love, though. If she were truly in love with Boyd, then she could never have responded in such a devastating way to another man's kisses.

"There's something I've got to talk to you about," she burst out impetuously. "Can we see one another this evening?"

He frowned. "Not a hope, darling. Sir Hugo's chasing me for the rehearsal schedules, and there are any number of complications to be ironed out."

"Tomorrow, then." When he started to shake his head, she added urgently, "Please, Boyd, it's important."

His handsome face darkened and he gave her an impatient glance. "What's more important than getting on with our careers?"

"But it's about our careers in a way," she persisted. "I mean, about our whole future. I feel that we really ought to have a talk about our relationship . . . get a few things sorted out."

Boyd stood up abruptly and gave her a quick kiss. "For heaven's sake, darling, don't start making problems. I've got too much on my plate at the moment.

Just be a good girl and leave everything to me. Now, I've got to rush. . . ."

During the next few days Nina tried several more times to pin Boyd down. She hated the situation of not being honest with him about her feelings. It wasn't going to be an easy encounter, she knew; Boyd had always been possessively jealous about her. She intended to make it clear to him that though she was no longer in love with him, she still felt extremely fond of him and wanted their close working relationship to continue as before. She just had to hope that Boyd would be understanding. However, he gave her no chance to have things out. Each time she tried to fix a date to see him alone, he became more and more irritable, scowling darkly and telling her that she simply had no conception of the workload he carried on his shoulders these days. In the end she gave up trying to force the issue, concluding uneasily that she'd have to wait until a suitable opportunity presented itself.

On Friday afternoon she was called to the phone at the rehearsal studio, and it was Dexter.

"Nina, I want to see you this evening," he said.

Her heart stampeded. But all the misery and tension of the past two weeks came bursting out of her. "Just like that! You crook your finger, and I'm expected to come running."

"Please don't be difficult."

"So I'm being difficult now! I'd have thought that after what happened between us last time, you'd have the common decency to leave me alone." Breathless with anger, she stormed on, "I don't know why you're wasting your valuable time on me. There must be plenty of more amenable females around."

"Agreed! So doesn't it mean anything, Nina, that you're the girl I'm phoning?"

"Am I supposed to be flattered? Bowled over by your gracious condescension? I suppose your plans have gone wrong somewhere, and you find yourself with a free evening on your hands. Well, it won't be me who fills it."

"I know that you're not dancing tonight," he said. "I checked."

"How clever of you. Not that it makes any difference."

"I'll call around at your flat to pick you up," he persisted. "Say about seven-thirty?"

"I won't be in."

"I'll come all the same, in the hope that you'll change your mind."

Zoe Gray from the *corps de ballet* was waiting to use the phone, making impatient faces at her. Nina seized the excuse, and said into the phone, "Listen, Dexter, I've got to go. Someone's waiting."

"Then good-bye for now. See you later on."

She sighed. "You just won't listen to what I say, will you?"

"I'll always listen to you, Nina. Only it isn't easy to discuss things on the phone. We'll go somewhere quiet for a meal this evening, and you can talk to your heart's content."

He had hung up before she could repeat her refusal. Well, it would serve him right when he turned up at the flat and found she wasn't home, she thought rebelliously.

But as the afternoon wore on—Boyd was putting together a new cast of *Les Sylphides*—Nina began to think again. It would be feeble, she mused, to exile herself from her own home, just because Dexter was calling around. And if he didn't see her this evening, he was certain to phone again. Or worse, he might decide to drop in unexpectedly at the rehearsal studios or the theater, and embarrass her in front of the other members of the company.

That evening she was firmly determined not to prepare in any way for Dexter's visit. Then, in an attempt to bolster her wilting confidence, she decided to change into a dress after all. She chose one in orange angora wool, very feminine and flattering to her coloring. Seated before the mirror in the bedroom, she arranged her dark hair in a loose coil and spent some time applying makeup.

Sitting back at last, she took a long appraising look at herself. Suddenly she felt gripped by revulsion at what she was doing. Dexter would think she had deliberately set out to make herself desirable to him. Ashamed, she tore off the dress and mussed up her hair, then started feverishly pulling on the jeans she'd abandoned earlier. At which point the doorbell rang. Trembling violently now, Nina half thought of keeping quiet and hoping that he'd give up and go away. Then, trying to inject some sort of briskness into her voice, she called that she wouldn't be a minute.

When she opened the door, the sight of him made her heart begin to hammer wildly. He looked so devastatingly attractive, immaculate in a light gray suit, white shirt and striped blue tie. She must look dreadful by comparison, in working jeans that were worn and crumpled, a shapeless sweater, and hair that was a mess from being too quickly rearranged.

Dexter's intent gaze swept over her, taking in every detail. Let him look at me, she thought with a flicker of her old defiance, and see how totally unglamorous I really am.

"It's good to see you, Nina," he said softly. Then,

because she still stood foursquare in the doorway, he added, "Aren't I allowed to come in?"

She hesitated a moment, then moved aside, saying ungraciously, "I suppose you might as well."

In the small living room, Dexter glanced around. "Mandy is always saying how much she likes your flat, with these quaintly sloping ceilings. But then, she approves of every single thing about you. You've become quite a heroine to that child."

"Big deal!" Nina said sarcastically. Then, because she felt ashamed to turn her anger at Dexter against his little daughter, she asked quickly, in a gentler voice, "How is Mandy?"

"Getting better, thanks."

"Getting better?" she echoed, concerned at once. "What's been the matter with her?"

"Just a touch of flu. The doctor said there was nothing to worry about."

"Oh, that's good. Well . . . give her my love, and tell her I hope she'll soon be quite well again."

"Right, I'll do that." He looked at her challengingly. "Aren't you going to invite me to sit down? And a cup of coffee wouldn't come amiss."

Nina was tempted to refuse both, but Dexter seemed to have the ability to put her in the wrong. Denying him a simple thing like a cup of coffee would make her look ridiculously petty.

"Oh, very well," she said reluctantly. "I won't be a minute."

When she reemerged from the kitchen with two mugs, he was settled in an armchair leafing through an illustrated book on the principles of classical dance.

"Looking at this," he said thoughtfully, glancing up at her, "makes me realize that although I enjoy watching ballet, my knowledge of it is very limited."

"Even a superman like you can't be expected to know everything," she cracked, and was annoyed because Dexter appeared quite unruffled. "Do you take sugar?" she asked, though she had already noted that he did.

"Two, please." He put the book aside, and took the mug she held out. Sipping it, he regarded her in thoughtful silence until Nina could contain herself no longer.

"You said you wanted to talk to me," she burst out. "So start talking."

"Let's go out for a meal," he suggested.

"Certainly not."

"Nina, we've both got to eat, so why not together? You wouldn't be so uptight in a public restaurant as you are here."

"I am not uptight," she snapped.

"Okay," he said pacifically, "I wasn't trying to get at you. But we've got things to sort out, and I just thought neutral territory would be best."

"I . . . I'm not dressed for going out to dinner. And," she added quickly, anticipating him, "I don't feel like changing."

"Why should you change? You look fine just as you are. In fact, Nina, you look more beautiful to me every time I see you, whatever you're wearing."

She sighed resignedly. "Look, there's a small restaurant around the corner—nothing fancy, but the food isn't bad. We could go there, if you like." It would be safer, she argued to herself, to get him out of the flat as soon as possible. She took just a couple of minutes to put on a clean sweater and brush her hair—but that was more than enough!

They didn't bother with the car, as the restaurant was only a block away. The moment they entered, Nina

77

realized with dismay that she'd made a bad choice. It was an intimate place, each softly lit table set in its own small alcove. But it was too late to change her mind now.

"This is nice," Dexter commented, glancing around as they took their seats. "Do you come here often?"

"On a dancer's salary? You must be joking." She made a quick choice from the menu, hardly interested in what she was going to eat.

"Here's to a new beginning for us," Dexter said a few moments later, smiling at her over the rim of his wineglass.

Nina pointedly put her own glass down, refusing to drink the toast. "The only reason I decided to be home when you called this evening was to make it crystal clear that there's to be nothing more between us."

Dexter's lips quirked as if he thought it was some kind of game they were playing. "Mandy will be disappointed."

"Stop using your daughter as a pawn," Nina flared angrily. "I'm very fond of Mandy, I think she's a delightful child. But that's no reason for me to have any sort of relationship with her father."

"So Mandy has to suffer?"

"I doubt if she'll suffer very much by being deprived of my company," Nina retorted. "That's not to say that I don't feel sorry for her . . . having no mother, I mean. It's tough on any child. But there are a great many children in this world with only one parent, and most of them haven't the material advantages that your daughter has. And what about those handicapped children in the home we did the gala performance for? So you've no right to try and make me feel guilty over Mandy."

Dexter's face sobered. "Fair enough, Nina, I admit

I was cheating by bringing her into it. So I'll pitch on my own behalf. Look, I'm sorry I upset you the other night when we were coming back from sailing—though, to be honest, I still think you overreacted. But can't we just forget that it ever happened and start afresh, as friends?"

For a moment Nina wondered if this disarming new approach was just another tactic designed to break through her resistance. But, meeting the steady, intent gaze of his tawny eyes, she decided that for once Dexter was being sincere.

"Well . . . I hate being on bad terms with anybody," she conceded.

His lean features relaxed into a quick, warm smile. "Now then, what have you been doing with yourself since I last saw you?"

She shrugged. "Working hard. What else?"

"I really admire you, Nina, for the dedication and effort you put into your career."

"Don't you do the same?"

"Certainly. But, unlike you, it's for financial gain, not purely for the sake of excelling in a form of artistic expression." He paused, twirling his stemmed wineglass between his fingertips while he considered. "Maybe that's being too hard on myself. I'm not motivated solely by cash rewards. It pleases me to think that my company's products are just about the best there are, known and respected all over the world."

"Was it you who started Rolfe Industries?" Nina asked interestedly.

"No, I'm third generation. I owe a lot to my father and my grandfather. They paved the way. But they didn't have the advantage of modern technology which has allowed me to expand so rapidly during these past few years. So many developments that we take for granted today were not even dreamed of in their time—things like computers and lasers and micro-chips. It's different with the ballet, though, isn't it? That book I was glancing at in your flat seemed to show that the great classical tradition goes on and on, unchanging through the decades."

"That's not really true," Nina said earnestly. "The classical tradition is very important, of course, and all dancing is based on the seven essential principles . . . stance and balance and coordination and transfer of weight and so on. But ballet is developing all the time. Dancers appear on the scene who defy tradition and explore new techniques, new ways of expression. People like Isadora Duncan and Martha Graham, for instance, who were savagely criticized for being so revolutionary, and are now regarded as visionaries. That's what makes ballet so exciting . . . the blending of the new with the old gives it a marvelous vitality."

Their conversation flowed on and on. Dexter was so open-minded, so ready to listen, Nina discovered, and so stimulating in what he had to say. On the subject of the graphic arts she found that he was far more knowledgeable than she was, despite her interest in costume and stage design.

"Do you do any drawing or painting yourself?" she asked.

He shook his head. "Not me. My sister-in-law, Phyllida, dabbles a bit. I can appreciate many forms of art, but I lack the creative artistic temperament."

"Still, you could say that building a great business empire is a form of creative art."

He flashed her a brilliant smile. "It would be nice to think so, anyway."

Nina was utterly astonished when the waiter hinted, with a discreet cough, that it was closing time. "Heavens above!" she exclaimed, "we've spent the entire evening here."

"I've enjoyed it enormously," Dexter said. "And you?"

Nina felt impelled to admit the truth. "Yes, very much indeed."

Outside the restaurant, the night air was soft and warm against her cheeks. Dexter took her elbow. "There's something I have to tell you," he said. "Can we stroll in the park for a little while?"

Nina hesitated, some of her old qualms returning. Was this evening, after all, going to end like the previous one she'd spent in Dexter's company? Perhaps he could read her thoughts, for he added persuasively, "It's something I should have mentioned earlier on, but somehow I didn't want to spoil things."

"What is it?" she asked, as they turned in among the trees.

"I'm afraid I have to go away for a couple of months, Nina."

"Go away?" she gasped, with a cold feeling of dismay. "When?"

"Tomorrow. I'm taking my senior sales team on an extended tour of the Far East," he explained. "I doubt if I'll be back before you go to Nice for the summer season."

"Oh, Dexter." It was a devastating blow, and she was past the stage of pretending with him.

"I wish now that I hadn't arranged this trip, but too many people are involved to cancel it. Even if I can't manage to get back and see you before you leave London, I'll definitely be coming to Nice for part of the time you're there."

The thought of not seeing him again for so long was unbearable. Eight weeks or so seemed like an eternity.

"I shall miss you," she said, making a big effort to keep it casual. But Dexter must have heard and understood the catch in her voice.

"You'll see, the time will quickly pass," he said softly, and slid his arms around her, drawing her close.

His kiss was long and sweet and achingly beautiful. As his hands slid down her back and across her waist, Nina clung to him in wild delight, matching his kindling passion. All her senses were tinglingly alive, and her lips parted eagerly to welcome the erotic inner kisses of his tongue.

"Oh, Nina, you're so lovely," Dexter whispered huskily, when he drew back at last. "I want you so much."

Held like this in his arms, molded against his long lean body, she could feel his pulsing desire and her blood seemed to be on fire with her own feverish longing. It would be so easy, so desperately easy, to abandon herself to the ecstasy of his lovemaking.

But another part of her was clamoring to be heard. If she were to give herself to Dexter now it would somehow spoil the loveliness of this evening, the exciting discovery of the unique meeting of their minds. Never before had she felt so marvelously in tune with another human being—not even with Boyd—when they were at their closest, dancing together. It was something she wanted to savor slowly.

In a sudden decision, she pulled back from his arms. "I . . . I must go home now," she said, and added on an urgent note, "Please, Dexter . . ."

He hesitated, and in those long moments she wondered if he would reproach her . . . storm at her again, perhaps. But when he spoke, his voice was calm and reassuring. "Come along, then. I'll walk you home."

Arms entwined, they made their way through the night quiet streets. When they reached the house

Dexter paused a moment, then he swiftly kissed her on the lips, tenderly, his passion restrained.

"Good night, Nina," he whispered softly. "You haven't seen the last of me, I promise."

"You've got visitors," announced Meg Fraser, the assistant stage manager, putting her head around the door of Nina's dressing room.

"Who are they?" asked Nina, who was peeling off the colored tights she'd worn in the matinée performance of *Coppélia*, which had just ended.

"It's a small girl named Mandy, who says she knows you," said Meg, "and there's a woman with her. Okay if I tell them to come in?"

Nina happened to be alone as neither Cheryl nor Lisbet, who shared the dressing room with her, were dancing this afternoon. Reaching for her jeans, she said, "Oh yes, sure. Just give me a couple of minutes to get dressed."

Nina wondered who the woman might be. Not Phyllida Hooper, Mandy's aunt, because Meg would have recognized her. It turned out to be Dexter's London housekeeper, Mrs. MacDonald.

"I do hope we are not being a nuisance to you, Miss Selby," she began apologetically as they came in. "But Mandy insisted that we must come around to see you before we left."

Nina smiled in welcome. "I'm glad you did, Mrs. MacDonald. Hello, Mandy. Did you enjoy the performance?"

"You bet! It was wonderful, Nina."

"Yes, indeed," concurred the housekeeper. "I've never seen a ballet before, and I thought it was just lovely."

"When you were dancing on your points," Mandy burst out excitedly, "I was holding my breath for you. I thought you couldn't possibly go on and on without stumbling."

"I have my partner to thank for that," Nina said, with a dismissive shrug. "Robin is very good. I rely on him to hold me firmly and see that I don't fall." She removed a costume from the back of a chair so that Mrs. MacDonald could sit down. "Are you staying in London, Mandy?"

She nodded. "Aunt Phyllida had to go to Paris, and I said I'd rather stay in London than at Haslemere Hall over the half-term holiday from school." She gave Nina a shyly reproachful look. "You promised that you'd come and see me again, but you didn't."

"I'm sorry, Mandy, but I've been rather busy . . . with various things."

It was a feeble excuse, but Nina didn't know what else to say. Four weeks had passed since her last meeting with Dexter, four long, dragging weeks for her. Away from him, away from his dynamic magnetism, she was able to view things a little more objectively. She kept asking herself what she imagined their relationship was all about, where she supposed it could possibly lead other than the obvious place—bed. She kept sifting through their various conversations, dissecting them word by word, searching for a sign that Dexter's intention was something more than a brief affair. Why, she asked herself, had he pursued her with such persistence when so many other women were only too eager to fall into his arms? Probably, though, to a man so devastatingly attractive as he was, any woman who rejected his advances represented a challenge.

It had been a clever move in Dexter's seduction strategy to seek her out that last evening before his departure to the Far East. Otherwise, she might have got over him completely by now. As it was, he dominated her thoughts entirely, and she yearned with a desperate longing to see him again. It was merely an infatuation, of course; she refused even to consider the possibility that she was seriously in love with him. Such a thing was unthinkable, ridiculous. Even though she knew now that she could never marry Boyd, it would be the height of folly to let herself start building dreams about any kind of future with a man like Dexter Rolfe. If she had any sense at all, she would forget about him, thrust him out of her thoughts.

But . . . oh, it was so difficult. Dexter's name was always being mentioned by someone or other in the company, and now, to remind her afresh, this visit from his daughter.

"I expect, Mandy," she said brightly, "that we shall see lots of one another when we're in France. I believe you're going to be staying at the Villa Mimosa with your aunt?"

"But that's weeks and weeks away," the girl protested.

"Only three-and-a-half weeks now," Nina pointed out. "The time will pass soon." But for herself, she thought ruefully, those three-and-a-half weeks would be unending.

"When Daddy phoned last night from Japan," Mandy went on, "he said why don't I invite you down to Haslemere Hall for a weekend. Will you come, Nina?"

"No!" The instinctive protest came out too sharply, from a sudden feeling of panic, and she tried to soften her refusal. "I . . . I'm afraid I shall be too busy, Mandy."

Mrs. MacDonald came to Nina's rescue, giving her an understanding glance. "What with all the dancing and practicing Miss Selby has to do, Mandy love, I don't expect she gets much spare time. And if she does have a weekend free, she'd want to spend it with her friends."

"But I'm one of her friends," Mandy objected.

"I meant grown-up friends," the woman explained patiently.

Poor Mandy looked so dejected, that Nina felt guilty. "As it happens," she said, "I'll be free for a few hours tomorrow afternoon. So if you're still in London, Mandy, perhaps . . . ?"

"Ooh, yes," she exclaimed, happy again at once.

"Would you like to come to the apartment for tea, Miss Selby?" invited Mrs. MacDonald.

"Please say you will," cried Mandy, jumping up and down. "Please say yes, Nina."

"Well then . . . yes, I'd like to come. Thank you."

The tea spread was delicious, and of a kind which betrayed the housekeeper's Scottish background. Well-buttered scones and rich shortcake. Nina ate very sparingly, mindful of that evening's performance at the theater. Mrs. MacDonald, it emerged, had a niece who was in a dance troupe which often appeared on TV and consequently she had a special interest in dancing herself.

"Mandy keeps on and on about being a ballerina when she grows up," she said, pouring tea. "I try to tell her that it's not easy, and that only a few of the very best dancers ever get anywhere."

"It's early yet," Nina said with a smile. "But keenness helps a lot. I was just like Mandy. Ever since I was a small girl, it was my one ambition to dance in ballet."

"There, you see!" said Mandy triumphantly, as if Nina's success answered every possible objection. Nina thought it necessary to add a warning note. "All the same, a dancer—any kind of dancer—has to work very hard indeed if she ever hopes to succeed. Years and years of real hard work, Mandy."

"I don't care how hard I have to work," she insisted.

"Let's try a little experiment, shall we?" Nina suggested on an impulse. "Come and stand here in front of me, Mandy. Now, I don't want you to strain in the least, but just stand with your heels together and with your toes turned out as far as they'll comfortably go."

"You mean in first position? Like this?"

Nina smiled. "That's right, in first position. And do you know what a *plié* is, Mandy?"

At once the girl bent her knees slowly, keeping her feet in the same position, with the heels lifting off the floor. She added a graceful arm movement to accompany the *plié*.

"That's really lovely," Nina said sincerely. "You're a lucky girl, you know. You naturally have what's called a good 'turnout,' which depends on the way your hip joints move in their sockets. And it's absolutely essential if you want to be a ballet dancer. But you *will* remember what I told you before, won't you? Never on any account try to go up on point until you're much older, or you'll damage your toes."

"No, Nina, I promise I won't," Mandy said earnestly. "I haven't, honestly, since you said."

"Good girl."

When they'd finished eating, Mrs. MacDonald wheeled the tea things out to the kitchen. While Nina was chatting to Mandy the telephone rang, and it turned out to be Phyllida Hooper, calling from Paris. Not wanting to appear to eavesdrop, Nina wandered out to the lobby. There, driven by an impulse she couldn't restrain, she opened the door of Dexter's bedroom and stepped inside. Crossing to where the Degas painting hung, she stood looking thoughtfully at the woman it portrayed . . . the likeness, Mandy had said, of her mother at the time Dexter Rolfe had fallen in love with her. Judith.

At that moment she heard the phone being replaced, and quickly left the bedroom, meeting Mandy in the lobby.

"Oh, Nina, I'm sorry. But Aunt Phyllida just kept talking and talking. She wanted to know all about everything and was I being good. Honestly, you'd think I was just a baby."

"Well, you are quite young, Mandy, and it's only natural that your aunt is concerned about you."

Mandy shrugged. "Mostly she doesn't take much notice of me. I told her that you were here, Nina," she added artlessly.

"Oh, what did she say about it?"

"She didn't seem very pleased. She can be really horrid sometimes."

Making no comment on that, Nina glanced at her wristwatch. "Mandy, I'd better be going now."

"Oh, must you?"

"I'm afraid so." She could have stayed for another half hour, but somehow she wanted to get away. It had been a mistake to come, and an even bigger mistake to succumb to temptation and go into Dexter's bedroom. Here, in his home, he became even more vividly alive in her mind.

The Regency Ballet's season in London came to an end in a blaze of glory. Sonia Lamartine seemed to be at the crest of her career, and her performance in the company's new version of *Sleeping Beauty* was acclaimed by the media as one of the most outstanding in the history of ballet. Nina was awed and even a little bit scared to think that it was to these dizzy heights of public adulation that she herself aspired.

Though there were now no performances to worry

about, the dancers were still kept busy. Apart from the daily routine classes and rehearsals, a TV company was making an hour-long documentary of a ballet company backstage, giving an inside view of all the hard work and dedication that goes into producing the glittering performances seen by the public on stage.

With Robin as her partner, Nina danced the Black Swan *pas de deux* before the cameras, and afterward they were interviewed. "I suppose," the friendly, fair-haired young woman began, "that when a couple have to work together as closely as you two, there must be a special kind of rapport between them?"

"It helps if you like one another," Robin agreed with a grin. "And luckily Nina and I do—a lot. But don't give the viewers the impression that it goes any further than that, or I'll be in dead trouble with my girl friend, Jilly. And Nina with her boy friend, Boyd Maxwell," he added, to Nina's dismay.

The interviewer laughed. "So a close professional relationship doesn't automatically lead to a romantic one?"

"It can," said Robin seriously. "Like Nina and Boyd. They used to be partners until Boyd gave up dancing last season to become the company's Assistant Director and choreographer."

"And you and Boyd Maxwell are still together, Nina? Splitting the dancing partnership didn't end your romantic partnership?"

This line of questioning was making Nina feel acutely embarrassed. How could she announce publicly that she and Boyd were no longer romantically involved, when she hadn't yet told Boyd himself of her change of feelings? Flushing, she said ambiguously, "Boyd and I are still very close, but there's nothing binding about our relationship."

Any possible chance she had of talking to Boyd

vanished when, a full week before the rest of the company, he and the administrator traveled to Nice. This was to check out the arrangements at the large villa Dexter had rented, so that daily classes and rehearsals could go on without interruption. With a week's holiday ahead, Nina gladly accepted Cheryl's invitation to join her in a last trip to her parents' home to see her young son.

"I wish I could take him to Nice with us," Cheryl said gloomily. "Poor Jeremy doesn't see all that much of me, and it will mean we'll be apart for nearly two whole months."

"I know how you feel," Nina said sympathetically. "But at least you don't have to worry about him being well looked after, Cheryl. Your parents are lovely people, and they have a marvelous way with kids. I should know! I'll always be grateful for the way they welcomed me into your home during vacations from ballet school, just because I was your friend."

The two girls took Jeremy out. One day they swam at a big open-air lido, and then had lunch in the cafeteria, Jeremy choosing hamburgers, with chips and baked beans, plus a glass of fizzy lemonade.

"This is scrumptious," he declared. "Granny always makes me eat lots of salads and veg'tables."

"Quite right, too," said Cheryl fondly, "or you'll never grow up big and strong. This is just a special treat."

"I like special treats," he said, beaming a gap-toothed smile. "Can I have treacle tart and custard for dessert?"

Allowing for the difference in age and sex, Nina thought, he was very much like Mandy Rolfe—an attractive, friendly child, and easy to talk to. Jeremy didn't seem in the least deprived because neither his mother nor his grandparents were blessed with much money. Conversely, she realized, Mandy wasn't in the least bit spoiled, even though she was the daughter of a wealthy man.

Nina and Cheryl returned to London on Sunday night. Next day there would be a hectic rush of getting packed and ready, and the flat left tidy. First thing Tuesday morning they were to meet the bus which was to take them to London airport. And five hours later they would be in Nice. What, Nina wondered with a little inward shiver, did those long-awaited weeks in France hold in store for her?

Chapter Five

*N*ina was walking alone in the terraced gardens of the Villa Mimosa. There was a special kind of tranquil beauty to be found here early in the morning, everything bathed in the Mediterranean sunshine, the air softly fresh and fragrant with the scent of countless flowers. She felt a need these days for her own company, which was something quite new to her.

Pausing by a graceful tree, whose long spikes of speckled pink blossoms were swaying gently in the breeze, she gazed back at the villa. It could be more aptly described as a palace—a pink and white extravaganza with a stone-balustraded roof and a hundred glittering windows. The Regency Ballet Company had been in residence for a week now, a week of grueling rehearsals, with one or two evenings spent in Nice as a relaxation, plus a preliminary inspection of the theater at which they would be opening for their short season in just under a fortnight's time.

Wandering on again past the marble-flanked swimming pool, she walked beneath a pergola of climbing roses, passed through an arched gateway in a jasmine-clad wall, then descended a shallow-stepped pathway that zigzagged down the steeply sloping hillside. She came to a pretty trellised belvedere, a viewing platform cut into the solid rock, that was overhung with purple bougainvillea. For long minutes she stood looking out across the tumble of craggy rocks and windswept trees to the glinting, sapphire expanse of sea. Somewhere on a nearby branch, an unseen bird shrilled its pure sweet song.

A scrunching sound of footsteps on the pathway above her made her frown in annoyance. She kept very still, hoping that whoever it was wouldn't spot her and want to chat. Then a voice called her name, and she swung around quickly.

"Dexter!"

His tall, striding figure loomed above her on the path, seeming to overwhelm her emotions. He looked even more devastatingly attractive than Nina remembered, and she felt suddenly breathless, her heart thudding wildly. He wore no shirt and his lean-cut white linen slacks accentuated the deep bronze of his naked chest and bare arms. A green towel was slung carelessly over one shoulder.

"I didn't know that you were here," she said, deliberately making her voice a little cool and aloof. "When did you arrive?"

As he descended the last few steps and stood beside her, Nina felt swamped by his nearness. She caught the faint musky odor that was uniquely Dexter and her senses whirled, making her dizzy with longing to be held in his arms.

"I flew in late last night," he told her. "I came straight from Tokyo, via Paris. I didn't bother returning to England. I was anxious to get here as soon as possible."

To see her, did he mean? Instead Nina asked matter-of-factly, "Has Mandy arrived, too?"

"Not yet. She and her aunt will be here tomorrow. It doesn't suit Phyllida's plans to come right away."

His tawny gaze, steady upon her face, held a question. Ignoring it, Nina turned and looked out across the sea again, her hands resting on the stone balustrade to stop them from shaking.

"Did you have a good trip to the Far East?" she inquired, frantically making conversation

"Excellent, from a business point of view. But I was glad when it came to an end."

"I'd have thought you liked traveling . . . going to all those interesting countries."

"I do, usually. Not this time, though."

Again Nina had to resist the urge to pin him down, to ask if it were really she who had brought him hurrying to the Villa Mimosa. In a strained, husky voice, she said, "I don't blame you for wanting to get here, Dexter. Everything is so lovely."

"Yes," he agreed softly. "Very lovely." And though she didn't dare to glance at him she could sense that Dexter was looking at her, not the surrounding scenery. After a moment he added in his richly timbrous voice, "It's wonderful to see you again, Nina. I've missed you. I was wondering how I was going to catch you on your own this morning, and I could hardly believe my luck when I came out for an early swim and spotted you standing here."

"I must go back in a minute," she said nervously. "They'll be starting breakfast soon."

"Must you? I was hoping that I might persuade you to join me for a dip. I remember, from when I came to view the villa, that there's another pool down these steps which is much more secluded. It's a natural, spring-fed rock pool, and an ideal spot for private swimming."

"No, I couldn't possibly," Nina told him firmly. "Anyway, I've no swimsuit with me."

"As if that would matter," Dexter said with a soft laugh. "The operative word, Nina, is 'secluded.' Never mind, perhaps tomorrow morning?" Seeing the start of a flush on her cheeks, he added dryly, "Both of us equipped with swimsuits."

"Oh, but I'm not sure that . . ."

"Yes," he said insistently. Laying his two hands on her shoulders he turned Nina to face him and gave her a long, compelling look. With the tip of his forefinger he gently traced down the curving line of her cheek and throat. Next moment he was striding on down the steps, calling back over his shoulder, "Don't forget, be here tomorrow—nice and early."

For long minutes Nina remained where she was on the belvedere, trying to get herself together. The imprint of Dexter's fingertip touch burned her skin and she was trembling in every limb. She had been expecting a passionate embrace from him and had steeled herself to resist it. But this tender little gesture had caught her off guard.

Perhaps, the thought stole into her mind as the sound of his footsteps died away, it had been Dexter's deliberate intention to unnerve her. A ploy in his campaign of seduction to weaken her defenses against him. Why wouldn't he leave her alone? She sighed wretchedly. But her thudding heart responded with a different plea.

In the absence of Sonia Lamartine, the company's prima ballerina, Nina, Cheryl, Lisbet and Elli between them were taking all the major roles in the Regency Ballet's repertoire. But the main attraction during the season at Nice was undoubtedly Boyd Maxwell's new ballet, *Summer Rhapsody,* featuring Nina Selby. As Boyd had said, it was a glorious opportunity for her to establish her position as heir apparent to the great Lamartine. It was a thrilling prospect, but a scary one, too—coming at a time when she found it difficult to give her unwavering attention to the demands of dancing.

The fact that she hadn't yet found an opportunity to talk to Boyd about her changed feelings toward him still weighed heavily on her conscience, but they never seemed to get a moment alone together these days. Boyd was always so hectically busy, and as the opening night drew nearer his volatile temper seemed on a dangerously short fuse. She found it easy to convince herself that this wasn't a good time to force the issue of something so important

Nina was painfully aware that her dancing at the daily rehearsals, though it might appear satisfactory to the layman, lacked the extra sparkle which could establish her in the "great" category. As a result, Boyd was constantly finding fault with her.

"For heaven's sake, Nina," he cried exasperatedly, "you're just not trying. Don't you realize how completely vital it is for you to shine in this role? I'm counting on you."

"I'm sorry, Boyd," she said miserably. "But don't worry, it will come right in the end."

He glared at her. "You talk as if there's all the time in the world. We open in just under a fortnight, Nina. Now come on, you and Robin had better go through the *adagio* again." Impatiently, he signaled the pianist to start.

Nina began to feel desperate. She was putting in every spare minute she could manage, running through the role and practicing the more difficult steps again and again, persuading Robin to join her for the *pas de deux* sequences. She knew, guiltily, that he would have preferred to spend his spare time with Jilly, but he was very patient and acquiesced without grumbling.

Dexter's arrival, far from making the situation better, had left her even more on edge. He was around a lot of the time that first day, generally making himself pleasant to everyone, watching rehearsals for a while, sitting with Sir Hugo for luncheon and dinner. Nina did her best to steer clear of him, afraid she might give away the fact that a special sort of relationship existed between them.

She agonized long and hard over whether to keep the date he'd insisted on making for the next morning. But when she awoke at daybreak she realized that she'd never had any doubt in her mind. The temptation was too strong to resist. She rose stealthily, not to waken Cheryl, donning her yellow bikini under jeans and tee shirt, and picking up a towel. She strolled slowly, as if casually, in case anyone should observe her from a window; then, once out of sight of the villa, she hastened through the arched gateway and down to the little belvedere.

It was a bitter disappointment to find Dexter not there. Had he forgotten, or never really meant it seriously? Either way, she'd made a dreadful fool of herself to have hurried here with such eagerness. Dispiritedly, she turned and began to make her way back. But Dexter's voice checked her.

"Hang on, Nina," he called. "Don't be so impatient. I'm just coming."

Peering over the balustrade of the belvedere, she saw him climbing a small path to her right. Next moment he had reached her, looking so incredibly attractive that her heart nearly stopped beating. "I was beginning to think you weren't coming," he said reproachfully. "I was just scouting around in case you'd gone the wrong way."

"Oh, I see."

Taking her hand, Dexter led her back the way he had come. "It gets a bit more overgrown lower down," he warned. "Nobody ever seems to come this way, which makes it very private. Here, careful of that branch—just duck your head. Now, a few more steps and through this creeper, and there it is!" He stopped, pointing dramatically. Nina caught her breath in delight.

"Oh, how pretty!"

The little rock pool lay cupped in a cleft on the cliff face, its limpid water sparkling where fans of sunlight struck through the interlacing branches of an acacia tree. Small birds flitted and twittered all around, and there was a heavenly scent of lavender and rosemary.

"Come on in and try it," Dexter said, kicking off his espadrilles. "I'm sure you'll find it warm enough for you. I thought so when I swam here yesterday."

Wasting no time, he peeled off his tan-colored jeans and stood before her in very brief swim trunks that were a dark navy blue against the golden bronze of his skin. It was all Nina could do not to stare at the sight of him looking so magnificently virile. Fortunately, Dexter didn't seem to notice her dazed reaction. Turning away, he at once plunged into the deep water, swimming below the surface.

Quickly, while he wasn't watching, Nina took the chance to throw off her own jeans and tee shirt. In her haste to reach the concealment of the water, she misjudged her dive and made a mighty splash. When she surfaced, Dexter was beside her, grinning sympathetically. He put his hands under her arms, as if helping to buoy her up, and his touch made her catch her breath.

"How's the temperature for you?" he asked.

"Lovely, just cool enough to be exhilarating." But the thudding of her heartbeat, which she felt sure he must feel, was not caused by the stimulating freshness of the water. She twisted away from his hold, making it seem like a game by splashing handfuls of water at him.

Nina was an excellent swimmer, despite her clumsy dive. She'd always found swimming a marvelous activity for general toning-up. Here, in the sparkling clarity of this spring-fed rock pool, she found it fascinating to dive down and study the clean pebbles and shells that formed a colorful mosaic on the bottom, sending reflections of sunlight shimmering magically through the water. Several times Dexter caught hold of her as they swam close, and always she succeeded in playing it lightly, splashing him or pushing his head down. Once when Nina was swimming underwater, he suddenly appeared just beneath her, face upward, and caught her prisoner in his arms. The sudden surge of longing that swept through her was electric, terrifying, and she struggled wildly until he released her. Surfacing, she gulped a breath and swam to the bank, levering herself out of the water. Choosing a grassy patch, she sat down and hid her confusion by vigorously toweling her long dark hair.

A few moments later Dexter too climbed out. He regarded her quizzically, but made no comment about her swift, panicky retreat from the pool. He lay stretched out on his back beside her, his hands linked behind his head. Surreptitiously, as she continued toweling her hair, Nina let herself study his superb physique, noting the muscled contours of his shoulders and chest, tapering to a narrow waist and slim hips. The briefly cut swim trunks revealed the taut flatness of his abdomen, the length of his powerful legs.

Dexter's observance of her was less secretive. His

tawny eyes sparked in unconcealed admiration as they slid over her shapely curves, lingering at the soft swell of her breasts.

"Can you be free any time during the day?" he inquired. "I'd like to drive you somewhere along the coast."

Nina shook her head. "No, I'll be tied up the whole time."

"This evening, then. We'll go somewhere for dinner."

"No, Dexter," she said decidedly. "I can't come out with you, not at all."

"For heaven's sake, why not? I know you're busy rehearsing, but you've got to relax sometimes."

"I . . . I don't want everybody talking about us," she faltered. "Gossiping about us." This was true, but even more she dreaded the thought of a confrontation with a furiously jealous Boyd.

Dexter's hand flashed out and caught her wrist in a sudden harsh grip. "Don't play games with me, Nina. I won't stand for it."

"I'm not playing games," she protested.

His eyes blazed into hers. "Are you saying that you'd be content to continue this way, just meeting me secretly for a swim in the mornings, and otherwise only seeing me in the company of other people . . . pretending that we hardly know one another? Because I wouldn't! If that's all you're willing to offer me, I may just as well clear right out of here."

"No," she protested, dismayed at the possibility that he might quit the Villa Mimosa. She glanced away from him, aware that her whole body was flaming with heightened color. "You . . . you can't leave," she faltered. "Mandy is due here today, with your sister-in-law. You couldn't walk out on her."

"It wouldn't be necessary," he stated calmly. "I'd suggest that Mandy and Phyllida come with me, to Monte Carlo or wherever. But it won't happen, Nina, because we're discussing a hypothetical situation. You and I would be fooling ourselves, fooling one another, if we pretended that we could part now. Maybe I'm at fault for having been too patient with you. Well, if so . . . not anymore!"

Before his intention could register in her brain, Dexter sat up and swung around to catch hold of her by the shoulders, his weight pressing her backward onto the sun-warmed, grassy bank. Nina was overwhelmed by the passion with which he kissed her, his mouth fastening on hers with a possessive demand that permitted no refusal. As the tip of his tongue parted her lips and thrust between them to make delicious circles inside her mouth, she felt a glorious exhilaration. Their swimsuits were so scanty that it was almost as if they were both naked. She felt the tautly muscled hardness of his chest crushing against her breasts, and she was gripped by a wild, flaring excitement. His lips began a sensuous journey, moving caressingly across her face, trailing tingling kisses around her jawline and down the smooth satin skin of her throat and neck. Then, tugging aside the fabric of her bikini, he released one breast and his mouth closed over its rosy peak, teasing it to a sharp pinnacle of longing and making her moan aloud in ecstasy. Involuntarily, her arms wrapped around him, her fingers raking his broad back with jerky, convulsive movements, then rising up still further to clasp about his neck and twist into the hair at his nape.

Dexter's hands now roamed her body freely, hungrily, sliding down her back and over her waist, following the soft curves, seeking out exquisitely sensitive spots. She felt the rapid pulse of his heartbeat thudding against her own. With deep, shuddering breaths, he muttered hoarsely, "My beautiful Nina, you're so utterly desirable. It will be wonderful, I promise you."

"No," she cried, alarmed. "You . . . you mustn't."

"Yes," he said huskily. "Of course I must. It's been too long, waiting for this moment, but now at last . . ." His fingers began to tug at the other half of her bikini, and as Nina felt it begin to slide away she jerked upright and forcibly pushed him back.

"I said no!"

"You can't mean that, Nina," he protested. "It will be so incredibly good between us. Just let me show you."

"Leave me alone," she burst out hotly. "I've given you no reason to think that I'd agree to let you . . ."

His tawny eyes, so near her own, smoldered with smoky fire. "You've given me every reason, you little witch. You've been saying yes in every way a woman can say yes, except in actual words . . . with your eyes, your hands, your soft lips, your glorious body. Can you deny that you have responded to me eagerly and passionately?"

His ardent gaze was upon her, devouring her, and Nina felt suddenly ashamed to realize that her bikini bra was still pulled aside, exposing one breast. She adjusted it quickly, but she still felt naked under the look of raw desire in his eyes. Hastily, unsteadily, she scrambled to her feet and dragged on her jeans and tee shirt. Dexter made no attempt to prevent her, though he watched her relentlessly.

"You haven't answered my question, Nina."

"It doesn't deserve an answer," she retorted.

"You mean because it would pain you to admit the truth?" he inquired ironically. "You want me, just as I want you. Yet you hold back. Why, for heaven's sake? Surely you aren't a silly little prude who would deny her own magnificent womanhood? You are a talented and intelligent young woman who can delight thousands of spectators by the skillful movements of your beautiful, sensuous body. So why not delight one man in a more intimate way? An activity at which, I'm certain, you would be just as skillful." His voice had by now adopted a hateful, lazy drawl. As if, Nina thought desolately, his words were meant to hurt and wound her as a punishment for refusing him what he wanted.

Stung, she threw at him, "Very well, Dexter, I'll answer your question. I feel ashamed that I responded to you just now. Ashamed, because I allowed myself to be sexually aroused by such a cynical man."

"Don't tell me," he said sarcastically, "that you permit yourself to be carried away by the romantic idealism of the ballets you perform? Do you see yourself living out the role of the sleeping Princess Aurora awaiting the chaste kiss of Prince Florimund? Or as Odette in *Swan Lake* with her Prince Siegfried?"

Nina stood looking down at him in brimming misery, seeing his lithe, superbly virile body stretched lazily on the grassy bank. Her voice, when she finally summoned it again, was almost inarticulate.

"Please, Dexter, let me go."

"I'm not preventing you walking away," he pointed out grittily.

"But I meant . . . leave me alone, don't keep forcing yourself on me."

"You call it forcing?" he scoffed. "Each time we've been together, you've come of your own free will. This morning you've displayed yourself to me in a very sexy bikini, knowing that it would drive me crazy with desire for you."

"I didn't," she cried. "I mean, not with that intention. You persuaded me into coming here to swim with you, though it was against my better judgment.

But . . . well, I was beginning to think that you had accepted the fact that we can't be more than just friends. I couldn't ever let myself indulge in the casual sort of affair that you seem to take for granted. Never!"

"The lady protests too much, methinks," he said dryly.

"Why are you so utterly hateful?" Nina demanded despairingly.

"I prefer to see myself as being honest," he returned. "I don't deliberately fool myself by donning rose-tinted spectacles whenever I take a look at life."

"Honest, you call it? I'd have thought deceitful was a more apt word."

"When have I been deceitful, Nina? When have I lied to you?"

"Perhaps you haven't actually lied to me," she conceded. "But you can't pretend that a life spent chasing one woman after another is honest and sincere. How many women have you taken up with, then just dropped when you've got what you wanted from them? What about when you were married, did you sleep around even then? Did you cheat on your wife? That wouldn't surprise me in the least. Nothing disreputable about you would surprise me."

Dexter sprang to his feet and stood towering above her menacingly, the sun sheening on the skin of his muscled torso. His face was dark with fury. Nina shrank back, half-afraid that he would strike her in his molten anger.

"Damn you, Nina!" he grated. "Damn you to hell!"

"I . . . I'm sorry," she faltered. "I shouldn't have said that. I didn't really mean it."

"Yes, you did. You meant every spiteful word." He bent to retrieve his jeans and snatched up his towel. Then, without as much as another glance at her, he turned and strode away up the path in the direction of the villa.

"Where on earth have you been, Nina?" asked Cheryl, breaking off from doing warm-up *pliés* with some of the other girls at one of the portable *barres* which had been brought out onto the terrace. "You didn't turn up at breakfast, and Boyd has been yelling for you ever since. He's really blowing his top. Didn't you remember that we were making an extra early start this morning, so we could finish early this afternoon?"

"Oh heavens, I completely forgot!" exclaimed Nina in dismay, and ran off upstairs to scramble into practice gear and bind up her long hair. Returning downstairs, she found that Boyd had already started teaching morning class in the villa's elegant, chandeliered ballroom.

"What the hell did you think you were up to, disappearing like that?" he demanded, swinging around on her angrily.

"I . . . I'm sorry, Boyd. I just wasn't aware of the time, I'm afraid."

"What was so important that it took your mind off dancing?" he asked with a glare. Thankfully, he didn't wait for an answer. "Oh well, now you're here we can all get down to some serious work." He clapped his hands in the air to get everybody's attention. "Now, I want some nice *grands battements*—toes pointed and knees straight, and don't forget to breathe."

For the next hour and a half they were all kept hard at work in class. Slowly, the professional in Nina took over, and she was almost able to drive Dexter out of her thoughts. But the instant they broke off for refreshments, the shaming memory of the scene by the pool came rushing back. As she headed with the others toward the coffee and cold drinks table set up in an anteroom, Boyd drew her to one side.

"Just what is going on, Nina?" he asked roughly.

An icy feeling shivered down her spine. "I . . . I don't know what you mean."

"I mean," he said grimly, "that your whole attitude seems to have changed lately. I find it hard to get any sort of response from you."

"That's hardly surprising," she retorted, with a catch of breath. "I've told you again and again, Boyd, I want to talk to you . . . about our whole relationship."

"I'm talking about *work*," he snapped. "Your dancing is way below the standard you're capable of, and I want to know what's up."

Nina sighed, feeling helpless. "It's just a temporary phase," she mumbled. "I'll snap out of it soon."

"You'd better, or this tour is going to be a disaster. Understand? Now, let's grab ourselves some coffee so we can get back to work."

Nina caught his arm. "Please, Boyd . . . I guess I need a break from all this concentrated rehearsing. You too. It's such ages since we've had a date together. How about us going into Nice for dinner tonight? My treat."

He frowned blackly. "For God's sake, Nina, don't push me. I'm too darned busy for that sort of thing."

Later, having changed for lunch, Nina was descending the grand staircase with Cheryl when a small flying figure charged at her.

"Nina, Nina, I've been looking everywhere for you."

"Hello, Mandy." She bent and hugged the eager little girl. "Have you just arrived?"

"Yes. Daddy fetched Aunt Phyllida and me from the airport. We only got here a little while ago." Bright-eyed, she glanced around. "Isn't this a super place?"

"Isn't it just!" Nina wondered anxiously how she was

going to avoid Dexter, when his daughter would be seeking her company at every opportunity. "This is my friend Cheryl," she introduced.

"Hi, Mandy," said Cheryl. "I gather that you want to be a ballet dancer one day."

"You bet! More than anything in the world."

Cheryl laughed. "Well, you've come to the right place to see what goes on behind the scenes."

They chatted for a few minutes until a distinctly irate Phyllida Hooper appeared and took Mandy away, barely even acknowledging Nina and Cheryl.

"You and that child seem to be very close," Cheryl observed, when they were seated at a white table on the terrace with their lunches of salad and yogurt.

Nina didn't try to deny it. "That's because Mandy is so starry-eyed about everything to do with ballet."

"Hm!" A thoughtful silence. "Where did you disappear to this morning? You were gone for ages. And yesterday morning, too."

Nina gave a careless shrug. "You know I like to go walking, and this morning I had a swim."

She hated being evasive with Cheryl, but she knew that if she admitted the truth her friend would castigate her for being so stupid as to get involved with a man liked Dexter Rolfe. As if she didn't already know that for herself! In any case, it would only complicate matters, since it was all over now between the two of them. The belvedere and the rock pool had become strictly off limits to her. And going for lonely walks in the beautiful garden of the villa was out, too. She would be careful to stay in the company of other people, for safety—though it was extremely doubtful if Dexter would want anything more to do with her now.

In fact, Cheryl was in no mood to follow through with her suspicious questions. A worried look in her amber eyes, she said, "There was a letter from Mum in the midday mail. She says that Jeremy is a bit poorly."

"Oh dear, what is it?"

"They don't really know. A couple of times over the last few months, apparently, he's been brought home from nursery school, so this time she thought she'd better get the doctor. He's advised her to keep him home for a few days."

"Too bad, he's normally such a lively little boy. Will you be telephoning him, Cheryl?" When she nodded, Nina went on, "Be sure to give him lots of love from me, won't you?" On an impulse, she added, "Look, since rehearsals are finishing early this afternoon, why don't we go into Nice and each buy Jeremy a little present to cheer him up? Something typically French that he wouldn't be able to get back home."

Cheryl brightened. "That's a nice thought, Nina."

"Maybe we could stay and have a meal out?"

"I suppose so—as long as it's somewhere cheap. Okay?" Cheryl grinned ruefully. "Don't forget I've got a small son to support, and on a dancer's salary it's really scary. You'd never believe how quickly Jeremy grows out of things these days."

Nina regarded her friend sympathetically. "I can imagine! But you do make life harder for yourself than it need be by never going out and having any fun. I mean, it's obvious to everyone that Alan is in love with you, yet you always give him the cold shoulder when he tries to date you."

"Oh, Alan!" said Cheryl scornfully.

"What's wrong with poor Alan, for heaven's sake? You make a lovely pair when you dance together, so why not try it offstage, too?"

Cheryl gave a deep sigh. "I suppose I can't expect you to understand, Nina. But when you've had my experience . . . getting pregnant like that, and then being abandoned by the man—well, it really turns you off the whole male sex."

"That was a long time ago," Nina said gently. "You can't go on taking that sort of attitude forever just because of one bad experience. So isn't it time you gave Alan—or somebody else—a chance?"

Cheryl shrugged her slim shoulders. "Don't push me, Nina. Let me get around to it in my own good time, right?"

Mandy crept into the ballroom rehearsal studio that afternoon and sat in one corner, keeping as quiet as a mouse. For once, Nina thought, she was living up to the nickname Dexter had given her. Afterward, though, the little girl pounced on Nina and bombarded her with keen, intelligent questions about what she'd been watching.

"What's it called when you jump up and quickly change your feet backward and forward lots of times?"

"That's an *entrechat,* Mandy."

"Is it terribly difficult to do?"

"Not really," Nina said with a smile. "It's just a question of practicing and practicing."

Mandy nodded solemnly. "Why do dancers keep doing *pliés* in all sorts of odd moments?"

"It's because bending the knees like that is such a very good way of keeping your muscles soft and supple," Nina explained.

"I see." Mandy had more than once studied the hands of her wristwatch, gravely working out the time. Now she announced, "Aunt Phyllida said I have to be back upstairs in our suite at four o'clock for tea. Why don't you come too, Nina?"

"Oh, no, I couldn't . . . not without being invited."

"Well, I'm inviting you." It was a simple statement, entirely without pertness.

"But I meant by a grown-up," Nina elaborated gently. Then, in case Mandy got the idea of rushing off to ask her father, she added hastily, "By your aunt."

Mandy nodded, clearly accepting the hopelessness of expecting this. About to run off, she said, "Can I come and watch you rehearsing again, Nina? You don't mind me being there, do you?"

"Of course I don't mind, Mandy."

"Daddy said this morning that I wasn't to be a bother to you," she explained with a little frown.

Which, being translated, Nina decided, meant that he didn't want his daughter keeping up a special friendship with the woman he had failed to seduce. But she didn't see why Mandy should be made to suffer because his overweening masculine pride had been dented.

"Well, you won't be a bother to me, however often you come and watch," she said firmly. "I don't mind a bit, Mandy—honestly. Nor does anyone else."

She felt, obscurely, that she had scored a tiny victory over Dexter.

In Nice that afternoon, Nina and Cheryl meandered around wherever their fancy took them, poking and probing in tiny shops for the presents they had come to buy for Jeremy. Cheryl chose a multicolored mosaic puzzle, and Nina bought a charming little fish toy that was carved out of wood having the spicy scent of oranges, the mouth opening and closing comically when you pulled a string.

Afterward they linked up by arrangement with a group of the other dancers, who'd traveled with them on the local service bus, including Robin, Jilly and Alan. They were all in a mood for a cheap meal, and started checking out the menus chalked up outside the bistros in the Old Town, comparing prices. The place they finally settled on was down a flight of worn stone steps to a candlelit basement with a vaulted ceiling. It was pleasantly cool after the heat of the streets, which had lingered even after sundown. Two of the tables were hastily pushed together to accommodate their party.

Sipping local wine, the young people leisurely discussed the elaborate menu. Eventually Nina and Cheryl both decided on chicken spit-roasted over a fire of vine wood, with an herb-flavored salad. It was absolutely delicious, but they didn't dare permit themselves to eat all of the vast quantity served. While they were drinking coffee, a gypsy accordionist and fiddler appeared and wandered among the tables playing their wild, soulful music. Alan swept Cheryl to her feet and they performed a frenzied dance, improvising from steps they used in the Czardas from *Coppélia*. They were accompanied by rhythmic handclapping from the other diners, which broke into loud applause when they finished. Eventually, laughing and just a bit light-headed from the wine, they all made a mad dash through the dark streets to catch the last bus back.

Jolting and swaying through the darkness, Nina suddenly felt the cold hand of depression descend on her again. For a while, in the cheerful company of her friends, she had almost been able to hold her misery at bay, but now she was once more in the painful grip of her tangled emotional problems.

Beside her, Cheryl was also silent and thoughtful. At length she said, "I know it's pretty late, but I think I'll call Mum when we get back, to see how Jeremy's been today."

"That's a good idea," Nina smiled. "I'm sure he'll be okay by now, and it will reassure you before you go to bed."

The bus stopped for them at the tall, wrought-iron

gates of the Villa Mimosa, and they walked down
the snaking driveway that was flanked by flowering
shrubs. The night air was laden with a heavenly scent of
jasmine and roses. Entering the foyer, they were greeted by the sound of their pianist playing popular numbers in the lounge and lots of singing and laughing.
The others all trooped off in that direction, but Cheryl
stopped at the phone lobby near the entrance, and Nina
stopped with her.

"There's no need for you to hang about," Cheryl
told her. "Sometimes it takes a while to get through. I'll
join you when I've finished."

"Okay." Nina strolled toward the lounge, thinking it
might be preferable to join in the singing rather than lie
restlessly awake in bed. But in the doorway she stopped
short, her glance riveting on the tall figure which
seemed to stand head and shoulders above everybody
else. At that instant Dexter turned to look in her
direction. For a long, pulsating moment they stared at
one another, their eyes locked, then his mouth creased
into a smile and he made a tiny beckoning movement
with his forefinger. Abruptly, Nina swung on her heel
and headed for the staircase, almost stumbling in her
haste to escape from Dexter's magnetic hold over her.

The faint sound of singing could still be heard
upstairs, but otherwise it was very quiet. Turning out of
the gallery, Nina entered the long corridor leading to
her bedroom. Farther along, nearer the end, a door
opened softly and a head peered out. It was Boyd, she
realized, and something oddly furtive about his manner
made her dodge out of sight behind a marble pillar.
After looking both ways along the seemingly empty
corridor, Boyd withdrew back into the room. Next
moment the giggling figure of a girl emerged, blowing a
kiss to him through the doorway. It was Zoe Gray, one

of the *corps de ballet* girls. Then she came hurrying along toward the spot where Nina was still concealed.

Stunned, unable to think clearly, Nina wondered frantically what to do. It was impossible now to remain undetected, so should she step out boldly and confront Zoe? But what would she say? She had no doubt at all what had just taken place in Boyd's bedroom; but even if she needed any confirmation it was provided by Zoe's sudden flush of high color when she drew level and spotted Nina.

Almost instantly, though, Zoe recovered her cool. Shrugging her shoulders, she threw Nina a glance of smiling defiance.

"Well, well, look who's here!" She chuckled softly in her throat. "I do hope you had a pleasant evening in Nice. Mine was wonderful, Nina. Absolutely fantastic." With a triumphant toss of her head, Zoe walked on along the corridor and vanished around the corner.

Chapter Six

Nina's first stunned reaction of shock and pain was quickly followed by a sense of relief. No longer need she suffer qualms of conscience over her feelings for Dexter, now that she had discovered Boyd was having an affair with Zoe. With her sense of relief came a feeling of anger, too. Anger at the realization that all the heartache and indecision of the past weeks could have been avoided if only Boyd had been honest and straightforward with her—as she had tried to be with him. If only he had told her that *his* feelings too had changed and that he no longer loved her. But one way and another he had evaded all her attempts to talk to him about their relationship; and even though they had not seen one another alone for ages, he had maintained the attitude before all their friends in the company that she was still his girl friend.

Next morning, to judge from Boyd's attitude during

rehearsals, Nina guessed that he must be unaware that she'd seen Zoe emerge from his bedroom the previous night. He was in a supercritical mood, intent on getting a flawless execution from her of every *pirouette* and *arabesque*.

During the lunch break, as soon as she'd finished eating, Nina decided to seize the chance of a little time on her own. But as she was slipping off she came face to face with Zoe in a doorway. Nina would have walked straight past without speaking, but Zoe barred her path.

"The way I see it," Zoe drawled lazily, "if a woman can't hold a man, that's her own stupid fault."

"Are you and Boyd in love?" Nina asked her.

"Love!" scoffed Zoe. "What's that got to do with anything? A girl's got to look after number one in this harsh world. Being involved with Boyd has paid off in your case, hasn't it, so why not for me?"

Nina refused to lower herself by engaging in a sordid verbal sparring match. She turned her back on Zoe and walked away, rounding the corner of the terrace. By bad luck, just a few feet from her, a clutch of people sat drinking coffee at a small white table—Sir Hugo Quest, Dexter, Phyllida Hooper and Mandy.

Before Nina could take evasive action the little girl had spotted her. Jumping down, she came running over. "Nina, Nina, I couldn't come and watch you this morning because Daddy and Aunt Phyllida took me out with them. But I shall this afternoon."

"That will be nice, Mandy," she said with a smile.

"Where are you going now?" the child demanded. "Can I come with you?"

"Well . . ." Nina shook her head helplessly, not having any good reason to refuse, but somehow thinking it would be tactless to agree.

"Mandymouse, I told you that you mustn't make a nuisance of yourself to Nina," Dexter reproved her, coming across to join them. But the full impact of his gaze was turned on Nina, seeming to burn right through her. "She might be intending to meet someone."

"But I could go along too," Mandy protested.

He shook his head. "There are times, pet, when—much as we all love you—the company of a little girl isn't quite what grown-ups want. Isn't that right, Nina?"

Furious that he should mock her, she deliberately contradicted him. "As a matter of fact, I was just going for a short stroll on my own. I should welcome Mandy's company."

"In which case," Dexter said smoothly, "there is nothing to prevent you sitting down with us for a few minutes first, and having some coffee."

"No thanks."

"Isn't that taking rather an unsociable attitude? Sir Hugo," he added enticingly, "has just been saying some very nice things about you. He might be persuaded to repeat them in your presence."

Nina hesitated—which was fatal. Dexter moved quickly between them, taking Mandy's hand in one of his, and putting the other under Nina's elbow. Unless she wanted to make a big fuss, she had no option but to go with him. As they neared the table, Sir Hugo made a polite token gesture of rising to his feet, while Phyllida Hooper glared hostility.

"I was just telling Nina, Sir Hugo, that you were praising her to the skies just now," Dexter observed, as he pulled out a chair for her to sit down.

"For heaven's sake," Phyllida protested, "you almost dragged it out of Sir Hugo."

"On the contrary, my dear," the old man corrected her. "I don't need any prompting to praise Nina Selby.

It is no secret that she is Regency Ballet's brightest hope."

"But I thought each of your soloists was handpicked for her all-around ability," Phyllida commented acidly. "They're all supposed to be capable of dancing the major roles in the company's repertoire."

Sir Hugo inclined his head in agreement. "That is so, and I have no wish to make invidious comparisons. But what is it that makes one diamond sparkle more brightly than another, one ruby glow more richly red than the rest? It is an indefinable something which the other gemstones, precious as they are, don't quite possess." He laid a graceful, age-veined hand over Nina's and pressed it affectionately. "Nina is our brightest star, after Lamartine, and it is in her unique talent that we put our hopes for the future."

Embarrassed, her heart brimming over at such extravagant praise, Nina murmured, "It's very good of you to say such nice things about me, Sir Hugo."

"I wouldn't be saying them if they weren't fully merited, my dear. How is *Summer Rhapsody* coming along? I haven't had a chance to look in on a rehearsal this past day or two."

"Oh, quite well, I think, Sir Hugo." At least, Nina realized thankfully, Boyd hadn't been complaining to the Director about her recent deficiencies. She still had time to get herself together and live up to the old man's faith in her.

"Watching Nina dance is Mandy's favorite occupation at the moment," Dexter commented laughingly. "We had quite a tough time dragging her off with us this morning, didn't we, Phyllida, when you decided you wanted to go shopping in Nice?"

Spite smoldered in his sister-in-law's green eyes, which were riveted on Nina. "For heaven's sake, don't encourage the child, Dexter. I'm sure that Miss Selby is

117

doing quite enough of that on her own account, without you making things any worse."

"I think," Dexter replied mildly, "that Mandy's interest in Nina is natural, under the circumstances."

"What circumstances?"

"The fact that she's so keen on the idea of becoming a ballet dancer."

"There are plenty of other female dancers in the company," Phyllida pointed out. "So why pick on just one and hang around her the way Mandy's been doing?"

"But I like Nina best." Mandy looked distressed, as if she feared that obstacles were going to be put in her way.

"And why shouldn't you?" her father said with a smile. "It shows that you have a most discerning eye, Mandymouse. An eye for the very finest there is."

Seeing Phyllida's expression of fury, Nina's heart sank. It seemed that there was no way of avoiding the hostility of Mandy's aunt. Though Phyllida didn't seem to enjoy Mandy's company herself, she was acting like a vixen jealously guarding her cub. But was it, Nina wondered suddenly, jealousy over something else? Did Phyllida have designs on Dexter? At once she felt surprised that it hadn't occurred to her before. What more obvious target for a divorced woman who was on the lookout for a new marriage partner than her dead sister's husband? Dexter was not only devastatingly attractive, but wealthy and influential too. It would explain Phyllida's readiness to stick around and take responsibility for Mandy, even though she had no particular liking nor aptitude for taking care of the child.

And what was Dexter's view of the situation? With a knife twist in her heart, Nina wondered whether he too accepted a match between them as a desirable move. Wasn't a man quite likely to find himself attracted to his sister-in-law, a woman who must have certain physical resemblances to his late wife? And the practical advantages of such a match were obvious. Well, she thought with a defiant tilt of her chin, Phyllida was welcome to Dexter, and he to her.

"You and I have got to have a talk," said Boyd that evening after dinner, taking hold of Nina's arm and leading her down the terrace steps into the sweet-scented darkness of the gardens.

"Isn't that what I've been telling you for ages now?" she returned, a bitter edge to her voice. "Only you've always been too busy to pay me any attention, Boyd. But it won't take long to say what has to be said and get things straightened out. It's clear now that we've both had a change of feeling toward each other. We can still continue to have a close working relationship, of course, but apart from that everything else between us is over and done with."

"You don't mean that, darling," he protested urgently. "Listen, I know that you're upset. Zoe told me about you seeing her last night, and it must have been a nasty shock for you. But you've got to understand . . . what happened isn't the least bit important. It doesn't need to make any difference between you and me, Nina."

"Didn't you hear what I just said?" she cried angrily. "*My* feelings have changed, too, and it has nothing whatever to do with you and Zoe seeing each other. I'd already made up my mind to tell you that everything was over as far as I was concerned. That's what I've been trying to talk to you about all this time."

Boyd plainly didn't believe her. "I can appreciate

that you must feel very hurt just now, darling. Women always look at these things differently from men. Only you've got to try to see it from my point of view. Zoe was right there, making it obvious that she was available. I've been working darned hard lately, and under a lot of pressure. It was just a form of release, nothing more."

How odd, Nina found herself thinking, that what had happened and Boyd's casual attitude about it could still hurt so much, even though she no longer loved Boyd— if, indeed, she ever had. Her hurt showed itself in heated words. "Is that how you regard lovemaking . . . nothing more than physical release from tension?"

"It depends on the girl," he said defiantly. "With a little tramp like Zoe . . . yes, that's all it means. But with you, Nina, it would be entirely different. I love you, so I'd feel a deep sense of commitment."

"And commitment is what you've always run away from, isn't it?" she flung at him. "You seemed to want to keep me dangling on a string."

He sighed exasperatedly. "I thought we were agreed about not getting too emotionally involved at this stage of our careers. Later on, when we're both more securely established, marriage would be just the thing to carry us to the very top of the tree."

Nina felt sickened. "You seem to view getting married as an exercise in public relations. 'Ballet Stars to Wed!'" she quoted ironically. "It would make a nice headline, wouldn't it, especially if you were able to choose the right psychological moment to spring the announcement on the media. Well, you can forget all about marriage as far as I'm concerned."

"All this stupid fuss about something so unimportant," he grumbled. "Can't you get it into your head that I don't care a damn about Zoe Gray?"

"Neither do I," she cried vehemently.

"So you'll forget about her?" he broke in quickly, before she could continue. "I swear it won't ever happen again, Nina. You mustn't let this spoil things between us. Together, you and I have got a terrific future. We could end up as one of the all-time great partnerships in the history of ballet, like Hugo Quest and Janina Silkova."

Nina sighed deeply. "It's what I used to dream of, Boyd. But all that's behind us now."

"Don't say that, darling," he begged, trying to draw Nina into his arms. "Come on, let's kiss and make up. If we just carry on as we are for a little while longer —say until we get *Summer Rhapsody* safely launched as a big hit in our next London season, then maybe we can start thinking about tying up our future together. How's that?"

She twisted away from him, saying fiercely, "No, Boyd! From now on we'll confine ourselves to a strictly working relationship. There can never be anything more than that between us."

"But, Nina . . ."

"I mean it, Boyd." To add greater conviction, she was half-tempted to explain that it was the intensity of her response to another man's kisses which had shown her that marriage between the two of them was out of the question. But remembering how jealous Boyd had always been where she was concerned, she knew he would probe until he found out the identity of the other man. She could just imagine Boyd's sarcastic remarks if he discovered that it was Dexter Rolfe, the company's wealthy patron. Now that everything was over between herself and Dexter, it would be wisest to keep their relationship a close secret. "I mean it," she repeated emphatically. "You'd better believe me."

For long seconds Boyd stared at her, his eyes gleaming in the faint glow of starlight. Then he shrugged. "If that's really how you want it, Nina."

As they walked back together in an uneasy silence, Nina suspected that Boyd hadn't fully accepted the finality of her decision. But what more could she say? She realized now with a sense of dismay that Boyd had never cared about her for herself, but had seen her all along as a potential ballet star who could further his own career. On his part, everything about their relationship had been calculating from the very beginning. Love just didn't enter into it at all.

Back at the villa, she didn't feel like joining the gang in the great salon. Instead, she went upstairs to her bedroom. For a long while she stood at the open window, staring out at the dark, iridescent sea, her conversation with Boyd churning over and over in her mind.

Presently she saw two figures emerge from the house and descend the terrace steps, taking a path that led toward a small, rustic-timbered pavilion, the man, tall and broadly built, the woman also tall, and slender. It was Dexter and Phyllida. They were laughing together, Phyllida holding onto his arm with both hands. Their intimacy brought Nina a terrible feeling of anguish and she turned away from the window, unable to watch another moment.

This afternoon, she had mentally accused Phyllida of jealousy. Now, that same ugly emotion was seething in her own heart, to a degree that she would never have believed herself capable of feeling. She hated Phyllida Hooper—yes, *hated*, it wasn't too strong a word. She longed to be in Phyllida's place at this moment, walking in the gardens with Dexter, cloaked by the fragrant darkness . . . to feel his strong arms enfolding her, and to experience the sensual delight of his kisses . . . to be caressed by his skillful hands into a state of rapturous desire. As Nina slowly began to undress for bed, she was tormented by the bitter knowledge that all this could have been hers had she not thrown it away. Dexter had wanted her, he had told her so again and again, and the quickening response of his body had blazed the truth of his words. And as for herself, she yearned for his lovemaking . . . she'd known that deep within her being since the first time she'd met him, and she felt it now with an intensified hunger.

But lovemaking was the wrong word for what would take place between them . . . on his side, at least. For him it would be comparatively trivial—a physical release, a pleasant pastime, without a trace of emotional commitment, just as Boyd had described his relationship with Zoe. Nina knew that she could never give herself to any man on such terms, not without love. And yet, despite all this, she still wanted Dexter, wanted him with a craving need which was stronger than any emotion she had ever felt before. How was such a paradox possible?

The answer came to her unaware, like an explosion in her mind. It was a terrifying, overwhelming answer, yet very, very simple. She was in love with Dexter. She loved him deeply and irrevocably . . . not because of what he was, but *despite* what he was.

Surely to love a man and not be loved in return should have plunged her into despair? Instead, Nina felt an incredulous sense of joy rising within her and spreading a golden warmth through her whole body.

Nina rose early when no one else was about, and walked in the dew-fresh gardens. Last night's champagne feeling of joy was still with her, but sobered now by the realization that nothing had really changed, nothing beyond this earth-shattering discovery of her love for Dexter.

Skirting a clump of crimson oleander bushes, she took the path into a grove of pine trees. Golden spears of sunlight lanced down between the tall, straight trunks to form mysterious patterns of light and shade that looked like a dramatic stage set for *Giselle*. Pine needles rustled dryly beneath her feet, and there was a sweetly resinous scent. The soft warm air was vibrant with the song of countless small birds. It was all so incredibly beautiful, and Nina unconsciously smiled to herself as she wandered onward.

"Nina!" It was Dexter's voice, calling after her. But was it just a trick of her imagination, conjured up out of her intense longing to see him? She stopped, standing very still, not daring to turn around. There were quick footsteps on the path, then his voice again, from near at hand.

"Nina, it's me . . . Dexter."

Still Nina hesitated, afraid to face him. He came right up behind her, and she reacted with a violent jerk when she felt the touch of his hands on her shoulders.

"There's no need to jump like a scalded cat," he said reproachfully. "I spotted you from my bedroom window. . . . I was restless and couldn't sleep. I thought I'd come and join you on your walk."

She turned slowly, uncertainly, stepping back a couple of paces to escape the contact of his fingers. He had a strained, hollow-eyed look about him, as if from a sleepless night. With Phyllida? she wondered bleakly, a sharp pain stabbing at her heart.

"I . . . I was just going back to the house," she said untruthfully.

"Must you?" Dexter sounded disappointed. "It's still

early, breakfast won't be for ages yet. Couldn't we just stroll together for a while?"

The thought filled her with an anguished pleasure. "What would be the point?" she temporized.

"I want to talk to you, Nina."

"Is there anything more to be said between us?" she asked wearily.

"A great deal, I'd say. The other morning, down by the rock pool, you and I threw some pretty nasty remarks at one another."

"You did to me, you mean," she flashed.

"And you hit back, Nina, you can't deny it. Listen, why don't we call it quits and go and have another swim together?"

"No!" she cried, beacon warnings flashing in her brain.

"Why not?"

"Because . . . well, for one thing I've no swimsuit with me."

"Would that still matter to you now, Nina?" he asked softly.

She shivered as if he had caressed her with a feather touch of his fingertip. "Yes, it would."

"You could always go back and fetch your swimsuit, if you must wear one. I will too," he added, "to spare your blushes."

"No, I . . . I might wake Cheryl, and . . ." Rather than making feeble excuses, she chided herself, she ought to be stating a firm and decisive no.

"Then let's make it tomorrow," Dexter went on insistently. "Same time?"

"No, it's not possible."

"Anything is possible, Nina. It's just a matter of wanting to enough."

"Well, I don't want to," she said, trying to make her voice sharp.

"We must hope that you'll have changed your mind by then," he continued with a coaxing smile. "I'll be down at the pool myself, just in case."

"You'll be wasting your time," she replied coldly, and turned back toward the villa.

"Nina, stop being so darn stubborn," he began, catching at her hand.

His touch seared through her like a scalding pain, and she wrenched her hand from his grasp. "Don't do that," she snapped, and broke into a stumbling run.

"Daddy's being ever so funny," said Mandy, her small face screwed up in puzzlement. She and Nina were sitting on a grassy bank from where they had a wonderful view across the treetops to the limitless blue of the sea shimmering serenely under the hot southern sun.

"What do you mean, Mandy . . . funny?"

"Since we've been here he gets funny moods," she explained. "Sometimes he goes all quiet and doesn't seem to listen to anything I say."

"Well, your father has a great many responsibilities," Nina reminded her. "There must always be various problems cropping up in Rolfe Industries."

"But he never lets business problems bother him at home," Mandy protested. "This morning he was quite cross with me, for no reason at all."

Nina gave her an uneasy smile. "I expect there *was* a reason, Mandy. Had you been naughty?"

"Well, only a little bit. Not naughty enough for Daddy to snap at me like he did. It's not fair!"

"I'm afraid grown-ups don't always manage to be fair," Nina said diplomatically. "I'd forget about it, pet, if I were you. It'll all blow over, you'll see."

Mandy nodded, then said in a confidential tone,

"Aunt Phyllida *often* gets cross with me. She thinks I'm a ghastly nuisance."

"Oh, no! You must have got things wrong, Mandy."

"No, I haven't, Nina. I heard her tell somebody on the phone once. She said, 'I've been out with the ghastly nuisance all morning,' and it was *me* she'd been with."

Nina's heart turned over in pity. Considering Phyllida Hooper's cold, selfish indifference toward her, it was very understandable that an affectionate child like Mandy was looking elsewhere for the loving attention she was supposed to receive from her dead mother's sister. But was it wise to let things continue like this? Nina thought worriedly. Mandy's childish devotion to her was fast turning into a fixation. At the Villa Mimosa, with them all living under the same roof, seeing quite a lot of Mandy caused no particular problems. But back in England, contact with the child would inevitably involve contact with her father. Even so, even knowing that she was only storing up trouble for herself in the future, Nina couldn't find it in her heart to reject Mandy's plea for friendship.

"Come on, pet," she said, getting to her feet and holding out a hand to the little girl. "It's time I got back for afternoon rehearsal. Are you going to sit in on it today?"

"You bet! I never get tired of watching you dance, Nina."

That afternoon Nina made more mistakes than ever; somehow she just couldn't seem to get anything right. Yet, strangely, this didn't earn her the acid rebukes from Boyd she might have expected. He was altogether gentler with her, ready to make allowances.

"Never mind, darling, it's not important," he said, loud enough for the others to hear. "Every dancer gets these bad patches. Just keep on trying, and it'll come right in the end."

Though relieved to escape so lightly, Nina guessed that Boyd was being very careful not to upset her any further. Presumably, he still had hopes of winning her back.

Next morning, the sun's golden brightness beckoned Nina irresistibly. She rose from her bed and quietly drew on jeans and a tee shirt; then, after a moment's hesitation, she slipped them off and donned a swimsuit, a one-piece black and white suit that she'd bought in Nice which was less revealing than her bikini, before getting dressed again. However, she still hadn't definitely made up her mind to meet Dexter for a swim this morning. With a last cautious glance at the still-sleeping Cheryl, she slipped out of the room and down the grand staircase. Not another soul was about.

Outside, the warm, fragrant air was like soft silk on her face. A faint breeze whispered through the trees, and the sea glittered green and sapphire all along the lovely curving coastline. For a while Nina strolled aimlessly, then found that her footsteps had brought her down the stepped pathway to the little belvedere. It was as if some compelling magnetic force was drawing her toward the rock pool.

At the foot of the pathway she parted the hanging tendrils of bougainvillea and pushed her way through nervously. Dexter was already in the water, swimming with a powerful, relaxed crawl. He noticed her at once and waved, then swam to the side and heaved himself out onto the bank.

"I'm glad you came, Nina," he said, the admiring look in his eyes and the low intimacy of his voice making the blood race in her veins.

"I . . . I can't stay," she stammered foolishly.

"Of course you can, for a little while."

He looked magnificent, the sun striking his wet sunburned torso and turning it to gleaming bronze. He was like a living statue, the sculpted muscles of his chest rippling beneath the skin as he inhaled. There was an athlete's strength about his leanly built physique . . . wide shoulders and slim waist, long legs and powerful, taut thighs. For all the concealment afforded by his close-fitting blue swimtrunks, he might just as well have been naked.

"Are you coming in?" he asked, flicking wet hair from his eyes.

"No . . . no, I don't think so," she faltered nervously.

"Why not? No swimsuit?"

"Yes, but . . ."

"No buts. Come on!" His eyes were teasing, challenging. "You don't want me to lay these wet hands on you, do you?"

Nina backed away quickly, then nodded in resigned agreement. "Okay, just for a few minutes. You get back in the water, Dexter, and I'll join you."

Though he did what she asked, Nina knew that he was still observing her intently as, in the grip of a feverish shyness, she peeled off her jeans and tee shirt.

"Very nice!" he called. "Mind you, from a man's point of view, the bikini was more . . . interesting."

Flushing, Nina once again made a clumsy dive, hitting the water with a mighty splash which winded her. Surfacing, gasping for air, she found herself imprisoned in Dexter's arms. She struggled in wild, panic-stricken protest, and as a result they both went under.

"Let me go!" she spluttered, as they bobbed up again.

"You don't look very competent in the water to me," he laughed.

"That's unfair. I'm a perfectly good swimmer, as you well know."

"Unfair, Nina?" He was treading water, keeping them both afloat, his legs moving against hers tantalizingly. "I'm only making the most of my chances, like any sensible man."

"Any *decent* man," she objected, "would let go of me when I want him to."

"But then you don't really seem to know *what* you want, do you? You came to meet me here this morning, but now you're turning all coy on me."

"But I only came because . . ."

"Yes," he prompted, "why exactly did you come?"

She could find no answer to give him. Instead, she replied weakly, "Let go of me, Dexter. Please."

His tawny eyes met hers. "You have nothing to fear from me, Nina. I won't expect anything of you that you aren't freely willing to give me."

"But . . . but I'm not willing to . . ."

"Are you sure of that?" he asked softly. There was a sudden breathless silence between them. The sun glinted on his wet hair, which was stuck to his forehead in a sort of fringe, making him look oddly boyish. She watched, mesmerized, as he licked away a bead of water from the tip of her nose. Then, moving swiftly, he pressed his mouth to hers in a thirsty, demanding kiss. Helpless against her surging emotions, Nina clung to him, her fingers sliding underwater across the smooth skin of his back, riding over the hard ridges of muscle, feeling the long channel of his spine.

The kiss intensified and, unheedingly, their tight-clasped bodies submerged once more, sliding down into a limpid world of light and shade, her long dark hair floating sensuously behind her, the crystal clear water enveloping them in a weightless, drifting dream. It was all unreal, and yet in Nina's confused mind it seemed oddly to possess the only true reality. Dexter locked her more tightly against his hard male body, crushing her soft breasts to his chest, encircling her legs with the vice grip of his powerful thighs until she was thrillingly conscious of his pulsing male arousal. The kiss went on and on, his tongue probing and searching, exploring the secrets of her mouth, lifting her to new and dizzy heights of longing. In this strange underwater world he could have possessed her right here and now with her joyful acceptance.

At long last they drifted upward again and finally broke the surface. Only then, it seemed, did either of them discover the desperate need of their lungs for air. They both gulped it in greedily, choking and coughing a little. At the same time Nina rediscovered her sense of shame. She thrust back out of his arms, and this time Dexter let her go. Turning quickly, she splashed her way in a clumsy stroke to the bank and clambered out.

Dexter watched her from the water as she hastily snatched up the towel he'd brought along, and dabbed herself dry. Then, trembling in every limb, she dragged on her jeans over her still-damp swimsuit.

"Nina," he said huskily, "I . . ."

She shook her head. "No, don't say anything. Just let me go."

"If that's how you want it. But meet me here again this evening, Nina, after dinner. You *must* come."

She gave him no answer, but turned away and began to mount the pathway back to the villa. He had no right, she thought angrily, to keep on expecting her to meet him like this. But more than her anger against Dexter, she felt a helpless fury against herself. Because she knew that, however much her reason and intelligence told her it was foolish, nothing could prevent her from keeping the secret tryst with him that evening.

Chapter Seven

The warm evening was heady with flower fragrance as Nina set out for her rendezvous. Above the silent treetops the stars glittered like a scattering of diamonds on jewelers' black velvet. The sounds of voices and laughter gradually receded, and the lapping of wavelets in the cove far below grew louder. She walked steadily, without hesitation, the leather soles of her sandals gritting on the rough-hewn steps. And then, still several yards from the rock pool, she sensed Dexter's presence reaching out and seizing her like a powerful magnet. She paused, her heart fluttering wildly, a hand to her throat to try to still the pulse that throbbed like a jungle drumbeat.

"Nina!" His voice was low and vibrant, floating to her on the silk soft air. "Nina, I'm here."

But her confidence had drained away by now and she stood there rigidly stiff, unable to take another step.

She tried to speak his name, but her voice was lost in the thickness of her throat.

Dexter came to meet her, and she caught the glitter of his eyes in the starglow. Close now, the aura of his potent masculinity was overwhelming, and when his arms closed around her she gave a little gasp of dismay at the sudden sensation of falling helplessly into a bottomless abyss.

Somehow, she summoned up a hoarse whisper. "Dexter, I . . . I . . ."

"I know," he murmured tenderly. "It'll be all right, darling." He bent and touched his lips to her hair, while the fingertips of one hand molded the outline of her face, as if he were conjuring up the image of her that was denied to his vision by the darkness. And where his fingertips had searched his lips followed, trailing caressingly across her brow, her eyes, touching the petal-soft lobe of her ear, following the curve of her cheek until finally his mouth came to rest on hers. And in that kiss every final shred of doubt fled her mind. She clutched him to her in a fever of emotion, fingers sliding across the smooth silkiness of his shirt to where the dark hair curled at the nape of his neck, twining and tangling into it convulsively.

Time winged by and still they stood there locked together. The present moment was a floating dream, in which past and future had no relevance. Just here and now, this secret place, and the two of them joined in a blissful embrace.

At last Dexter moved, half-releasing her so that he could gather her up in his arms. He bore her weight as if it were less than nothing, carrying her down the remaining few steps to the poolside and laying her gently on the grassy bank. Her nostrils caught the sharp sweet redolence of wild thyme where he had crushed it underfoot.

"Let me undress you," he murmured, kneeling down beside her, and Nina found herself making no demur. In the starlight she watched his face as he began to undo the tiny buttons of her cotton blouse, deftly freeing each one from its buttonhole until he was able to slide the garment over her shoulders and draw it completely away. Then, leaning forward, he laid his lips against her bared skin, sending shivers of delight radiating through her. Next, with careful, unhurried movements, he removed her jeans. When he gently tugged away her panties, Nina uttered a low moan, but whether in instinctive protest at such intimacy or in joyful anticipation she could not have said. Of their own accord her hands fluttered upward to help as he searched for the fastening of her lacy bra.

Dexter gave a deep sigh of pleasure when at length she lay there quite naked. Slowly, almost reverently, he slid his hands over her soft curves, making her flesh come tinglingly alive.

"You're so beautiful, Nina," he whispered. "Quite utterly perfect. When you dance, you must send every man in the audience wild with desire to possess this lovely body of yours. Doesn't that knowledge give you an exciting sense of power?"

Weakly, she shook her head in protest. In the starglow he saw the movement and gave a quick, throaty half-laugh of the triumphant conqueror. "At any rate, you've driven me nearly out of my mind, Nina, and you've gloried in that, haven't you?"

His fingertips traveled her soft skin upward from her waist, circling each breast with a feathered touch, then his hands closed to cup them warmly, possessively. With his two thumbs he teased at her nipples, coaxing them to hard peaks of blissful torment. He explored her body slowly and searchingly, inch by inch, first with his hands, then with his lips, his questing tongue adding to her sensual delight. On and on the exquisite caresses continued until she was in a daze of quivering excitement, frantic with her need of him.

"Dexter," she murmured into the fragrant darkness. "I . . ."

"Say it," he whispered. "Tell me that you want me, Nina."

"Yes, yes, I want you."

He touched his lips to hers in a brief, soft promise. Then quickly he stood and stripped off his own clothes, tossing the garments carelessly aside. Fleetingly, Nina glimpsed him standing above her, magnificently naked, the starlight sheening on his skin and turning him into a sculpted silver statue. Then in a swift movement he was beside her, molding his lean length to hers, thigh to thigh, stomach to stomach, his hard chest pressed against the softness of her breasts, mouth joined to mouth, while his hands roamed her back, savoring the firm, yielding contours. He endlessly caressed her, circling and searching over her lovely dancer's body, skimming the firm buttocks, reaching down to stroke her thighs. Nina drifted off into a dreamworld in which they were joined together like this forever and always, in a sort of perfect limbo where no one else intruded. She felt a marvelous sense of having become a complete woman, as if her entire life until now had been building up to this supreme moment, this magnificent discovery of the ultimate ecstasy. Uncounted minutes went drifting by until, with a thrill of intoxicating joy, she felt the throb of Dexter's renewing desire. This time, because she knew how it would be, because she could anticipate the wonderment, their loving was even more intensely perfect. And when at last it was over, they remained welded together, both of them replete and satiated, their limbs heavy with a delicious languor. Dexter tenderly kissed her eyelids, then laid his lips against the dark spun silk of her hair as he held her enfolded in his arms. Nina hung suspended in a half-world between waking and sleeping, and Dexter's soft voice, murmuring endearments, was like a lullaby.

Nina roused, slightly dazed for a moment; then she remembered, and felt a glorious sense of exhilaration. Everything was still, and she wondered how late it was. Dexter's arm had fallen limply to his side, and she could see the faint luminous glow of his wristwatch. Moving a little, she saw that it was long past midnight. She would have curious questions from Cheryl to face, but she didn't care.

Dexter seemed to be asleep, and she was reluctant to disturb him. She trailed her fingertips along his arm with a feather touch, loving the feel of his warm, taut skin, riding smoothly over the muscled contours. A lock of hair had fallen across his brow and she reached up to brush it aside, then touched her lips to the spot.

He opened his eyes, and Nina saw in them a reflection of the starglow. "I think I must have dropped off to sleep."

"I know you did," she laughed, "and so did I." She felt no shyness, no shame, to be lying there naked with him like this. Such emotions would be out of place in the new and wondrous closeness between them. "It's time I went back," she said reluctantly.

His arms came up and tightened around her. "Must you?"

"Yes, I must! I'll have some explaining to do, as it is."

"So explain," he said, and kissed the tip of her nose.

"It's not so easy," Nina objected. "If anyone got a hint of our relationship, it would spread like wildfire."

"I don't see how you're going to prevent people knowing. Nor why you should want to. There's sure to be someone still around when we get back to the house, and the two and two they add up will make a very conclusive four."

"But we mustn't be seen together," she said in alarm. "I'll go first, and you follow after a little while."

"Are you ashamed of being seen with me?" he remonstrated.

"Of course not. But . . . well, surely you can understand? In your case, maybe it wouldn't matter. But for me, what are people going to think?"

"Let them think whatever they like. Why should it bother you? You don't regret what's happened, do you, Nina?"

"No, but . . ." She shifted uneasily, and when she started to rise to her feet Dexter didn't attempt to stop her. She was suddenly overcome with shyness and she hastily gathered together her clothes and started to put them on. Neither of them spoke until they were both fully dressed, then he said in a low-throated voice, "You still haven't answered my question, Nina. Why are you ashamed to admit to your friends what's happened between us?"

She stood facing him, feeling cornered. Why couldn't he understand that what had been a wonderful, beautiful experience for her wouldn't look at all the same way to the other members of the ballet company? Yet it was something she couldn't possibly try to explain—either to him, or by way of justification to her friends. Suppose she were to say to Dexter, "I let you make love to me because I *love* you. Without that it would have been unthinkable. I could never engage in sex without love." He would think her incredibly naive and unsophisticated. Suppose she were to say to other people, "Yes, Dexter and I are having an affair, because I love him, even though he doesn't love me." It would be good for a giggle, she guessed, and plenty of snide remarks. They would see her relationship with

Dexter as opportunistic, sleeping with a wealthy, influential man for what she could get out of it. She just couldn't bear that.

"I've nothing more to say," she faltered. "I'm going back now—alone."

Dexter took hold of her by the shoulders. "So it's to be a hole-and-corner relationship, is it?" he asked, and she could detect a note of anger in his voice.

"It . . . it might be better if we didn't let things go any further. If we ended it right here and . . ."

"End it," he grated, really angry now. "How can we possibly 'end it'? You know as well as I do that it's beyond us, either of us, to go back now. We are way past the point of no return."

She felt a spark of rebellion that he was taking too much for granted. "If I say it's to end here and now, Dexter, that's that!"

"Very well, then say it! I challenge you to tell me that you want me to walk right out of your life." He stood before her with his arms akimbo, his stance aggressively masculine. Nina shivered, biting down on her lower lip, afraid lest her impetuous pride should fatally betray her into saying just that. In the silence that throbbed between them, she could feel the warmth of Dexter's breath on her cheek, could sense the pulsing maleness of him. She yearned to reach out to him and feel the reassuring comfort of his embrace; she ached with a need to have those strong hands running over the soft contours of her body.

"You see, you can't say it," he cried triumphantly. "Because you know as well as I do, Nina, that we're so right for one another. Tonight we achieved perfection, and we will again—many, many times. It would be a crime against nature to deprive ourselves of something so wonderful."

She bowed her head, accepting the truth of what he

said. Dexter's voice suddenly gentled, all the harshness gone. "Come, darling, kiss me good night and we'll go our separate ways . . . on *your* terms."

Momentarily, Nina remained frozen. Then with a rush she went into his arms. His lips covered hers and they clung in a kiss of sweet passion. With her arms about his neck and their bodies pressed close, she thrilled to the swift response of his virility. At last he broke away, laughing huskily. "Get going, you wicked temptress—while I'm still able to let you go. And be here again tomorrow night, without fail. Promise?"

"I promise," she whispered.

With a low laugh Dexter turned her and, placing the broad spread of his hand where her jeans were tightly stretched across her hips, he gave her a little push.

On wings of happiness, Nina ran lightly all the way back to the villa. Luckily, although she heard voices in the salon, she encountered no one as she slipped inside and hurried up the staircase. Reaching her bedroom door, she tried to make no noise as she crept in, but Cheryl stirred sleepily.

"What time d'you call this, for goodness' sake?"

"I call it bedtime," Nina answered chirpily.

Cheryl propped herself up on one elbow and glanced at her wristwatch. "Where on earth have you been till this late?"

"I went for a stroll," Nina told her, making it clear that she didn't intend to say any more. She wished that she could have confided in Cheryl and admitted the truth, but she knew what her friend's attitude would be.

"Well, I just hope you realize what you're getting yourself into," Cheryl said warningly.

"Don't worry, I can look after myself."

"I wish I could be sure of that. The way you've been

dancing lately, it looks like you're set on a disaster course."

"For heaven's sake stop fussing," Nina protested. "You're acting just like an old mother hen. I'm a big girl now."

Cheryl didn't answer. Turning over pointedly, she pulled up the covers and settled back to sleep. Nina regretted their tiff, but nothing could spoil the perfection of the evening for her. She felt blissfully happy, more vitally alive than ever before in her life. She felt charged with a wondrous new energy, and longed to express it in her dancing. Tomorrow, she would show them exactly what she was made of; she would demonstrate to everyone that Nina Selby would be a worthy successor to Sonia Lamartine, when the time came.

And tomorrow, when it grew dark, she would meet Dexter again, and they would share once more those magical moments of passion.

"Whatever's come over you, Nina?" asked Boyd, with a puzzled frown. "You suddenly seem to be full of the joy of spring."

"Why not?" Nina called back happily. "Isn't that what dancing is all about?"

He looked at her strangely for a moment, then shrugged his shoulders and smiled. "Well, whatever the reason, it's really great, darling. You're getting it all together at last."

The transformation was so dramatic that everyone noticed, and Nina received numerous compliments, from her partner, Robin, and from other members of the company. At one point, after she had flawlessly executed a sequence of rapid, intricate footbeats, she received the rare accolade of having her fellow dancers break into warm applause. The only exception was

Zoe, who regarded her with eyes that smoldered hatred. But Nina cared nothing for Zoe's hostility. In her newfound happiness she was brimming over with self-confidence, her body responding with delicate lyricism and faultless technique to every instruction of her brain.

Just once that morning did she falter, when she caught sight of Dexter. She was at that moment on point, spinning in a series of rapid *pirouettes,* fixing her eyes at each full turn on a marble statue outside on the terrace to prevent herself from getting dizzy. Dexter's sudden appearance with Mandy at one of the open French windows caused her to shift her gaze fatally. She stumbled and broke off.

"Sorry," she stammered in dismay.

"Not to worry, love," said Boyd, and called to the ever-patient Charles at the piano, "Pick up about eight bars back."

Dexter seemed to realize that he was the cause of her mistake. With a wave of his hand, he turned away and led Mandy out of sight. Then a few minutes later Mandy crept into the big room to take her usual place in one corner, carefully out of everybody's way.

When they broke off for lunch, Boyd came over and laid his arm across Nina's shoulders. "Apart from that one slip, you were magnificent this morning, darling. You showed all the brilliance I've always believed you capable of."

"Thanks, Boyd," she said, with a happy smile.

"I don't mind admitting," he went on, "that I'd been getting really worried about the way you were dancing. You seemed to have lost your touch completely. But now I think we're all set for a fantastic debut of *Summer Rhapsody* next week."

"You bet!" said Nina, unconsciously adopting

Mandy's favorite expression. But she felt uncomfortable with Boyd's arm about her, and she twisted away from him and stepped back.

His glance was reproachful. "You're not going to keep me in the doghouse forever, are you? I mean, that business with Zoe was nothing."

"It isn't because of Zoe," she said. "I told you the other night, Boyd, it's all over between you and me."

"Please, Nina, give me a break. Look, I'm sorry I've not managed to see more of you recently, but what with this and that . . . you know how it's been. How about this evening, though? I've got the rented car, so why don't we go for a drive along the Grande Corniche road? You get fabulous views of the whole coastline, all the way to Monte Carlo, and then we can find a nice place to have dinner."

"No, Boyd," she said with an emphatic shake of her head.

"There's no need to slap me down quite so hard," he protested, looking hurt. "We've got so much going for us, Nina, surely you can see that? It would be crazy to throw it all away just because of something so trivial and unimportant. I've always said that you and I make a terrific team."

"On a professional basis, I agree," she said earnestly. "The days of our dancing partnership built up a tremendous rapport between us and I know that we can help one another in our careers. But as for our private lives, Boyd, that's all finished." The ballroom was empty now, apart from one small figure waiting patiently by the door. Nina seized her excuse, and said, "Look, Mandy Rolfe is waiting for me, so I'll have to go now."

"The kid can wait! Surely you're used to small girls getting a crush on you by now."

"I know, but Mandy is different. She's a very lonely child."

"For heaven's sake," Boyd flared angrily, "she's got her father, hasn't she, and her aunt. So why should *you* feel under any obligation to the kid, Nina?"

"I don't feel under an obligation to her, as you put it. But I like Mandy, and . . . and she's terribly keen on the idea of becoming a ballet dancer when she's older. So a little encouragement from me won't do any harm."

Boyd's eyes narrowed with suspicion. "It's not her father you're aiming to encourage, is it?"

"What do you mean?" she asked, nervously.

"I didn't think anything of it at the time, Nina, but when we did the charity gala at Haslemere Hall, I heard talk that you'd managed to waylay Dexter Rolfe on the grounds."

"That's not true," Nina objected, and went on in a carefully level voice, "I did happen to meet up with him and Mandy when I was having a stroll around, and we all walked back to the house together. But it was quite by chance. I certainly didn't waylay him." Though her words were no more than the truth she could feel her cheeks grown warm, and she hoped desperately that Boyd wouldn't pursue the matter. It was cowardly, she knew, but she didn't want the true nature of her relationship with Dexter to come out. She guessed that Boyd would create a scene, which would spoil everything, casting a dark shadow over her happiness.

To her relief, Boyd accepted what she said with a muttered, "Okay, sorry." Shrugging, he went on, "If you're determined that I've got to be made to suffer for a bit longer, I'll just have to put up with it. But don't sulk for too long, will you?"

"I'm not sulking, Boyd," she stated flatly. "Why

won't you believe what I keep telling you? My feelings have changed, even if yours haven't. From now on our relationship is on a strictly professional footing. Okay?"

He sighed resignedly. "If you insist! But just remember, darling, as long as you dance like an angel I'll still keep on loving you."

Perhaps that was much closer to the truth than Boyd meant to convey, Nina thought ruefully, as she left him and went over to join Mandy. Just how deep had his affection for her ever gone? Merely as deep as his valuation of her as a ballerina?

"Nina, can I eat my lunch with you today?" Mandy asked plaintively.

"Oh . . . but what about your folks?"

"Aunt Phyllida won't miss me."

"But your father, Mandy. He'll expect you to eat with him."

"Daddy isn't here now."

"Oh, where's he gone—into Nice or something?"

"No, he's gone back to London. He had a phone call this morning from one of his managers."

Nina stopped dead in her tracks. "Back to London? How . . . for how long, Mandy?"

"As long as it takes, Daddy said. I wish he hadn't had to go, Nina, but I don't really mind as long as you're here."

The pain of it was unbearable. Dexter had gone off without even troubling to say good-bye to her. Last night, those blissful midnight hours which had so completely overturned her whole world, couldn't have been very important to him. Would he even care if they never shared the experience again? Maybe overcoming her resistance and finally seducing her had been his one objective all along. Some men were like that, repeatedly scoring new conquests in order to foster their macho image; and Dexter Rolfe had quite a reputation for sleeping around.

What had she really expected from him? Nina asked herself fiercely. True and everlasting love? She had known from the very beginning that Dexter couldn't be expected to fall in love with her; he just wasn't that sort of man. So what was she whining about? She'd learned a bitter lesson the hard way—one that thousands of women learn about men every single day that passes.

Blinking hard to hold back the tears that pricked behind her eyelids, she smiled at Mandy and said, "Of course you can have lunch with me, pet. Would you like to come upstairs while I have a shower? I feel so sticky, I must change into fresh clothes."

"You bet!"

Cheryl was in the bedroom, releasing her fair hair from its bandeau and shaking it free. "Hi, Mandy! How's things?"

"Okay, thanks." She settled herself on the window seat. "Wasn't Nina wonderful this morning, Cheryl?"

"Terrific! I've never seen her dance better." Cheryl glanced at Nina with the shrewd insight of a close friend. "I guess it's the result of being happy. All the same, Nina, you look a bit down in the dumps at the moment. Perhaps it's just gnawing hunger. By the way, you hadn't collected your mail, so I brought it up for you." She gestured toward the dressing table.

Nina's wretchedness over Dexter's departure had wiped from her mind the daily routine of checking the mail slots in the entrance hall. Uninterestedly, she gathered up the three envelopes. A reminder from her dentist, sent on from the London flat, that she was due for a checkup. Well, that would have to wait until she got back. Pausing in the act of slitting open number two, which looked like a bill, she glanced at the third envelope. Thick cream-laid paper, it hadn't been through the mail, just having her name written in a firm, bold hand.

From Dexter! Her heart faltered and her legs felt suddenly unsteady. She couldn't bear to read whatever he might have to say except privately, so she grabbed up a towel and her robe, saying, "Stay and talk to Cheryl, Mandy. I'm off for a quick shower."

Sitting on the edge of the bathtub, she pushed her finger under the envelope's flap and clumsily ripped it open. As she unfolded the letter inside, the writing seemed to shimmer on the paper.

If you receive this note, it will mean that I haven't had the chance of a quiet word with you. In view of what you said last night, I shan't draw attention by interrupting if you happen to be dancing. You may have heard already that I've had to return post-haste to London. I'm not sure for how long. There's a crisis blown up about a new export regulation which calls for some top-level handling. I'm devastated that it should happen now, and I was very tempted to say what the hell! But too many jobs are at stake for me to play fast and loose with Rolfe Industries. I'll be back, if it's humanly possible, for the opening of Summer Rhapsody. *Meantime, I'll have to keep myself going on a wonderful memory . . . and the thought of you waiting for me. Don't let Mandy be too much of a nuisance. She'll fasten on like a limpet and spend every moment of the day with you . . . wise child! Meanwhile, until I see you again, all my thoughts and good wishes are with you.*

D.

The tears Nina shed were tears of relief, tears of joy. She read the letter through again and yet again, then held it cradled against her heart. As she showered, she reminded herself cautiously that although Dexter had written wonderful things, he had not said "I love you." He did not love her, she knew that; she had known it all along. She would never expect him to love her, never grieve over the lack of love. It was enough that she loved Dexter and that he needed her—for the time being. She must treat the present as very precious, savoring to the full each silver moment, each golden hour.

And when it was over . . . but no, she refused to let her mind think ahead to that bleak time. Life was about *now* . . . today, tomorrow, the next few weeks. Who in the whole wide world could be sure of more than that?

And last night . . . nothing could ever steal the beautiful memory from her.

Chapter Eight

During the following days Nina glowed with her secret happiness, which seemed to lend everything around her an added beauty. Her dancing continued at a brilliant level, reflecting the inner radiance of her love for Dexter.

Because rehearsals for *Summer Rhapsody* were going so well, the pressure of work eased a little. This enabled her to spend more time with Mandy. Being in the company of Dexter's daughter somehow brought him closer, and Phyllida Hooper seemed glad to have her little niece happily occupied, allowing her to drive into Nice—where, Nina gathered, she spent most of her time at one or other of the casinos. Nevertheless, Phyllida never lost the chance of making a sarcastic remark whenever she and Nina met up.

"Trying to dig yourself in?" she inquired nastily on the fourth morning after Dexter's departure. It was during the coffee break, and Nina, having spotted

Phyllida reading a magazine on the swing hammock on the terrace, had gone over to ask where Mandy was. "Perhaps you're hoping to make a good impression."

"I don't know what you mean, Mrs. Hooper."

Delicate eyebrows arched ironically over the rim of her sunglasses. "No? Perhaps you just adore small children, is that it?"

"I happen to like Mandy, in any event."

"And you think that a demonstrative display of your affection will go down well with her father? But you're wasting your time, Miss Selby." She gave Nina a sugar sweet smile. "Just a friendly warning, my dear."

Friendly! Phyllida Hooper didn't know the meaning of the word where other women were concerned. If Phyllida guessed just how far the relationship with Dexter had actually gone, Nina thought with a shiver, her claws would really be out. To a woman like her, there would only be one conclusion—that Nina Selby was chasing Dexter for his money. Phyllida would be the last person in the world to believe that she loved Dexter and wanted nothing from him . . . except, against all hope, his love in return.

Despite Phyllida's provocation, Nina managed to keep her cool. "We've just been told that we'll have an extra-long break at lunchtime today, so I was wondering if Mandy would like to come down to the cove with Cheryl and me. If that's okay with you," she added diplomatically.

Phyllida's beautiful features tightened in a spiteful, ugly expression. "No, it's not okay with me. I'm taking Mandy out myself today."

"Oh, I see. That will make a nice change!" Immediately, Nina felt like biting her tongue off. She hadn't intended to sound so rude.

"Are you trying to be offensive?" Phyllida demanded sharply.

"No . . . I just meant . . . well, that you'll be able to give Mandy a really nice treat, and . . . and not have to bring her back as early as we would."

Phyllida was in control again, smiling unpleasantly. "I'm sorry your little plan has misfired, Miss Selby. I think perhaps I've been unwise to indulge Mandy's childish desire for your company, but that will have to end. I can't permit you to make use of her in the way you've been doing."

"Make use of her?" Nina echoed in protest. "That's a ridiculous thing to suggest. What harm can it possibly do Mandy to be with me if she wants to?"

Phyllida looked impatient. "To put it bluntly, Miss Selby, I consider you a most unsuitable person for her to associate with. Now, if you don't mind, I'd like to get back to my magazine."

Nina went back to join Cheryl, boiling with anger. It was wickedly unfair of Mandy's aunt to deprive the child of something she enjoyed, just out of spite. She wondered what Dexter would have to say when he returned. But instantly she realized that she couldn't possibly complain to Dexter about his sister-in-law.

At lunchtime the two girls went to the big kitchen and persuaded a friendly cook to pack up a picnic bag for them: crusty French bread and yellow farmhouse butter, some mild creamy cheese and two luscious peaches to follow.

It was yet another glorious day, hot and cloudless. The rest of the company were content to splash around in the swimming pool or laze on the terrace. Nina and Cheryl soon left everyone behind as they began the winding descent down the tumbled cliffs to the villa's private cove, a small crescent of smooth, sea-washed pebbles which they had entirely to themselves.

Peeling off their outer clothes, they plunged into the beautifully warm water, swimming and floating lazily.

It was heavenly, like drifting in a sea of molten gold, and the world seemed far away. Afterward, they allowed the hot sun to dry them off while they fell eagerly upon their picnic. Their swim, following an energetic morning's dancing, had made breakfast a distant memory, and they finished every last crumb.

"It's a pity Mandy couldn't come along," said Cheryl. "Where's her aunt taking her, Nina?"

"She didn't say."

"If you ask me," Cheryl continued, "the kid would have been far happier with us. From the little I've seen of them together, I get the distinct impression that Phyllida Hooper regards poor Mandy as a pain in the neck. I wonder why she ever took on the job of looking after her." She paused in the act of fishing in her bag for a notepad and pen, and looked questioningly at Nina. "D'you think she's aiming to step into her sister's shoes and become the second Mrs. Dexter Rolfe?"

"I wouldn't know," said Nina shortly.

"You have to admit," Cheryl went on, with a warning note in her voice, "that she's in a good position to get him, if that's what she's after. I mean, she's right there on the spot, looking after his child. And she's certainly got the looks and style to attract a man, if Dexter ever decides he's had enough of the playboy life and gets around to marrying again."

Nina tried to conceal her heightened color by turning away and packing up the picnic remains. When she turned back, Cheryl was beginning one of her long letters to Jeremy. Happily, her son's bout of ill health just after their arrival here had soon cleared up. Feeling disturbed and restless, Nina slipped on her sandals and began strolling along the beach, stopping now and then to peer into little rock pools at the tiny fish darting among the fronds of seaweed. Her wandering took her to where the cliffs ran right down to the sea. With the special caution that was second nature to a dancer she clambered a little way up, aiming for a wide, flat ledge. She sat there, leaning back, and gazed out across the sun-silvered water. From around a jagged promontory a yacht had appeared—a ketch, she was now able to recognize. The white sails formed three graceful curves, leaning slightly in the breeze. Her mind drifted back to the afternoon she'd spent sailing with Dexter off the Sussex coast in just such a boat as this. She hadn't known, then, that she loved Dexter, but she was drawn to him by a strange fascination. In her more lucid moments, she had recognized that he spelled danger for her, but she'd believed that she could combat the danger and emerge unscathed.

Now, she no longer saw Dexter as dangerous. He would eventually bring her heartbreak when the day came that he grew tired of her. But the greater heartbreak would be to give him up now. She was entitled, surely, to the happiness he could bring her while their relationship lasted—and later, when she was compelled to face the future without him, at least she would have some wonderful memories to help her loneliness. Dexter . . . what was he doing at this precise moment? Was he thinking of her, as she was of him? If only he were here with her . . . if only they could have been sailing together in that yacht, drifting endlessly across the calm, placid ocean . . .

A scream of terror rent the silence, snatching Nina back to startled awareness. Her first thought was for Cheryl, but her friend was still there on the beach below, writing her letter. She too had heard something and was looking around to see what was wrong. Could it have been the shriek of a seabird? No, that had been a human voice—a child's voice.

Jumping to her feet, Nina stared all around her, then gasped in horror as she caught sight of Mandy clinging to the steep rockface some twenty feet or so higher. The child was obviously terrified and in great danger; she swayed alarmingly on her insecure perch, and below her was a chasm of jagged rocks. There was no time to waste wondering how Mandy had got there. She had to be rescued instantly.

"It's all right, pet," she called out, making her voice sound calm and reassuring. "I'm coming, don't worry. Just stay right where you are and keep as still as possible."

A quick glance over her shoulder showed her that Cheryl was already on her way to help. Nina turned and began clambering with all the haste she could manage, slipping and sliding on the rock, gaining a few precarious inches at a time. All the while she was pressured by the heart-rending sound of Mandy's sobbing. She kept calling in reassurance. "Just hang on for another few minutes, and I'll be there with you. I'm coming as fast as I can. Don't worry, Mandy, I'll soon have you safe."

A last feverish effort brought her almost to within reach of the child. But they were still divided by a vertical slab of smooth, unbroken rock almost three feet across which offered Nina no hand or foothold. There was no time to be lost in going back to try and find another route that would take her closer. Mandy was in a real panic now, and she might easily fall at any moment, to be smashed on those ugly rocks. Bracing herself, Nina reached as far as she could and gripped tightly with her fingertips, then swung herself sideways until she was right behind Mandy, pressing the child's body against the rockface, while she scrabbled wildly with her free left foot to find a toehold. Mercifully, she managed to get her foot into a small cleft.

"You're all right now, Mandy," she said soothingly. "I'm here, so don't worry anymore. You're quite safe now."

But this tenuous position was impossible for Nina to hold. She was spreadeagled, and her arms screamed out with the strain of bearing too much weight. She yanked herself across to get a better purchase, and as she did so the foot which was lodged in the cleft shifted and pushed in deeper. She felt a terrible wrench, and needles of fire shot up her leg.

Closing her eyes, Nina bit down against the agonizing pain. Mandy was a little quieter now, somewhat reassured by her presence, and Nina struggled to remain calm and sound normal.

"You're quite safe, honestly. Cheryl's coming, and it'll be easier when she's here, so we'll just wait quietly." She didn't add that there was no alternative course open to them.

"I . . . I'm frightened, Nina," Mandy said chokily.

"There's no need to be, pet. Just keep still. There, I can hear Cheryl now. She's coming up a different way."

A few moments later Cheryl's head appeared just above them. "Luckily there's a good, wide ledge here," she said. "I can give Mandy a hand up, if you can lift her a bit, Nina. Okay?"

"Okay." As Cheryl reached down an arm to get a tight hold on Mandy's small wrist, Nina made a supreme effort, letting go with one hand in order to take some of the child's weight and help raise her. "Right, up you go, Mandy. Heave-ho!"

Mandy cried out again in panic as, for a moment or two, she was hanging in space. Then Cheryl had her safely on the ledge beside her.

"Sit there, Mandy, and don't move," she ordered crisply. Then to Nina, "Now for you, only you'll be a lot heavier, so you'd better try and climb a bit your-self."

"I'm stuck," Nina whispered in horrified dismay a moment later. "You'll have to go and fetch help. My foot's wedged in a cleft and I can't get it out."

"Oh, Nina, that's awful! Will you be able to hang on for that long?"

"I . . . I think so. But please be as quick as you can."

A voice from below was suddenly shouting at them. "What on earth do you think you're doing, letting Mandy climb the cliff like that? Are you both out of your minds? Bring her down at once."

Phyllida Hooper! She and Mandy must have been on the public beach just around the small headland, Nina realized, and she'd allowed Mandy to wander all this way alone.

"Nina is stuck," Cheryl called down to her. "Please go and get help, Mrs. Hooper."

"I'm not leaving that child in your incompetent hands," Phyllida protested. "Bring her down to me at once, d'you hear?"

"For pity's sake, don't argue," Cheryl shouted furi-ously. "Can't you understand—Nina is injured. She did it rescuing Mandy. So get going at once and be as quick as you can."

The urgency in Cheryl's voice at last got through to Phyllida and she hurried off at a stumbling run. Cheryl reached down and gripped Nina's hand, giving her comfort and courage.

"Is . . . is Mandy all right?" Nina asked from be-tween clenched teeth.

"She's fine, aren't you, Mandy? Tell Nina, so she won't worry about you."

"Yes, Nina," the tremulous little voice gulped. "I'm all right."

Nina concentrated all her thoughts on the job of hanging on until help arrived. Without Cheryl there, taking some of her weight and murmuring encouraging words, she probably wouldn't have managed. Her consciousness seemed to ebb and flow and she fought desperately not to faint. As a fierce wave of nausea hit her, she started counting off the seconds, but she lost the thread and found herself gabbling numbers at random. She had a tantalizing vision that Dexter had come, that his arms were about her ready to lift her gently to safety. In a daze of pain she almost loosed her grip . . . but then snatched back just in time as she began to slip. She was fighting a battle against her own weakness, her longing to succumb to the blessed oblivion that promised a respite from this agony in her leg—and the fear of what it might portend for her future.

Finally there was a sound of people coming, a medley of voices. Were they calling to her, instructing her? She didn't know, and she could only hold on grimly. Soon there were hands upon her, lots of hands, supporting her weight. Someone eased her foot from the cleft which held it prisoner, handling it delicately, with tender care, yet the pain was like nothing she had ever experienced before. It was then that she fainted, giving way at last and sinking into a twisting whirlpool which swallowed her into its dark depths.

Very slowly, Nina drifted upward to the surface. Her first conscious realization was that, blessedly, the pain was gone. She let her eyelids open, and saw Cheryl's anxious face beside her.

Dazedly, Nina looked around. A small, clinically white room, with yellow curtains. She lay in a narrow bed that had a pale green cover.

"Where am I?" she murmured, her voice emerging from somewhere far off, and echoing in her ears.

"You're in a hospital, in Nice," Cheryl explained. "You were brought straight here, so they could set your ankle."

"Set my ankle? Why, what happened to it?"

"Don't you remember? Your foot got stuck when you were rescuing Mandy, and you . . . well, your ankle was fractured."

It still didn't make sense. She had no pain, she was floating comfortably on a bed of softest down. How lovely, she thought drowsily, to let herself sink back into a delicious sleep. And then, striking her with a terrifying horror, came the full import of Cheryl's remark.

"My . . . my ankle?" she gasped. "I fractured my ankle?"

Cheryl's eyes misted, and she glanced away. "By a fantastic stroke of luck, there was a doctor near at hand when . . . when it happened. He took charge and made sure no further damage was done."

"But will it ever heal properly? Will I ever be able to . . . ?" The thought was too terrible to express in blunt words. Would she ever be able to dance again? It was the dread of every ballet dancer who suffered physical injury.

Cheryl was looking back at her now, but didn't quite meet her eyes. "They say it's a fairly straightforward break, Nina. Of course you'll be laid up for a while, but afterward . . . hopefully there won't be any restriction of movement in your ankle."

Soothing words, Nina knew, which meant nothing. She fell back listlessly against the pillows and gazed at the ceiling in blind despair. Her career was finished, the one thing that gave meaning and purpose to her life. In her weak, half-drugged state, her eyes flooded with tears, and the image of Cheryl's face became blurred.

Cheryl remained with her until she was politely asked to leave. "Your friend should rest now," Nina heard the nurse say. "You may come and see her again tomorrow, *n'est-ce pas?* Do not worry, *mademoiselle*. She is in good hands, and all is well."

All is well, the nurse could say blithely, yet her whole life had been shattered. "Is Mandy all right?" she asked, as Cheryl rose to leave.

"Sure. She seemed to be slightly in shock, and a bit confused about what happened. But she's okay."

"And Phyllida Hooper, what does she have to say?"

Cheryl looked glum. "She's been trying to make out that it was all your fault . . . that you enticed Mandy away from her. According to her version she was painting on the beach, and told Mandy to stay close. She says you must have called or beckoned the child to go up on the cliffs with you."

"But that's not true," Nina protested. "I didn't even see Mandy until I heard her scream out."

"I believe you," Cheryl assured her, with a comforting smile. "I heard Mandy scream, too. But it's not going to be easy to prove unless Mandy herself can give a clear picture of what happened. I'll talk to her when I get back."

"Oh, but you mustn't upset Mandy," Nina said quickly. "Anyway, what does it matter what Phyllida says about me? The damage is done now, and nothing can alter that."

The next day Nina was discharged from the hospital, it being decided that she would be more comfortable among her friends. An ambulance transferred her to the Villa Mimosa, and a daybed was placed near the window of her room so she could look out. Presently, a tap on the door announced Boyd.

"Well, this is a fine mess," he said frowningly, as he bent to plant a brief kiss on her forehead. "You ought to have known better than to clamber about like that on dangerous rocks, Nina."

"But I had no alternative," she protested, astonished and hurt beyond measure by his tone. "I only went up there to rescue Mandy."

"That's not the way Phyllida Hooper tells it," Boyd commented. "According to her, you beckoned the child to join you up on the cliffside."

"So you'd rather take her word than mine, would you?" Nina choked.

Boyd shrugged away a specific answer. "The fact remains that if you hadn't been on the beach in the first place, you wouldn't have become involved."

Nina stared at him aghast. "Are you seriously suggesting that it would have been better if I hadn't been there on the spot? Mandy could be dead now, Boyd, or terribly injured."

"Maybe, maybe not," he grunted. "As it is, *you're* the one who's been injured, and it couldn't have happened at a worse moment. God knows where we'd be now if Cheryl had hurt herself too—it might have meant canceling the season here altogether. With you completely out of the picture, the other girls will have to take over your roles between them, and it's going to mean a lot of rearranging. As for *Summer Rhapsody,* it's a calamity. I've decided that Cheryl had better do the premiere, as she's coped the best in the understudy rehearsals. But I never intended her to actually dance the role, only you and Lamartine. Cheryl will never make a good showing with all that delicate footwork, and I'll need to simplify things for her. She'll have to be partnered by Robin, because he's better than Alan, and it's going to mean a hell of a lot of work in the next couple of days to pull it all into shape."

Nina blinked frantically to hold back tears. Despite the change in her relationship with Boyd, she'd expected sympathy from him over what had befallen her. He, who had encouraged her dreams of becoming a prima ballerina, could understand more than anyone else what this accident would almost certainly turn out to have cost her. But Boyd's only concern seemed to be the inconvenience to himself. Of course the show had to go on, she fully realized that, and it was Boyd's job as Assistant Director to make immediate plans regarding all the other dancers. But in any ballet company sprains and injuries necessitating changed schedules were a regular fact of life. It was unbelievably cruel of him to take this attitude.

"You mustn't let me keep you, then," she told him bitterly. "You'd better hurry off and get on with all the things you've got to do." Boyd shot her an uneasy glance, and she could tell that he was wondering how to get away without displaying indecent haste. "Well, go, if you're going," she snapped.

"There's no cause to take that tone," he muttered. "After all, I can't help it that you've put yourself out of action."

"Of course not," Nina said with heavy irony. "The accident was entirely due to my own stupidity, right? I've only got myself to blame for the fact that my whole career is in ruins."

"You'll be okay, given time," he said quickly. "As good as new."

"That's a lie and you know it, Boyd. If I ever dance again, I'll never reach the level I did before."

He glanced away, looking embarrassed. With his

thumbs stuck in the waistband of his jeans, he stared out through the window. "Look, you're getting the very best treatment possible, Nina, Sir Hugo insisted on that. I gather that the orthopedic man at the hospital is absolutely tops. When the plaster comes off, they'll give you physiotherapy to restore full movement, and there's every chance that you'll hardly notice any difference."

Listening to his stream of platitudes, she felt a bitter sort of sympathy for him. Boyd was terribly ambitious, and until yesterday Nina Selby had nicely slotted into his vision of a glittering future. Now, she was useless to him. Someone that he'd have to unload just as soon as possible.

Could the man she had once expected to marry really be so coldly calculating? Nina asked herself bleakly. Looking across at his handsome profile now, seeing his hard expression, the sulky set of his mouth, she realized that he could. She had believed, during the time they had danced together, that she and Boyd had a unique empathy, that they knew one another through and through. But now the cloak had fallen from her eyes and she realized that in reality they were poles apart.

"Stop trying to kid me, Boyd," she said wearily. "We both know the score, so we might as well be honest about admitting it. Now, you'd better go and get to work rehearsing Cheryl."

Nina was thankful when the door closed behind him, but she was not alone for long. Her next visitor was Phyllida Hooper.

"I hope you realize," she said coldly, looking down at Nina with hard eyes, "that it's your own fault you're in this predicament. I shall never forgive you, Miss Selby, for enticing Mandy up on those rocks and exposing her to such terrible danger."

"You know very well that's not true," Nina retorted furiously. "I did nothing to entice Mandy. The first I knew was when she screamed out."

"Rubbish. Mandy was playing happily on the beach, right by my side, while I was painting. Then suddenly I was aware that she'd disappeared, and I hurried to look for her. I'm very cross with her for sneaking off with you, of course, but in fairness one cannot wholly blame a six-year-old child. The fault was yours—ninety-nine per cent at least."

Nina was silent, shocked to the core of her being. If she tried to defend herself now, she would appear to be laying the blame on Mandy. Phyllida was desperately trying to cover up her own negligence in permitting Mandy to stray, and she had been very clever in spreading her version of the story around like that. The real truth might never emerge. Poor little Mandy was probably hopelessly confused now about what actually *had* happened, and no doubt she was full of remorse for the accident she had unwittingly caused.

"How is Mandy?" she asked Phyllida in a quiet voice.

"Very upset, naturally. It was a shocking experience for her."

"I'd like to see her."

Phyllida's eyes glittered. "I've no doubt you would—so you can feed her mind with lies and persuade her to say that you *didn't* beckon her to join you on the rocks."

"What *does* she say about what happened, then?"

"I haven't even asked her," Phyllida said in contemptuous dismissal. "Nor will I. She'll be punished, of course, for being so naughty, and she most certainly will not be allowed to come running to you. Let that be clearly understood."

"It's not fair to punish Mandy," Nina began in protest, but Phyllida cut across her.

"I shall decide what is fair and what is not fair. In future, Miss Selby, you will refrain from trying to drive a wedge between me and my niece. In any case, it's all been a waste of time because you've totally failed in your attempt to make use of Mandy to ingratiate yourself with her father. Dexter, I'm sure, will be no more forgiving than I am when he hears that you heedlessly risked her life in the first place—even if you did manage to prevent disaster by a dramatic rescue."

Would Dexter not be even just a tiny bit concerned about what had happened to her? Nina thought wistfully as Phyllida swept out of the room. Certainly not if his sister-in-law could help it. She would feed him lies and completely poison his mind in order to protect herself from his wrath.

The afternoon dragged on interminably, though Nina wasn't short of visitors, from Sir Hugo downward. Everyone was very sympathetic and full of praise for her bravery; and thankfully the members of the company all seemed to accept Cheryl's version of what had happened, rather than Phyllida Hooper's. Nevertheless, Nina could sense an uneasy air in her visitors' attitude toward her. The reason for this wasn't difficult to understand. They all guessed what she herself knew with such terrible certainty—that she would never dance a major role again. However well her broken ankle mended, she was doomed to be relegated to an insignificant status in the company's ranks, just one of the *corps de ballet* girls. To hope for more than that was to hope for a miracle, and Nina didn't believe in such things where she herself was concerned.

Robin turned up when Nina was drinking a cup of tea. Looking embarrassed, he apologized for not being able to come and see her any sooner, but explained that all afternoon Boyd had kept him and Cheryl busy rehearsing *Summer Rhapsody*.

"I realized that," Nina told him. "I could hear the music. How's it going,. Robin?"

"Okay, I suppose," he said uneasily. "Only . . . well, it's not the same as partnering you, Nina. It seemed as if I just couldn't put a foot wrong when I was dancing with you, especially these past few days."

Poor Robin, he looked terribly uncomfortable, and she knew that he felt disloyal to be partnering another dancer in the starring role designed expressly for her. How different from Boyd's attitude, she thought bitterly, and hastened to console him.

"I'm really glad it's Cheryl who's going to take over the role," she said, with a warm smile. "I'll be rooting for you both, Robin, and I hope it's a terrific success."

Brought down to recline on the terrace the next morning, in the fragrant shade of an orange tree, Nina was never short of a companion for long. The various members of the company came up for a few minutes' friendly chat. Yet there was no escaping the sense of isolation, of being an outsider now. Through the open French windows the sound of the rehearsal piano reached her, and Boyd's voice calling instructions. None of it had any relevance for her now. She felt like giving up and just drifting through time.

A footstep heralded yet someone else approaching, and she turned her head to see who it was. The sight of Dexter's tall figure made her gasp out loud. With dismay, with hope? . . . She didn't quite know what it was she felt. He came to her side swiftly, and perched on the edge of the daybed, taking her hand in his.

"Nina, this is a terrible thing to have happened."

Was he just being kind? she wondered bemusedly. Was he curbing his anger because she had been so badly injured? Nina searched his lean features for an answer as he went on, "I only heard this morning and I came at once. I phoned to tell Mandy to let you know that I'd definitely be back tomorrow to see you open in *Summer Rhapsody*. When Phyllida told me what had happened, I got the first available plane."

"What . . . what did she tell you, Dexter?"

"That's not important," he said dismissively. "Whatever led up to the incident, I realize that Mandy must have been in a perilous situation, and you almost certainly saved her life, Nina—at a terrible cost to yourself. I shudder to think what might have happened if you hadn't been close by when she got into difficulties."

"Mandy mustn't be allowed to suffer, Dexter," she said, looking up at him earnestly.

"Why should she suffer?" he asked, seeming puzzled. "She's perfectly all right . . . not a scratch."

Nina hesitated. "I think perhaps Phyllida thinks Mandy should be punished for disobedience."

"I'm sure you're wrong about that, Nina," he said, frowning. "As a matter of fact, Phyllida was being rather especially sweet to Mandy when I arrived just now. Very gentle and motherly. I suppose she realizes what a traumatic experience it must have been for the poor child."

Nina closed her eyes to keep back the tears that pressed against her eyelids. Phyllida held all the aces, and she was playing them so cleverly. But at least, Nina consoled herself, Dexter wasn't heaping blame on her for what had happened, as Phyllida had so confidently predicted. Whatever he believed in his heart, he was being tender with her and showing great concern. That was something to be thankful for. When she opened her eyes again, she met Dexter's steady glance.

"Dearest Nina," he murmured, leaning forward to kiss her on the cheek. "I owe you so much. More than I shall ever be able to repay."

Chapter Nine

$\mathcal{D}$exter flew back to London that same day, explaining to Nina that the business negotiations were at a delicate stage which required his presence. He had asked her if she wanted to attend tomorrow night's opening at the theater, but she firmly shook her head. She told Dexter what she'd told everybody else, that she didn't think she'd be able to sit still for any length of time with her leg in plaster. In truth, though, she feared that her fragile emotions would disgrace her. She couldn't face the poignancy of watching the premiere of the ballet that should have been her personal triumph.

Dexter nodded sympathetically. "If that's what you think best. If you *had* intended going, I'd stick to my original plan to come over tomorrow in time for the performance. As it is, I'll call it off. Sir Hugo will understand." He hesitated, then went on, "Nina, I want you to have every single thing you need to make you as comfortable as possible. You only have to say the word, and it'll be provided. I'll tell Sir Hugo when I speak to him."

"Thank you," she murmured.

"No, you mustn't thank me. The debt is entirely on my side, and always will be."

Nina deliberately stayed outside on the terrace until he went, to make sure that their parting was in public. Dexter pressed her hand warmly, and touched her forehead with his lips. Nina was careful not to meet his glance, afraid that she would betray too much. An hour later, a florist delivered a bouquet of exotic orchids from the airport.

"From Dexter?" queried Cheryl, when she came to sit with Nina during a break in the rehearsal.

"Yes."

There was a brief silence. Then, "What exactly is going on between you two, Nina?"

"How do you mean?"

"Oh, come off it! You and I live in each other's pockets, and I'm not blind. From the time he phoned you after that charity gala at Haslemere Hall, your moods have been up and down like a yo-yo. I know you've been seeing him, even though you tried hard to conceal the fact from me. Are you in love with the man, Nina?"

The point-blank question caught her unprepared and she glanced away. "I . . . I suppose I might be."

"Might be?"

"All right then, I *am*." Nina looked up and met her friend's challenging gaze. "I wish I didn't love him, Cheryl. But I just can't help myself."

"What about him? How does he feel toward you?"

Nina spread her slender fingers in a defiant gesture. "You needn't worry; I'm under no illusion that it's for keeps. We both know Dexter Rolfe's reputation where women are concerned. I don't blame you for trying to warn me off him."

"I still would, if I thought it would make any difference," Cheryl said wryly. "But you two have obviously got the sort of chemistry which made it inevitable that you'd burst into flames when you came together. Has the affair burned itself out now, Nina, or is it likely to continue?"

"With me like *this?*" she said, with bitter irony.

"He could hardly toss you aside like a worn-out old slipper when you've been injured as a result of saving his child's life. Not unless the man is an out-and-out heel."

"He isn't," Nina insisted. "I mean, I'm sure he wouldn't be, not intentionally. But I don't know what Dexter really feels about me, deep down." She took a breath to steady her emotions. "At least he doesn't seem to have bought Phyllida's version of the accident wholesale. He's not holding me to blame for Mandy being on those rocks in the first place."

"I should think not," Cheryl said vehemently. "I haven't told you yet, Nina . . . Dexter had a word with me while he was here. He thanked me for my part in the rescue and so on, and of course I made it my business to give him the correct version of what happened."

Nina twisted one finger into her shining dark hair, and asked lightly, "How did he take it? Did he seem surprised?"

Cheryl mused. "It's hard to tell. My guess is that he's shrewd enough to realize that Phyllida is trying to cover up for her own shocking negligence. But the main thing is that Dexter has nothing but praise for your bravery. He feels deeply indebted to you."

"But I don't want that," Nina protested.

170

"Want it or not, you've got it." Cheryl gave an exaggerated sigh. "I must admit that he's a terribly handsome man, Nina. I suppose I can't altogether blame you for going overboard about him." She became serious. "What about your relationship with Boyd? I know that you and he haven't been dating lately, but . . . well, it doesn't seem to stop him from acting just as possessively about you in front of other people."

"There's nothing between Boyd and me anymore," Nina told her. "I've known for some time that my feelings for him had changed . . . or rather, that they were never quite what I imagined. Meeting Dexter showed me that what I'd felt for Boyd just wasn't enough—only Boyd never gave me a chance to talk things over with him. We finally had it out the other night."

"I see! Well, I can't say I'm sorry, Nina. I always did think that Boyd was just using you to help build his own career," Cheryl paused, then went on in a little rush, "I might as well tell you, I suppose. After you'd gone to bed last night Boyd made a strong pass at me. He started talking about how he could build me up into a world-famous ballerina, if he and I teamed up. Not quite knowing how you two stood these days, I wasn't sure what to say—whether to play it cool and simply tell him that I didn't fancy the idea of getting to the top that way, or really slap Boyd down for being so disloyal to my best friend."

"So what *did* you say?"

"Sort of half and half," Cheryl said, with a rueful smile. "I was quite tough, but not nearly as tough as I might have been. Boyd got the message, all right! This morning I saw him looking soulfully into Elli Kyle's eyes."

"Elli?"

"That's right. My guess is that she's next in line for being coached to stardom the Boyd Maxwell way. Boyd may be a good artistic director and a brilliant choreographer, Nina, but I'm fast coming to the conclusion that as a man he's an out-and-out rat."

By mutual agreement, the two girls decided that the subject had been talked out.

"I hope you don't mind me not coming to see you open tomorrow night," Nina said apologetically a few minutes later when Cheryl got up to return to rehearsal.

Cheryl laughed. "To tell the truth, Nina, I'm relieved. I wouldn't want to have you in the audience thinking how much better you'd have danced the role."

"Huh! You're a nice liar. But I'll be thinking of you and keeping my fingers crossed, be sure of that. Honestly, I'm really glad you've taken over the role and I hope it goes splendidly for you. Grab this chance with both hands, Cheryl. *Summer Rhapsody* is a marvelous ballet, and it could really lift your career."

"Oh, Nina!" Her eyes misty with emotion, Cheryl bent and gave her a hug. "What a way to achieve success, stepping into *your* shoes. Life is horribly unfair, isn't it?"

Nina swallowed down a lump in her throat. "You've had your share of life's unfairness, Cheryl, so you needn't feel guilty about this. Believe me, I'll be rooting for you like mad. I've told Robin, too, and it's the truth."

The opening night of the Nice season was quite a big success. *Summer Rhapsody* was given a warm reception in the press next morning, Cheryl Wyatt being commended for the grace and poignancy of her dancing. After breakfast the whole company was gathered on the terrace, excitedly translating the reviews from the

French. Though Nina tried hard to join in the chatter, her sense of isolation increased. Her ankle, under the weight of the plaster cast, seemed to throb unbearably.

The following morning brought a letter from Dexter. Nina waited until she was left alone before daring to slit the envelope. Her hands were trembling so much that she could hardly make out the words. What she was expecting, she didn't quite know, but she felt a chill of disappointment. Dexter referred to his great concern about her, and his deep sense of gratitude. He fervently wished, he said, that the export problems which had taken him back to London could be solved quickly, but unfortunately it looked like a long haul. Very probably, he would need to make a trip to Australia to get things sorted out, so it was likely to be some time before he would see her again. Meanwhile, he was most anxious that she shouldn't have a moment's worry about her future financial position. *For the moment, of course, there's no problem. But I want you to know, Nina, that I'm going to work out an arrrangement that will give you permanent security. The very least I can do is to make sure that you don't have any money worries as an added burden to the pain you're already having to suffer because of your bravery in rescuing Mandy.*

It could, Nina supposed with a sigh, be regarded as a considerate letter. But to her it read suspiciously like the carefully worded epistle of a man who felt himself trapped. His latest conquest, at the first passionate culmination of their affair, had got herself involved in a tragic accident which left him tied to her through a sense of gratitude and obligation. There was a hint, in Dexter's reference to her permanent financial future, that he was attempting to buy his way out. Just what had he in mind, she wondered . . . paying her some kind of pension as the price of his freedom? Nina rejected the idea contemptuously. He could have his freedom for nothing, she wouldn't make any emotional demands on him. Dexter could go his own way, and she would grieve silently for the loss of her lover and the loss of her future career. Despite everything, she had no regrets . . . she would live on the memories of those halcyon early mornings at their secret rock pool paradise, and that one perfect midnight when she and Dexter had shared ecstasy together. Nothing would ever make her stop loving him.

The succession of gloriously sunny August days dragged by in a gray dream for Nina. The nightly ballet performances continued to go well, and without the need for so many rehearsals her friends had free time to come and chat with her. But Nina felt more and more isolated, unable to join in their constant shop talk. Ballet dancers, she realized now, lived in a world apart from other people; there was little else they ever wanted to talk about except dancing. Boyd was obviously keeping his distance. The few times he did force himself to come over and speak to her, Nina was careful to make it easy for him to escape quickly—to his obvious relief.

After the first few days, she did at least have the pleasure of Mandy's company. Not, Nina guessed, because her aunt had relented and lifted the ban on them meeting, but because Phyllida had grown bored with the day-long care of a child, and was only too glad to have Mandy happily occupied so that she was free to go off to Nice. It was clear that the little girl didn't appreciate the devastating effect of a broken ankle on a dancer's career, and Nina took pains to leave her in happy ignorance. They didn't refer to the accident directly as Nina thought it best to keep off the subject, but she was very touched by Mandy's affectionate concern for her comfort, and the genuine pleasure she registered each time Nina reported feeling a little better than the day before. They fell into the habit of reading aloud together, taking turns, and always the books Mandy voted for had a dancing background. Mandy was as single-minded in her love of ballet, Nina thought, as she herself had been at the age of six.

Dexter phoned now and then, and always asked to speak to Nina. Though the sound of his low, vibrant voice coming over the line from Australia made all her nerve endings tingle with excitement, the enormous distance between them somehow created a barrier. Whatever they said seemed stilted and awkward. Hanging up, Nina was left with a sense of depression. She found herself wondering anew how genuine this urgent business of his was, or how much Dexter was using it as an excuse to keep away from her.

Nina's plaster cast came off on schedule, and further X rays showed that the bones were knitting well. It was still forbidden for her to put any weight on her foot, and she was given crutches. A physiotherapist, who'd been engaged to come to the Villa Mimosa during the company's stay to treat any sprains or whatever that might arise, gave her daily massages and taught her a series of therapeutic exercises.

"Bon!" she said after her eighth visit, having watched Nina perform the range of joint movements. "It goes well, I think."

"Not well enough, I'm afraid," said Nina.

The pleasant, middle-aged woman sat down with a starchy rustle of her white coat. "But you are so impatient, *mademoiselle*. In all such matters, time is needed. There must be no haste."

"No amount of time will help me to dance properly again," Nina murmured chokily.

"You must have courage, and persevere with these exercises, *n'est-ce pas?* A few weeks more, a few months perhaps, and your ankle will be fully restored to mobility. You will have no limp to worry about."

"It's still not good enough, in my job," Nina told her ruefully. "The slightest residual weakness is fatal in a dancer." At least, Nina might have added, at the level to which she had aspired. Those exciting days when she'd stretched her body to the limit in a struggle for perfection, fired with ambition to get to the very top, seemed so far away now. Back in some lost limbo of time.

It wasn't until the Regency Ballet's final performance that Nina found the courage to attend the theater in Nice. She had no wish to go, but felt that it would be disloyal to Cheryl if she didn't. Using her crutches, and carefully helped onto the bus by her friends, she sat back heavily in her seat and listened to the laughing chatter all around, not feeling a real part of it. Arriving at the theater, Nina declined Cheryl's suggestion that she should go backstage and limped her way to the empty auditorium settling down to wait. She had been there ten minutes or so when Sir Hugo arrived and came to join her, taking the next seat.

"How are you feeling today, Nina, my dear? I keep hearing reports on your excellent progress."

She forced a smile. "I've had wonderful treatment, Sir Hugo. I'm grateful for that."

"But . . .?" His pale gray eyes were shrewd. "I detect a note of reservation in your voice."

"But will I ever, *ever* be any good again?" she said, her fears coming out in a rush of words.

"Of course you will, of course." The kindly old man patted her hand. "You don't suppose that we could contemplate losing such a valued member of our company?"

"But in what capacity, Sir Hugo? Not as a principal dancer."

He stroked his beard, looking uncomfortable. "It's still much too early to be talking like this, my dear girl. There are instances of dancers making the most miraculous recoveries from serious injuries. In a few more weeks you may find . . ."

"You know the answer now, Sir Hugo," she said sadly. "The odds against me ever being good enough to dance a leading role again are a thousand to one."

He was too honest to deny it. "All the same, my dear," he went on reassuringly, "there are other fields open to you in the world of ballet—not necessarily involving dancing at all. For someone of your great talent, there will always be a place in the Regency Company. Remember that, Nina, and remember too that everyone admires you for your unselfish bravery."

A door at the rear of the auditorium opened and Nina glanced around, thinking that the audience must be starting to arrive. To her astonishment, it was Dexter. Her breath caught in her throat and her heart was hammering wildly as he strode briskly toward them down the carpeted aisle.

"I arrived at the villa an hour ago," he explained, after greeting them both. "I just dropped my stuff off and had a quick word with Mandy, then came straight here."

"I'm so glad, my dear fellow, that you could manage to come in time to see our final performance," smiled Sir Hugo.

Dexter slipped into the seat beside Nina and took her hand in his. "How are you feeling?"

"Not so bad," she stammered, still trembling from the shock of his presence. He looked even more incredibly handsome than the image of him imprinted on her memory, and her heart ached with love and longing. The touch of his warm, firm fingers caressing hers, was filling her with delight, reassuring her, to her infinite joy, that he still wanted to make love to her.

"You look pale," he stated, studying her face intently. "Have you been eating properly? Resting enough?"

"I'm okay," she insisted nervously. "Really I am."

"It's rather a pity," Sir Hugo Quest remarked, "that the company is returning to London so soon. A little longer in this beneficial climate would do Nina the world of good."

Dexter nodded. "That's precisely what I've been thinking myself, Sir Hugo. So I've arranged to continue my lease of the Villa Mimosa for the time being. I've finally straightened out the problems of Rolfe Industries and I consider that I'm entitled to a holiday in the sun. So we'll stay on here, Nina . . . you and me, Mandy and Phyllida."

While Nina stared at him in amazement, Sir Hugo chuckled. "An expensive holiday, leasing a vast place like the Villa Mimosa for a party of four."

Dexter shrugged. "It's convenient, it suits us." He smiled secretly into Nina's eyes, sending a thrill of delight skittering through her. "And we've been happy there. There's no better place for us to be, really."

"It would certainly solve a difficulty," Sir Hugo observed. "Back in London, Nina would inevitably feel somewhat isolated with Cheryl and her other friends all busy at the theater. I shall be relieved to think that she's in such good hands." The old man rose stiffly to his feet and left them then to go backstage.

"You haven't said what *you* think of the idea yet," Dexter reminded her. "You will stay, Nina, won't you?"

"Oh, Dexter . . ." she choked.

His glance met hers. "What kind of an answer is that?"

"Phyllida . . . what does she have to say?"

"I haven't mentioned it to her yet," he said. "If she doesn't like the idea, she's free to return to England."

But Phyllida would never do that, Nina thought wryly; she'd never leave Dexter alone with someone she saw as a rival. What did it matter, though, having to put up with Phyllida's enmity? The only thing that counted was that she would be close to Dexter; able to see him, able to touch him. And the unmistakable message in his eyes was that he still found her desirable and wanted to resume their love affair. Nina felt a wonderful flooding of joy within her body, like basking in the warmth of the first spring sunshine after a long hard winter.

It was strange to be at the Villa Mimosa now that the ballet company had gone. With only a skeleton staff remaining, the huge house seemed empty and hollow. Dexter and Mandy and Phyllida still kept to their rooms in the luxurious upstairs suite, but at Dexter's suggestion Nina moved into the spacious bedroom which had been occupied by Sir Hugo, with its spectacular panoramic view all along the sweeping coastline.

The days passed, falling into a pattern. Nina breakfasted with the others on the balcony of the suite, by which time the physiotherapist would have arrived to give her an hour of massage and exercises. Phyllida avoided outright hostility in front of Dexter, but otherwise she made her resentment very clear to Nina. Except when Dexter was safely occupied on the phone talking to one of his various executives, which he did for a little while each morning, Phyllida clung to him like a leech, right through until the time that Nina retired to bed. It was obvious that she didn't intend to leave Nina and Dexter alone for a single minute.

One morning after her massage session, Nina wandered into the ballroom. The *barres* had been taken away, of course, so she held on to the lid of the piano as a support. After a few warm-up *pliés*, she tried a *developpé*, unfolding her leg in front of her and swinging it at the hip in a *rond de jambe*, moving her leg on around to the back and finally letting go of the piano, finishing up in an *arabesque* with her arms gracefully extended. There was a sound behind her, and she turned to see Mandy skipping into the room.

"I wish you'd teach me how to do that, Nina," she said eagerly.

Nina shook her head. "I'm sorry, pet, but you're too young for ballet lessons." Then, seeing the child's crestfallen expression, she went on, "Maybe we could try something that wouldn't do any harm. Let me think a moment. I know . . . we'll pretend that you're Little Red Riding Hood, and you can be going to see your grandmother through the wood. Every now and then you stop to pick flowers and put them in your basket. And I'll pretend to be the wolf. We'll take off our shoes and do it in bare feet. No speaking, mind, just miming and dancing. Okay?"

Mandy took up the idea enthusiastically, and was imaginative in her interpretation. Nina contributed a few suggestions, showing her some simplified ballet steps that wouldn't strain the child's tender muscles.

After that they regularly had what Mandy stubbornly insisted on calling her ballet lesson each morning, and Nina got one of the house servants, Pierre, to carry a record player into the room so they could dance to music. There was a large selection of records in the suite and she picked out ones that were suitable.

Most afternoons the four of them would all go out on some expedition, Dexter driving his hired Citroën along one of the spectacular coastal roads, or inland to the mountains. One such afternoon they went to the little hill town of Grasse, the center of the French perfume industry. It was set among vast fields of growing flowers, and the fragrance as they drove past was heavenly. They visited a perfumery, and Nina was fascinated to see the exacting care with which the essences of hundreds of different flowers were blended together into masterpieces of the *parfumiers'* art. Dexter bought expensive bottles for Nina and Phyllida, and something less exotic for Mandy.

By this time Nina was beginning to walk more normally, using just a rubber-tipped stick, but when they came to a flight of unevenly worn stone steps leading up from the vat-room, she leaned heavily on the handrail. Dexter quickly slipped his arm about her waist, saying, "You must be very careful not to injure that ankle again."

"Thanks." Shivering in response to his touch, she babbled nervously, "It's improving fast, isn't it? I'm not limping nearly so much now, am I?"

Behind them she heard a cluck of impatience from Phyllida, making it clear that she thought Nina was exaggerating her need for Dexter's support. And in truth it was a temptation Nina found hard to resist. It was marvelous to feel the warm strength of his arm about her, the caressing touch of his fingers against her flesh each time he helped her out of the car. Nina longed for closer physical contact with him. She imagined that Dexter must be able to feel her body trembling with the intensity of her leashed emotions. When they exchanged glances she could read the naked desire in his eyes, and sometimes it was all she could do not to blurt out that she was ready to make love as soon as he wanted . . . that he need not be so solicitous and go on treating her like a fragile invalid.

"Take care, Nina," he kept saying. "You're too impetuous."

She was through being careful and cautious. That would mean denying herself the bliss his lovemaking could bring, on the reasoning that it could only lead to eventual heartbreak. She faced heartbreak either way, and if for a brief time she could snatch a little happiness, why not? When Dexter grew tired of her would be time enough to end their affair. Until then she would have no shame, no pride . . . just the overwhelming love she felt which was too intense to be denied.

One morning Nina became aware that Dexter was standing in the doorway of the ballroom while she and Mandy were dancing together. She broke off, but he said with a smile, "No, don't stop. I was through with my calls sooner than I expected, and I thought I'd come downstairs to watch you."

Nina found it difficult to continue unselfconsciously while he was there. But she did her best. "Mandy, let's try you being a butterfly hatching out of its chrysalis. You unfold your beautiful wings very carefully and let them dry off in the sun, and then you flit from flower to flower searching for nectar. It will give you an opportunity to show your daddy how nicely you can use your arms in those *port de bras* I taught you."

Dexter stood looking on quietly, but they were not left in peace for long. There was a sound of hurrying footsteps on the stairs, and Phyllida appeared.

"Oh, here you are, Dexter. I wondered where you'd got to."

He gave his sister-in-law an absent smile. "Mandy's dancing very nicely, don't you think? Nina is giving her real style and grace."

"Really, a six-year-old child! Now, Dexter, I want you to take me into Nice to do some shopping. These two seem to be amusing themselves, so they can stay here."

"No, we'll all go to Nice. And while you're shopping, Phyllida, I'll take Nina and Mandy to look at the flower market. If that's okay with you, Nina," he added.

"Sounds great! Just give me a few minutes to get changed, and I'll be ready." It gave Nina a secret glow of pleasure to see the sour expression on Phyllida's face at the failure of her little ruse.

They had lunch in Nice at a seafood restaurant near the harbor, and afterward Dexter drove them to a small village along the coast where there was a traveling fair. It was a happy day for Nina, marred only by the constrained atmosphere of yet another evening spent with Phyllida making it a threesome. Nina felt so on edge that she went off to bed early, pleading tiredness. But she didn't sleep. She felt as if a steel spring inside her was being wound up tighter and tighter. It was a hot, breathless night, and after a few hours of fitful resting she came fully awake to the tense, waiting hush just before sunrise.

Under a strange compulsion she rose from her bed and pulled on jeans and a sleeveless cotton sweater, quickly brushing her long dark hair. The house was utterly silent, with not even the servants stirring. She descended the wide staircase slowly, pausing every few steps to rest, still finding stairs a particular problem. At the foot she turned toward the entrance lobby, then froze in her tracks. Dexter was standing in the archway, watching her.

"Hello, Nina," he said, smiling.

"Dexter! I didn't know you were there."

For long, pulsating seconds they stood looking at one another, as if caught up in a spell of doubt and uncertainty. Then in the same split second each of them moved, drawn irresistibly together. Nina's stick clattered to the floor as Dexter's arms folded around her, enclosing her in the magic of his embrace. She thrilled to the achingly familiar pressures of his hard, virile body, went weak at the touch of his warm hands which molded her to him, felt her senses swirl as his mouth covered hers in a long kiss. It was a floating infinity of time before he let her go, his breath shuddering with the release of long pent-up desire.

"Oh, Nina, I've wanted you so badly," he murmured, his voice husky in his throat. "Ever since . . . oh God, what torment it's been."

"I know," she whispered. "I know."

Gently his hands cupped her face and he gazed down at her, smiling deep into her amber gold eyes; then he leaned forward and kissed her on the forehead, his mouth moving in a sensuous trail to her left temple and slowly across her cheek to halt at her lips in another deep kiss, his tongue thrusting in to taste the inner sweetness. His hands slid around to the nape of her neck, pushing beneath the dark mane of her hair, and Nina held her head back as his kisses, becoming more and more passionate, rained upon her face and the creamy length of her throat, as if he were in a fever to rediscover and imprint his mark on every tiny part of her . . . on and on until she gasped for breath.

"Oh, Dexter!" she moaned deliriously.

His hands roamed over her slender body in a ceaseless caress, moving down across her back and into the curve of her waist, spreading across her hips, gripping the soft warm flesh of her buttocks and smoothing over her thighs. Then they swept up again to slide beneath her sweater and cup the roundness of her breasts. Through the lacy fabric of her bra he found their hard buds and teased them into a state of tingling ecstasy.

"Nina, my beautiful Nina," he whispered hoarsely.

"I want you, I want you." Then, drawing back to look deep into her eyes again, he asked, "May I . . . shall I come to your room tonight?"

"Yes," she told him, and it was a cry of thankfulness and joy. "Yes, Dexter, yes."

From far off, somewhere in the kitchen regions, a door slammed. They drew apart, though Dexter still kept her imprisoned in the circle of his arms.

"People will be around soon," he said. "Let's go into the garden for a while."

The sun had risen by now, lifting itself above the mountains, and the sky was a beautiful pearly pink with gossamer veils of cloud. The sea glistened, tiny white wave crests dancing at the caprice of a warm breeze. Now that it was September the days weren't quite so hot, but it was still undeniably summer. An Indian summer, Nina thought as she walked with Dexter's arm about her waist. And like an Indian summer, this magical spell of happiness would be all too fleeting.

With unspoken consent they made for the little belvedere, their first meeting place at the Villa Mimosa. Sitting on the carved stone seat, they gazed out across the shimmering sea. The feverish white heat of their passion was gone now, its urgency damped down by the pact they had made for tonight. Dexter held her close, tenderly, his lips against the silken softness of her dark hair, while his fingers playfully intertwined with hers.

"When I watched you dancing with Mandy yesterday," he said, "I thought how wonderfully lithe and graceful you looked. It's incredible your ankle has mended so well that you can actually dance already."

"I was being very careful not to put too much strain on it," Nina explained. "But . . . I just had to try. Not being able to dance is like being only half-alive."

Dexter nodded somberly, then said, "The orthopedic man at the hospital told me that he's very pleased with your progress."

"You talked to him?" she asked in surprise.

"Of course. It's important for me to know about you."

For a few golden moments Nina basked in the thought of his concern for her. *It's important for me to know about you,* he'd said. And then, from nowhere, came a chilling draught of doubt. Dexter wanted and needed her, he had demonstrated that just now. But was he already thinking ahead to the time when he would cease to want her? Was he anxious to establish the fact that when his passion faded, he would no longer be obliged to demonstrate his gratitude to her for rescuing Mandy?

"What is it, Nina?" he asked, sensing her disquiet.

"Nothing," she lied.

Dexter studied her face gravely, his tawny eyes somber. "What are your plans for the future?"

"How can I possibly answer that?"

He was thoughtful, idly putting out a hand to pluck a sprig of wild thyme from where it grew in a rock crevice and releasing its sharp sweet fragrance. "I talked to Sir Hugo before he left. He told me that you are bravely facing the cruel fact that your career as a leading ballerina is over."

"I have no choice but to face that fact," she murmured chokily. "It's only too obvious."

"So what do you hope to do?" he pressed.

Until this moment Nina hadn't really known the answer to that question. Wild ideas had flitted through her head of leaving Regency Ballet and finding some different kind of work altogether . . . wouldn't it be too unbearably painful to be only on the outer fringe, after all her hopes and dreams of being a prima ballerina? Now, in a sudden blaze of truth, she knew that she loved ballet far too much ever to abandon it voluntarily. As long as she *could* work in some capacity with the company, she would. She would humbly accept whatever was offered.

"With any luck, I'll be able to dance in the *corps de ballet*," she told him. "Or maybe I could specialize in mime and do character parts."

"There are always nondancing jobs, too," Dexter pointed out. "Administration, artistic direction, publicity, all kinds of things. You probably know far more about the possibilities than I do. There's bound to be something you'd find satisfying and worthy of your talents, Nina."

She couldn't hide her bitterness. "Exactly what are you suggesting? A few quiet words in the right ear from the Regency's sponsor?" Anticipating his protest, she went on quickly, "But it wouldn't be necessary, would it? Sir Hugo already knows that it would please you if I were offered something. But don't worry, there'll be no need for them to *create* a job for me. I'll make it clear that as soon as I'm fit enough, I'll be seeking a place in the *corps de ballet*. And I shall never give up the struggle to dance leading roles again, however hopeless it might seem. But wherever I end up, Dexter, however high or low in the company's hierarchy, it's going to be by my own unaided efforts."

His mouth tightened. "There's such a thing as possessing too much pride, Nina."

"For a woman, you mean?" she countered, her anger flaring. "Females should docilely accept any helping handouts that men are good enough to offer them?"

Surprisingly, Dexter looked slightly shamefaced. "I'm sorry if it sounded like that. Believe me, Nina, I admire your sense of pride as much as I admire your courage. It's just that it hurts me so much to think of

187

you struggling bravely to get a foot on the bottom of the ladder, when once you were poised only one rung from the very top."

Nina turned her head and looked at him. "Tell me, Dexter, what would *you* do if, through some unforeseen disaster, Rolfe Industries came crashing down?"

He grinned ruefully. "I'd get a hut for a workshop, a couple of machine tools, and a lad to help me."

"Well, there you are, then!"

The tension between them suddenly relaxed, and Nina felt a warm glow of happiness as they sat there hand in hand in companionable silence. From the branches lacing overhead an autumn-tinted leaf came shivering down, to settle on the flagstones at their feet, a reminder that the Indian summer would soon be over, perhaps? Nina shut the thought away.

"Daddy! Nina!" It was Mandy, calling from somewhere in the gardens nearer the house. "Where are you?"

Dexter's fingers tightened on Nina's. "If we keep quiet, she'll go back indoors," he suggested.

"No, that's not fair." She raised her voice and called, "We're here, pet. At the belvedere."

A few moments later the little girl appeared, breathless from running. "Aunt Phyllida's still in bed, and when I couldn't find you, Daddy, I went to Nina's room. But she was gone, too."

"It's such a beautiful morning, we thought we'd come outside," he told her. They made room between them, and Mandy wedged in happily.

"What are we going to do today, Daddy?" she asked.

"We haven't decided yet," he said. "Is there anything special you'd like to do, Mandymouse?"

They fell to discussing plans, and finally settled on a trip along the coast to Monte Carlo. Just for this fleeting moment, Nina luxuriated in the feeling that they were a close-knit family group. Then, with a glance at her wristwatch, she realized it was time to go back for breakfast.

The return to the house was uphill all the way, and she was glad of Dexter's hand under her elbow on the steps. At one point she placed her foot unevenly and felt a sharp stab of pain in her ankle that made her wince.

"Are you okay?" asked Dexter, concerned.

"Yes, I'm fine."

"Shall I carry you?" he suggested.

"No, really . . ."

"What do you think, Mandymouse? Perhaps Nina is afraid that I couldn't manage to hold her safely."

His daughter scorned the idea. "Robin can lift Nina right over his head ever so easily; I've often seen him do it. And you're a lot stronger than Robin is, Daddy."

"What a challenge to throw a man," Dexter laughed. "Now I'll have to prove it, won't I?"

Instantly Nina found herself scooped up off her feet and held in the cradle of his arms. Her protest was merely a token and she happily relaxed against the solid wall of his chest, slipping her arms around his neck, delighting in the sense of intimacy. Dexter bore her weight without the slightest sign of effort, walking with long, easy strides. Mandy danced along beside them, carrying Nina's stick, laughing gleefully.

Entering the house, he didn't set Nina down, but insisted on carrying her all the way upstairs. Mandy, eager for her breakfast, raced on ahead. On the landing outside the private suite Dexter halted, but he continued to hold her. With their faces only a few inches apart, they gazed deep into one another's eyes and Nina thrilled to see the look of urgent desire that he didn't try to conceal. He smiled faintly and touched the tip of her nose with his in a playful gesture. Then, as he carefully let her slide down against him to find her feet, his mouth covered hers in a kiss that was tenderly soft yet full of the promise of passion.

With a happy sigh, Nina turned and went in through the door that Mandy had left open. Phyllida was standing in the lobby of the suite, her face a frozen mask. Though she greeted Dexter with a light "Good morning," the look she threw at Nina was venomous.

Chapter Ten

*D*inner was delayed that evening because Dexter had arranged a coast-to-coast phone conference with his American distributors—a discussion which he'd said might take some time. With Mandy in bed, Nina wandered downstairs rather than be left alone with Phyllida. Idly, she opened the double doors to the ballroom and went in. With the glittering chandeliers unlit the huge, empty room looked mysterious and ghostly, silver moonlight slanting in through the long windows and glinting on the mirrored walls. Humming softly to herself she began to dance, slowly, carefully, loving the feel of spreading her limbs and letting her body sway in fluid, graceful movements.

A switch clicked, and the ballroom was suddenly flooded with a dazzle of brilliant light. Nina blinked and turned around to see Phyllida advancing toward her.

"So this is where you hid yourself away," she said coldly.

"I wasn't hiding away," Nina protested. "I was just . . ."

"Calculating your next move, perhaps? I think, you know, that it's high time I put you fully in the picture."

"What about?"

"About Dexter, naturally. I hate to shatter your romantic dreams, Nina, but you really ought to be aware of the kind of man you're dealing with in my brother-in-law."

"Look, I don't think I want to stay and listen . . ." Reaching for her stick, Nina turned and began to limp away. A hand on her arm checked her, the grip harsh and surprisingly strong.

"You're going to stay and hear what I have to say," Phyllida said.

Nina shook herself free angrily. "Very well," she said in a tone of weary resignation. "I'm listening."

"You think you're very clever, don't you?" Phyllida spat out, her green eyes narrowed with hostility. "I've watched you acting the poor, helpless little bird with a broken wing for Dexter's benefit. I notice, though, that you can get around all by yourself very well when you have to."

"I don't pretend that I can't," Nina protested. "I use my ankle as much as possible because I can't wait to get back into action. But I know that it would be fatal to overstrain it."

Phyllida's short laugh registered total disbelief. "It's not difficult, of course, for an attractive girl to play on a man's pity in order to soften him up, but whatever fancy ideas you've got floating around in your pretty little head, I'm afraid you're going to be badly shaken up. In other words, my dear Nina, don't imagine for a single moment that Dexter is playing for keeps. He just isn't that sort of man. Besides, he's too shrewd to let himself be trapped."

Nina gasped. "You can't seriously believe that I'm trying to trap him?"

"What else? You're turning that unfortunate mishap of yours into a weapon against Dexter. Right now he feels sorry for you—and grateful, because of Mandy. But don't make the mistake of thinking that his feelings go any deeper than that."

Faced with Phyllida's venomous spite, Nina wondered what she could say in self-defense. There had been one reason and one reason only that she'd accepted Dexter's invitation to stay on at the Villa Mimosa. It was because she loved him. She could never have found the strength of will to tear herself away from the chance of spending a little more time in his company. She knew, though, that when they returned to London, her relationship with him would probably come to an end. She accepted that—and firmly shut it out of her thoughts. But she certainly wasn't about to explain her feelings to Phyllida.

"It was good of Dexter to suggest that I stay on here," she said, choosing her words with care, "and I was glad to accept his offer. I've no parents, you see, and . . . and Sir Hugo thought it would be a good idea, because Cheryl Wyatt, with whom I share a flat, would be out all day. So I'm grateful to Dexter for this opportunity to convalesce in comfort. But as for the future, I expect nothing from him."

"Very wise of you," agreed Phyllida. "Because nothing is what you'll get. Or to put it another way, you might get more than you bargain for."

"I don't wish to stay and hear any more of this," said Nina, and again made a move to go. This time Phyllida didn't lay a hand on her but brought her to a halt with words.

"I don't expect Dexter has ever mentioned how he caused my sister's death?"

"What . . . what do you mean?" Nina asked dazedly.

"Oh, I'm not suggesting that he actually killed his wife with his own two hands. But Dexter sent Judith to her grave, all right, by breaking her heart."

"I . . . I don't believe you," Nina faltered in horror.

"Whether or not you believe me won't alter the ugly facts. Dexter Rolfe is one of those men who spend their time chasing after women. You, my dear Nina, are just one of a long, long line stretching way back over the years. And you're no more important to him than any one of the others has been."

"Are you saying," Nina asked in a strangled voice, "that Dexter carried on like that even when his wife was alive?"

Phyllida's derisive laugh seemed to set the crystal drops of the chandeliers tinkling. "Of course he did, you little idiot. Don't you understand a word I've said? It's Dexter's way of life. He's always been the same, and he'll never change. My sister was a romantic idealist, poor darling, and she could never realize that to Dexter marriage was simply a convenient cloak of respectability. He blithely went his own way, leaving Judith at home to pine her heart out. He made use of her to run his home, to act as hostess to his business associates, and to provide him with a child. But he sought his pleasures elsewhere. The doctor gave a long name to the illness which killed Judith, but in simple truth she died of a broken heart."

Shocked and bewildered, Nina struggled to fight back. "You . . . you're sure that you're not making all this up, because you see me as a rival?"

"If you don't believe me," Phyllida said scornfully, "I suggest you ask Dexter himself—if you dare! As for me seeing you as a rival . . . the thought is laughable. My own relationship with Dexter is on an entirely different level. We understand each other perfectly. To me, his fooling around with other women is entirely unimportant. I have my painting, and I regard sex as a greatly overrated pastime. If Dexter wants to keep on proving what a virile fellow he is, why should I care?"

"According to you," Nina pointed out, "your sister cared."

"Yes," Phyllida agreed. "Sadly, she did. Poor Judith should never have made the mistake of marrying Dexter Rolfe. The wife of a man like him needs to be a very different kind of woman from my sister. Someone far less emotionally vulnerable, and a lot more secure in her own self-evaluation."

In her misery, Nina was stung to fling out sarcastically, "A woman like *you*, perhaps?"

"Exactly." Phyllida was entirely unruffled. "I shall give Dexter precisely what he needs, and leave him free to pursue his little conquests without letting myself be hurt by them. When we decide the time is right, we'll make an excellent partnership."

"You speak as if . . . as if it's already decided."

The smile on Phyllida's face was smug and self-satisfied. "I doubt if you'll welcome an invitation to the wedding, Nina. How would I introduce you to the other guests? Plaything of the bridegroom, now discarded?"

For long, agonizing moments, Nina felt Phyllida's triumphant gaze sweep over her, assessing the amount of pain she had inflicted. Then, briskly, Phyllida turned for the door. "I think I'll go back upstairs now and leave you to think things over."

The moon was lower in the sky now, sending its slanting rays across the gardens, brushing the trees with silver light and casting dense patches of shadow.

Nina stood at her bedroom window, filled with a wistful yearning to be able to go back in time, to return to that blissful night when she and Dexter had made love beside their secret pool. Now, since this evening's horrible conversation with Phyllida, she could no longer delude herself. She knew that Dexter was even more to be condemned than she had ever let herself believe. He was utterly ruthless in pursuit of his selfish pleasures and cared nothing for who might be hurt in the process.

It was very understandable, considered from all angles, that Dexter had chosen Phyllida as his second wife. She would make the ideal marriage partner for a man like him. Aside from the advantage of being his sister-in-law and already installed in his household, caring for his child, a woman with her attitude to sex would enable Dexter to carry on in his usual promiscuous way without creating problems for himself at home. In other words, he would be able to have his cake and eat it, too.

Any minute now Dexter would be coming to her room, and she would have to confront him with what she knew. Nina trembled at the prospect, remembering his terrible anger on a previous occasion when she had accused him of being unfaithful to his wife—though at the time not really believing it to be true. Dexter had sworn at her, before striding off in a fury. Would he react with the same violent temper tonight?

But there was an easier way, Nina decided, of putting an end to the relationship which she couldn't possibly allow to continue now, knowing what she knew. She would merely tell Dexter, firmly and flatly, that she wasn't prepared to go back to where they stood before her accident. Having had an enforced break in their affair for several weeks, it would be best not to resume something that couldn't last much longer anyway. Yes indeed, she resolved, unconsciously clasping and unclasping her hands in her agitation, that was the best way to handle the situation.

The softly shaded light at the bedside, she decided, gave too intimate an impression for the sort of scene she had in mind. Instead, she switched on another lamp on a small table across the room. Then she sat down on the padded window seat and awaited Dexter's arrival.

In the night silence, Nina caught the soft thud of his footsteps in the carpeted corridor. Then a faint tap at her door.

"Come in," she called.

Dexter entered quickly, closing the door behind him. He wore jeans with a white shirt unbuttoned to the waist, and his hair was damp from a recent shower.

"Nina, what is it? You look upset."

As she rose to face him, her limbs were trembling uncontrollably. She found herself staring in fascination at his open shirtfront, white against the vee of bronzed skin beneath. The urge to slide her hands into the gap and across his naked chest was almost too strong to be resisted.

"For heaven's sake, what's the matter?" he asked again, frowning. "You look so strange. And it's not at all cold, but you're shivering."

"I'm not shivering," she denied. "Dexter . . . I know I said that you could come to my room tonight, but it was a big mistake. You can't . . . well, you can't expect us to pick up where we left off. I've decided that it's got to end."

He came forward slowly until there was scarcely a foot between them. Holding her gaze, he said, "It's not a question of what I expect or what you decide, Nina. We can no more stop this happening, either of us, than we could stop a meteor falling from the sky. You know that's true."

"No . . . no!" With a little strangled cry she broke

away from his hypnotic spell, turning and moving behind a small armchair, making it a barrier between them. She clenched its high back with nervous fingers and stared fixedly at a point on the carpet.

"Look at me," he commanded, and with reluctant obedience she lifted her gaze to meet his eyes. Above the lamp, his face looked gaunt and shadowed, sculpted out of stone. "You can't run away from yourself, Nina," he said in a low-throated voice.

"Please go," she stammered. "I want you to leave, Dexter."

He shook his head in emphatic refusal. "Why are you lying to me, Nina?" he demanded. "This morning you were giving me the truth. This morning you were gloriously responsive in my arms, not ashamed to admit how much you wanted me. And now you've suddenly turned into an ice block." He drew a ragged breath. "Okay then, we'll put it to the test. Let me kiss you, just once. Then tell me to go away, if you still can."

"No!" The sharp cry of protest came bursting from her lips in panic. "You . . . you mustn't touch me, Dexter."

"Because you're afraid?"

"Why should I be afraid?" she parried.

"No reason at all," he said softly. "You know that, Nina. I want to make love to you, not rape you. So we're going to talk about this." As he spoke he came towards her, moving very slowly, mesmerizing her. Taking hold of her shoulders he gently pushed her backward until she was sitting on the edge of the bed. Then he sat down beside her, his arm around her waist, his other hand resting lightly on her thigh.

"I just don't understand it," he continued, shaking his head with a bewildered expression. "I thought you seemed very odd at dinner—tense and withdrawn, and you kept avoiding my eyes. But I put that down to a sort of nervous shyness. Now, though, you seem scared to death of me. I can feel you shaking like a leaf. What's it all about, darling?"

"Nothing," she stammered. "I . . . I just . . ."

"What has happened since this morning to change your attitude toward me?" he asked.

This was her opportunity to confront him with what Phyllida had told her, and challenge him to deny it. But it was already too late; she was trapped once again in the powerful magic of his charisma. His closeness, the sensuous warmth of his touch, the clean masculine scent that was uniquely his, had robbed her of all reason. All she could think now was that if she charged Dexter with infidelity to his wife, he would draw back from her in a fury . . . that the arm encircling her waist, the fingers caressing her thigh, would be snatched away, leaving her cold and desolate. Wanting desperately to cling to his nearness, his touch, his tenderness, she shook her head and whispered the lying words, "Nothing has happened today. I still feel the same toward you."

For a few throbbing seconds neither of them moved, both sitting very still. Then slowly Dexter folded his arms about her, holding her close, pressing his face into the fragrant softness of her hair. Nina surrendered the last feeble strand of resistance and let herself lean against his comforting, rocklike body. A traitorous voice within her asked temptingly why she shouldn't let him stay with her tonight, just for a little while. Happiness was going to be such a rare thing in her life from now on, it was senseless to throw it away willfully. At this moment, the only thing that mattered in the whole wide world was that she wanted the bliss of melting against Dexter, of being transported to paradise by his lovemaking.

Outside there was a silent moon, shedding its silver

magic; and here in the room muted lamplight cast a gentle, rosy glow. Tomorrow, when the harsher light of day returned, would be the time for facing up to the truth. Her original plan still stood firm. But tonight she could allow herself the joy of being in the arms of the man she loved. Perhaps—although the thought was too unbearable to contemplate—it would be for the very last time.

"You can't know how much I've enjoyed this time with you," Dexter said, taking her hand and caressing the inside of her wrist with his thumb. "It's been wonderful, a magical interlude from ordinary life. I only wish it hadn't come about for such a tragic reason."

"I've been happy, too," Nina murmured, saying no less than the truth.

"I hope you're not finding Mandy too much of a nuisance," Dexter went on, with a rueful grimace. "She's being very demanding, I realize that, but she does admire you so much. If it gets too much of a strain, though, I'll tell her to lay off a bit. And we could put a stop to the dancing lessons you've been giving her."

Nina shook her head. "No, please . . . I wouldn't want that. I love having Mandy's company, and it gives me enormous pleasure to help keep her interest in ballet alive until she's old enough for formal training."

"If you're sure, then."

"Quite sure. She's a sweet child."

Dexter smiled his pleasure. "It's lovely to see the two of you together. Anyone not knowing could very easily think . . ." He broke off abruptly. His voice changing to a lower timbre, he went on after a moment, "In another way, these past few days have been sheer hell . . . seeing you there so temptingly close. Every minute of the time I've had to restrain myself from carrying you off and making love to you. Oh, my beautiful Nina. I've wanted you so much . . . it's been so long. Please . . . don't refuse me now."

"Oh, Dexter," she murmured, feeling every nerve in her body coming tinglingly alive.

He put fingertips beneath her chin and tilted it up, leaning forward to touch featherlight kisses to her lips, moving on in a sensuous and lingering exploration of her face. Time seemed to come to a halt and there was a waiting, breathless stillness all around them. Nina rolled back her head in delight as his kisses trailed the length of her slender neck and he buried his face in the soft valley between her breasts revealed by her dress's scooped neckline. With heart thudding wildly, her fingers dug into the springiness of his dark hair and she held his head pressed against her bosom, wanting this heavenly moment to continue forever, yet already stirred by an urgent need for more and yet more.

With a sudden cry of impatience, Dexter felt for the zipper of her dress, drawing it down in one steady purring movement until the garment could be pushed from her shoulders.

"Let me look at you, Nina . . . let me see your lovely body," he breathed. "I've dreamed about this moment night after night ever since I had to go back to London and leave you. I've lain awake, tormented, desperately wanting to hold you in my arms and possess you again. I've never known such feelings of desire for any other woman."

With gentle insistence he pressed her back on the bed, pulling her dress away and casting it aside. Deftly, he unhooked the clasp of her bra, and freed her small, firmly pointed breasts; then his fingertips slid under the band of her panties and he peeled them off slowly until she was revealed to him in glorious nudity. For silent moments he stood drinking in her loveliness, his eyes glowing molten in the lamplight. "You're exquisite," he murmured at last, throatily. "Sheer perfection."

Sitting beside her outstretched body he allowed his fingertips to trail exotic paths across her skin, bending to touch his lips here and there in a reverent gesture. Nina felt a delicious agony as those fingertips circled her breasts, tracing out the perfection of their shape, then moving on to the two rosy peaks, hard and exquisitely responsive when he rolled them gently between finger and thumb.

"Beautiful Nina," he said thickly. "I want you, I want you."

The tiny voice of her assent was lost in the tightness of her throat. Yes, her intoxicated senses beseeched him silently . . . now, now!

With urgent impatience Dexter threw off his own clothes and stretched his long length beside her, pulling her to him with rough tenderness as he took plundering possession of her mouth, forcing her lips to open and welcome the sensuous probe of his tongue. She clasped her arms about him and clutched convulsively at the hard muscles of his back and shoulders, drawing him closer, wanting him to crush her beneath the weight of his virile body. Dexter murmured her name deep in his throat as he eased himself onto her, his hard flesh sliding against her softness. Then his hands began a ceaseless exploration of her body, molding the warm curves and seeking out the ultrasensitive places, sweeping her along at an unbelievable pace to a blazing need for fulfillment. She exulted in the urgent throb of his desire, becoming bolder in her caresses as her excitement grew to fever heat. He moaned with pleasure as she arched herself against him, thrusting her breasts against his chest, and Nina reveled in his shuddering responsiveness aś her hands rippled down the long channel of his spine.

Though Dexter had shown her before the supreme joy of unhurried lovemaking, it was an agony to contain her impatience for instant gratification. Surely it was impossible that he could raise her to even greater heights of longing than this? Yet as his hands and lips continued their coaxing arousal of her body, wave upon wave of sensual sweetness surged through her until she lost all awareness of time or place. She was consumed by a great flame of longing which flared higher and still higher, ecstasy building upon ecstasy. Then suddenly it felt as if the swirling heaven in which she hung suspended was exploding in a shattering of brilliant stars.

Dexter's breath rasped in his throat as his body relaxed. "Darling, wonderful Nina," he murmured, and pressed his lips to hers in a tender kiss. They lay clinging together, arms wrapped around one another, their legs entwined, in the delicious lassitude of spent passion. As the minutes drifted by, Nina felt herself floating in a dream of love, responding when Dexter kissed her or murmured soft endearments into the tousled mane of her dark hair. There was silence all around them, the fragrant stillness of a Mediterranean night. Until, joyously, she felt the idle caresses of his straying hands grow purposeful again, felt the throbbing stir of his reawakened desire. With a wondrous feeling of closeness she let him carry her again on the journey to paradise, pausing in a lingering exploration of every byway until the final culmination could be delayed no longer and for a second time that night she knew the ultimate ecstasy.

It was full daylight when Nina awoke, alone in the bed. Her memory of last night was instantaneous, bringing with it a rush of wonderment and joy. Something red on the pillow caught her eye and she turned her head to see a single, perfect rosebud, its dewy petals just beginning to unfold. She smiled at the thought that Dexter had been out to the garden to fetch it for her, and she pressed the fragile blossom to her lips, inhaling the delicate perfume.

During the daytime Phyllida still doggedly refused to leave Nina and Dexter alone together for more than a few moments at a time. But she could do nothing to spoil their nights together. Whether or not she guessed about them, Nina neither knew nor cared. On several occasions, Phyllida invited friends to the Villa Mimosa. They seemed to be people she had met at the casinos in Nice, and by and large Nina found them brash and uncongenial.

More welcome guests were Patrick Farr, the publicity director of Rolfe Industries, and his wife Marjorie, who were motoring through to Italy and stopped off overnight at the Villa Mimosa. Nina was happy to see them again, having greatly liked Marjorie when Dexter had taken her to the party at their home in Islington despite the fact that she hadn't enjoyed the evening.

After dinner, the two men withdrew to another room to talk shop, and left the three women sitting on the balcony over coffee.

"It's a real tragedy about your ankle, Nina," said Marjorie sympathetically. "I can imagine what a terrible blow it's been to you."

Nina smiled and shrugged dismissively. "I'll survive."

"I think you'll agree," said Phyllida, her eyebrows arching ironically, "that Nina is 'surviving' very comfortably."

"You mean, staying here?" queried Marjorie, her gauntly attractive features creased in a frown. "I'd have thought, after what Nina did, that she deserves all this and a darned sight more. When Dexter was in London he told Patrick and me all about the way she rescued Mandy. He was full of praise for your bravery, Nina, and said how indebted he feels to you."

"There's no need for him to feel like that," Nina murmured uncomfortably.

Marjorie gave her a shrewd look. "How exactly do things stand between you and Dexter now? When he brought you to our party that night, he appeared very keen, I thought. I seem to recall that I had to break you two up and make you circulate."

Phyllida's laugh tinkled. "Isn't Dexter always the same when he finds himself a new girl? Suddenly everything is very intense and obsessive, and then when the victim is still in a daze about her good fortune . . . bingo, it's all over. You must have seen it happen often enough, Marjorie."

"Dexter gets around, sure. Only this time it doesn't appear to be over so soon, if I can read the signs right."

There was a contemptuous shrug from Phyllida. "That's merely because of the regrettable mishap to Nina's ankle. It's brought out all Dexter's instincts of male chivalry and so on. But knowing my brother-in-law, his obsession with Nina won't last long."

Marjorie looked embarrassed. "Isn't that rather un-called for, Phyllida?"

"Don't worry, Nina and I understand one another perfectly. Fortunately, she's under no illusions about Dexter."

To Nina's intense relief, they dropped the subject there. Her cheeks burned and she would have liked to say something crushing in response to Phyllida's taunts.

But she feared that even if she could think of a suitable retort, her trembling voice would betray the raw state of her emotions.

Later, when the two men had joined them again, Marjorie drew Nina aside. "Phyllida was being terribly catty about you and Dexter, but you mustn't let her upset you."

"Oh, I don't," Nina said, striving to sound confidently unconcerned.

Marjorie regarded her thoughtfully. "She makes Dexter out to be an unscrupulous Don Juan. Which he isn't! All the same . . ." She hesitated, and Nina held her breath, praying that Marjorie wouldn't snap the tiny, slender thread of hope to which she clung . . . a less than one percent chance that Dexter might view her in a different light from his countless previous girl friends. "All the same, Nina, I'd hate you to be hurt," Marjorie went on, choosing her words carefully. "Patrick always says that in business matters Dexter Rolfe is the straightest man he's ever encountered, and in other ways he's generous to a fault . . . witness his support for the Regency Ballet, and various charities. But when it comes to women—well, I've got to admit it, Dexter is something of a taker." She gave Nina a faint, anxious smile. "It's bad enough that you've broken your ankle. You can do without having your heart broken, too."

That night when Dexter came to Nina's room it was later than usual because he'd stayed chatting with Patrick. He immediately threw off his clothes and slid naked into bed beside her. As he drew her into his arms and kissed her, he must have tasted the saltiness of tears on her cheeks.

"Darling, you've been crying. What is it?"

Unguardedly, she said with a tremor in her voice, "It's all going to be over so soon."

"All over? What do you mean?"

Nina hastily pulled back from the brink of spilling out her misery. She would hang on to her fragile happiness right up to the bitter end, not take risks with it by forcing things to a head with Dexter. "I just meant that we only have another four days here."

"Don't be depressed, darling." He hesitated a moment, then added, "I know that life will be pretty dull for you in London, not dancing, but we'll be able to see quite a lot of one another."

To Nina the hesitation seemed more significant than his reassuring words. Was this the beginning of the end of their affair? Would Dexter want out, just as soon as he could decently disentangle himself?

Thrusting the painful thought from her mind, she clung to him ardently and thrilled to the feel of Dexter's stirring desire as he drew her close against his hard-muscled body. While his mouth covered hers possessively, his hands slid sensuously over her naked flesh, bringing forth the most exquisite sensations and setting her blood dancing. Once again Nina was swept along on the gloriously familiar route of passion, and all her doubts and fears were left behind. The past and the future had no relevance compared with the wondrous here and now. It seemed golden eons of time later that she and Dexter together reached the final rapturous explosion of their loving. Afterward, they were both very still, their limbs sweetly entwined, her cheek against the warmth of Dexter's chest. She felt him relax as the tension left his muscles and he drifted into sleep. But tonight Nina remained awake for a long time, staring blindly at the ceiling, while tiny ice needles of doubt pricked at her heart.

"Nina, I couldn't bring myself to tell you last night, but . . ."

Only half-awake, she stared up at Dexter uncomprehendingly. He was sitting on the edge of her bed, fully dressed in a pale gray business suit. Nina sat up, dragging the covers over her naked breasts.

"What . . . what is it, Dexter?"

"I'm afraid I've got to leave you, darling."

"Leave me!" she cried in startled dismay.

"Only for a short time," he said quickly. "I'll be back tonight if I can possibly make it. Otherwise, it'll have to be tomorrow. Something Patrick told me last night needs my urgent attention in London. In fact, I've got to hurry now to catch my plane." He kissed her, then lightly ran his finger down the curve of her cheek, and hurried out. Nina was left with a leaden sense of desolation. It was stupid to feel like this, but having a whole day—and possibly a precious night—snatched away from the little time they had left of their idyll at the Villa Mimosa seemed too cruel.

As things turned out, it was a better day than she could have expected. The Farrs departed en route to Italy soon after breakfast, and Marjorie warmly invited Nina to visit them in London. Phyllida, with Dexter not there, drove off on her own—to the casino in Nice, Nina guessed, leaving her and Mandy to their own devices. Planning what they would do, Mandy opted for taking a picnic lunch up in the hills behind the villa, and the hours passed pleasantly. After Mandy was in bed, though, and the evening wore on with no word from Dexter, Nina resigned herself to the fact that he wouldn't be returning till the next day. She went to bed shortly before midnight and was still not asleep when she heard Phyllida arriving home an hour or so later.

Nina surfaced from an uneasy dream to hear the whisper of Dexter's voice in the darkness. "Nina, are you awake?"

"Y . . . yes!" She sat up and fumbled for the bedside lamp, blinking in the soft glow it shed. Dexter cupped her face between his two hands, caressing the line of her jaw with his thumbs, then leaned forward and touched his lips to hers.

"Hello, Sleeping Beauty!"

"What . . . what time is it?" she asked smilingly, still a bit dazed.

"Almost two-thirty. I've had the devil's own job getting back tonight. I was forced to shuttle around via Paris and Geneva."

"But why . . . ?"

"I needed to get back to you," he said. "I had to talk to you, Nina."

"What about?" she whispered, the serious tone of his voice sending flurries of alarm through her.

"About us, what else? We can't go on as we are. Being away from you today, I had a chance to see things in perspective . . . a chance to think."

"And what did you decide?" A pulse beating in her throat made it difficult to breathe.

"I decided," he said levelly, "that we ought to get married, Nina."

She felt a shock wave jerk through her. She stared at him speechlessly, her heart thudding. After an eternity, it seemed, she managed to get out the words, "No, Dexter, that's impossible."

"But why?" he demanded, looking totally bewildered. "I don't understand, Nina. I thought that you . . ." Dexter broke off, leaving the sentence unfinished. When he began again there was an edge of resentment in his tone. "It seems to me that the suggestion makes a lot of sense, but you appear to hate the idea."

"In what way does it make sense?" she asked shakily.

"Do I have to spell it out? You and I really set one another alight. I've never felt such desire for any woman as I feel for you."

"You think that physical attraction is a sound basis for marriage?" she demanded, a pain curling and knotting in her stomach.

"There's more to it than that, obviously."

"Such as?"

Dexter gave her a strange, long look. "We can't dismiss the fact that your whole life has been changed because of what you did for Mandy."

Her pain turned swiftly to anger. "You feel you owe me, is that it? You pity me, and you want to appease your conscience with an offer of marriage? Well, I don't want your pity, Dexter. I can do without it, thank you."

"You've got me all wrong, Nina," he protested.

"Have I? Suppose I'd never had that accident, would you still be asking me to marry you? Had the thought of marriage once crossed your mind before it happened?"

He was silent for several moments. Then, reluctantly, he said, "How can I answer that honestly? Before, we'd only just got to know each other . . . our relationship had only just started."

"And how long would *that* have lasted?" Nina challenged. Rising from the bed, she drew on a robe over her nightdress, to feel less vulnerable and more able to face up to him.

"You don't seem to understand," he said in a cool, impassive tone. "How things might have worked out between us if you'd not had the accident is entirely beside the point. Everything is different now . . . we've had the chance to get to know each other in a special sort of way. The chance to find out how well suited we are to one another. So now I'm asking you to be my wife, Nina."

"And just what would be my role if I did become your wife?" she threw at him. "Would you remain faithful to me for a day longer than it suited you? Any more than you did to . . . to Judith?"

Dexter's face turned to stone, his whole body became rigid. Only his eyes were alive, burning suddenly with angry fire.

"So it's true, isn't it? You can't deny it, can you?" Nina gasped in a breath and went on recklessly, "You made your wife utterly wretched with your blatant infidelity, and . . . and you finally broke her heart. You're ruthless, and selfish, and . . . and cruel."

Dexter reacted by taking hold of her shoulders and shaking her. "Stop it, Nina. You're getting hysterical."

"No, I'm not. I'm just coming to my senses. I've been allowing a smooth seducer to break down my defenses, and . . ."

"I don't seem to remember that I found it very difficult," he rasped. "You were only too willing."

Nina flinched under the impact of his sarcasm, but she made herself hold his gaze steadily. "Not anymore, Dexter. What has happened, nothing can alter . . . but I bitterly regret every minute I've been with you. I'm deeply ashamed."

For long moments their eyes locked and they glared at one another in a fierce duel, the night silence seeming to press in from all around. Then somewhere outside an owl screeched, breaking the deadlock between them.

"I must say," Dexter remarked ironically, with a shrug of his broad shoulders, "that you're reacting very strangely to a marriage proposal, Nina. Not many women would have the nerve to throw it back in my face like that."

"More fool you," she retorted. "You shouldn't have been so careless as to expose yourself to the humiliation of a refusal. But I'm sure you'll have no problem fixing yourself up with the sort of wife you're looking for . . . hostess and housekeeper, surrogate mother for Mandy, and bed-partner whenever you happen to fancy the idea. And all without the embarrassing need to feel permanently grateful to her, as you seem to think you'd have to be to me."

"Why do you keep on and on about me being grateful to you?" Dexter snapped. "As if that was the main issue."

"Well, isn't it? Isn't that what this whole charade is about?"

His eyes were rock hard now, his face a mask, and suddenly he seemed a complete stranger. "I'm to take it, then, that you prefer the prospect of going back to London and struggling to rebuild your career, rather than the idea of marrying me?"

"Dead right! The choice is infinitely preferable. So you can rest easy in your mind that you've done your duty by the wretched girl, can't you? Then you can forget me and turn to the next in line." Nina lifted her chin. "We might as well say good-bye, Dexter. I shall be leaving here in the morning, the first plane I can get."

Even now her treacherous body longed for him to brush aside her protests, to take her into her arms and kiss away her misery, to sweep her along in a whirlwind of passion. Nina hated herself for wanting a man she so deeply despised. But nothing could ever stop her from wanting Dexter.

It seemed an age before he turned and walked slowly to the door. When he glanced back at her, his eyes glittered in the lamplight and his voice was cold and hard. "As you wish, Nina. Just let me know your travel plans, and I'll arrange transport to the airport. Good night."

Chapter Eleven

$\mathcal{N}$ina was lying curled up against the cushions of the sofa when she heard Cheryl's key in the lock, sometime after midnight. Sleepy as she was, she'd thought it only fair to wait up for her friend.

"Nina! What a surprise. I wasn't expecting you for another couple of days. Sorry you found the place in such a terrible mess."

"I . . . I just decided that I wanted to get back," Nina had carefully rehearsed a plausible story, but now the words fled from her mind.

"Nothing's wrong, I hope?" said Cheryl, frowning, as she slipped out of her coat.

"No, I'm fine. My ankle is improving fast. Any time now I'll be able to get down to some serious practice."

"I meant," said Cheryl, with an intent look, "is there anything wrong between you and Dexter? Have you two quarreled?"

She was far too perceptive. Nina tried to shrug away the need for a full explanation. "Heavens above, it's nothing to be so surprised about. You knew as well as I did that it was only a temporary thing. Ships that pass in the night and all that."

"So he's dropped you, has he? The rat!"

"As a matter of fact," Nina corrected, "I was the one who did the dropping. You ought to be glad, Cheryl, considering the way you tried to warn me off Dexter Rolfe."

"Things are a bit different now, aren't they? I mean, right at this moment you need a broken romance like you need a hole in the head."

"I think I must already have had a hole in the head to get mixed up with him in the first place," Nina responded chokingly. "Shall I make you some coffee?"

"Thanks." Cheryl followed Nina out to the kitchen and leaned against the fridge. "Aren't you going to tell me all about it?"

"What is there to tell? Dexter asked me, and I said no. Finish!"

"He asked you . . . what, exactly?"

Nina bit her lip. That had been a stupid thing to say, and she tried to backtrack. "Isn't it obvious, a man like him?"

"Listen, Nina," said Cheryl impatiently, "if you're meaning to imply that you split up with Dexter because he wanted you to start an affair with him, then please don't insult my intelligence. Okay, you were very discreet about it, but to someone who knows you as well as I do, it was obvious that it had happened already. So come on . . . explain!"

"If you must know, he suggested that we get married, and . . ."

"Married! Dexter Rolfe proposed to you and you turned him down?"

"Don't sound so dumbfounded, Cheryl, it isn't very flattering. Considering all the things you said about him, I should have thought you'd be relieved."

"I'm only astonished that you could find it in your heart to refuse him," she explained. "You admitted to me that you were in love with the man, remember."

"But Dexter doesn't love *me.*"

"All the same, Nina, he must think an awful lot of you to propose—which might even be preferable to having him besottedly in love with you. He obviously fancies you like mad . . . and, sensible man that he is, he realizes that you'd make a terrific wife. How much more do you want?"

Nina felt choked with angry resentment. She'd been counting on support from Cheryl, not criticism. "Just fancying me a lot wouldn't have made Dexter propose," she said. "He's fancied any number of women in his time, and there'll be plenty more in the future. I gather that Phyllida Hooper was previously lined up as the second Mrs. Rolfe . . . and she probably is again by now. But in between Dexter had this brainwave that I'd do as well as Phyllida for the wifely role he had in mind—with the added advantage that it would cancel out the need to feel obligated to me about Mandy."

"He told you that?" Cheryl looked incredulous.

"Not in so many words, but that's the gist of it. Dexter doesn't see fidelity in marriage as sacrosanct—at least, not on his side. By marrying me, he'd be seen by everybody as making superbly generous amends to the girl who ruined her career in an accident involving his daughter. And just as soon as the honeymoon was over, he'd continue to go his own sweet way."

The kettle came to the boil and began to whistle. Cheryl asked in a low voice, "And how about you, Nina? Do you still love him, despite everything?"

Darn her for homing in so accurately on the truth,

Nina thought with a sigh. She said firmly, "There's no sense in talking about it, Cheryl. How're things going for you?"

"Not bad. We are playing to full houses at Wimbledon this week, and Boyd has persuaded Sir Hugo not to do *Summer Rhapsody* again for the time being, but to save it until we do our next West End season and Sonia Lamartine can dance it. Which is lucky, because I need to take some time off."

"Time off?" Nina looked at her sharply. "What's up, Cheryl?"

"It's Jeremy," she explained unhappily. "He's not been at all well lately, and when I was home last weekend the doctor said that he'd have to go into the hospital."

"Oh, Cheryl, I am sorry. What's the trouble, exactly?"

She shrugged wretchedly. "One of those things they can't quite pin down. That's why they want Jeremy in the hospital, to have him under close observation and give him tests."

"I see! When are you going?"

"Tomorrow, actually. I was planning to scribble a note to you, explaining the situation. I hate leaving you on your own just now, Nina, especially after what you just told me. But it can't be helped."

"Don't worry about me," Nina said quickly. "I'll be fine. Give Jeremy my best love, won't you, and perhaps I could come up to Nottingham sometime to visit him."

"Oh, he'd like that. He's very fond of his Auntie Nina." Cheryl smiled reflectively. "You've got a wonderful way with children, you know. Mandy Rolfe was always following you about like a devoted puppy. How did she take your going away?"

Nina hesitated. It had been a distressing scene this morning at breakfast, when she had told Mandy about her imminent departure. "But I thought you were staying here until we went home too, Nina, so we could all travel back together."

"I'm sorry, pet, but . . . things have changed. I've got to get back to London at once."

"Why?" Mandy demanded, adding with a child's embarrassing directness, "If you can't dance yet, what do you have to go back for?"

Dexter stood with his back to them, looking out of the window, his arms folded across his chest in an implacable stance. Nina was aware of Phyllida's intrigued gaze flitting between the two of them. Though puzzled, Dexter's sister-in-law was clearly delighted by this turn of events.

"Don't ask so many questions, Mandy," she reproved, though in an unusually gentle voice. "Nina isn't part of our family and it's entirely her own business how and when she goes back to England."

"But when shall I see you again, Nina?" the child asked plaintively.

Feeling helpless and somehow a little ashamed, Nina made a vague sort of gesture. "I . . . I don't really know, pet."

Mandy turned to her father. "Daddy, make Nina promise to come and see us when we're back home."

"I can't *make* Nina do anything. She has a mind of her own." With a dark look he quelled Mandy from pressing the matter any further. Half an hour later, with the taxi waiting to take Nina to the airport, Mandy had been in tears as they said good-bye.

In response to Cheryl's query, Nina muttered offhandedly, "Children soon forget. In no time at all, Mandy will have a crush on someone else."

"But will *you* forget *her* . . . or her father?" Cheryl asked shrewdly. "That's the real question, isn't it, Nina?"

"The real question," Nina retorted, attempting a feeble joke, "is where the dickens you've hidden the sugar. The bowl's empty."

The weekend, especially, was a desperately lonely time for Nina. Despite knowing that she wasn't really fit enough yet, she went along to the Regency's rehearsal studios on Monday morning and tried a little gentle work at company class. Everyone was kind and helpful . . . or almost everyone. Boyd was clearly ill-at-ease, though he tried to treat her presence matter-of-factly; from Zoe she received a sneering remark about how the mighty were fallen!

During the coffee break, Sir Hugo took her aside for a chat. "You mustn't overdo things, my dear," he warned. "I was watching you dance with Robin just now, and I must confess that I felt anxious for you."

Nina flushed, aware that her pathetic attempt at a *pas de deux* must have been almost an outrage to someone with Sir Hugo's high standards. "I didn't like to say no to Robin," she mumbled. "It was kind of him to suggest we try it together."

Sir Hugo nodded sympathetically. Fingering his beard, he went on, "Have you given any thought yet to the future, Nina?"

She had done little else, seeing only a bleak grayness ahead of her. But she said with a bright smile, "I'll just try and work my way back into the company at whatever level I'm capable of, Sir Hugo."

"As long as you don't rush things," he said, a worried look appearing in his gray eyes. "Perhaps a happy niche will turn up for you, my dear."

A niche, protected from the true reality of life? What sort of substitute was that for a dazzling career as a prima ballerina, achieved by sheer merit and ability? But she had to keep smiling, and look grateful.

Later that day Alan seized the chance of a private word with her, asking if she'd heard from Cheryl about how her son was getting on.

"Yes, I talked to her on the phone last night," Nina told him. "There isn't any real news. They're just doing lots of tests and things. But Cheryl is obviously terribly worried about Jeremy."

"Poor Cheryl! Next time you talk to her, Nina, will you tell her . . . well, just that I'm thinking of her and hoping that there'll be some good news very soon? You know the sort of thing."

"Okay, Alan, I'll tell her."

"And promise to let me know how things go, won't you?" he persisted, with a concerned look on his face.

All that week Nina persevered, attending class each day. Often she felt so depressed about her ankle and the way it kept letting her down whenever she tried anything but the simplest movements, that she just felt like slinking away to the washroom and having a good cry. The company was currently performing a week at each of various theaters on the outskirts of London, this week at Greenwich, and she could have gone along with the others on the bus. But she just couldn't face being merely an onlooker. So instead she went home and spent the evenings alone, time dragging by with interminable slowness.

At about nine o'clock on the Thursday of that week, when Nina was wondering whether to go to bed and try to get some sleep, the doorbell rang. Wondering, she went to answer it . . . then stepped back in shock, feeling all the color drain from her face.

"Dexter!"

"Hello, Nina. May I come in?"

"I . . . I suppose so." She stood well aside, but even so his arm brushed against hers as he stepped inside. Nina recoiled from his touch as if she'd been stung, dismayed at the flame of longing it sent licking through her. Noting her reaction, Dexter's tawny eyes darkened and his mouth went taut.

In the living room, he turned and faced her. "How are you, Nina?"

"I'm okay."

"Your ankle—is it still improving?"

"Yes, I'm hardly aware of it anymore." Hardly aware . . . when its inadequacy mocked her every hour of every day! She put on a bright smile and added, "I've started dancing again, in class. I'm getting along really well."

"Good." Dexter seemed strangely ill-at-ease. Giving her a long, measuring look, he went on, "I can't help feeling worried about you, Nina."

"There's no need," she countered. "In fact, I'd rather you didn't."

His lips curved in a faint, unamused smile. "Always so fiercely independent! Can't you ever accept other people's concern about you? The occasional helping hand?"

"Not from you, in any case."

"Nina, please . . ." He reached out and touched her shoulder, but she jerked fiercely away.

"Don't do that," she snapped.

Overruling her objection, Dexter purposefully slid his arms around her and drew her against him. To have struggled, Nina knew, would have been useless, but she made her body rigid and unyielding. He sighed.

"Why must you act like this? Can you possibly deny that you still want me, just as I want you? The flame of passion between us hasn't burned itself out."

Nina felt her traitorous body begin to tremble and it took all her willpower to remain calm. "Just what are you suggesting, Dexter?" she challenged in a cold voice. "That even though I've turned down your insulting proposal of marriage, there's no need for us to end our relationship? Is that what you've come here to say?"

"Nina, please . . ." His tawny eyes were vividly intent as he looked at her. "What we had going between us . . . it mustn't be allowed to die."

"It's already dead," she insisted. "Over, finished. Can't you understand?"

"I don't believe it's finished," he said flatly. "And I don't think you do, either."

"I do! I do!"

His lips parted in a coaxing smile and his voice became soft and low, vibrantly enticing. "And if I were to kiss you now, you would be totally unmoved? Is that what you're saying?"

"Don't you dare try to kiss me."

"Answer my question, Nina. Forget what your brain tells you, and take heed of your body's responses." His hand moved down in a sensuous trail across her back and waist, and he pulled her more closely against his hard frame. She responded with a gasp of arousal which she was unable to stifle, her heart thudding in a wild flutter of anticipation. The next instant his mouth came down and covered hers, his lips urgent and demanding, with none of the tenderness he had always shown before even at the very height of passion. And yet Nina exulted, her resistance melting like overnight frost before the bright morning sunlight. Dexter's fingers clenched convulsively into her firm soft flesh, drawing her closer to him with searing intimacy.

"God, how you torment me with your beautiful body," he groaned, pressing his mouth to the hollow of her throat. "I want you, Nina, and you want me. Isn't that enough? Isn't that the only thing that counts?"

He drew back a little, and with feverish impatience felt for the zipper of her dress, sliding it down smoothly. The action brought Nina abruptly to her senses; she felt shocked and sickened at how nearly she had succumbed to temptation. But when she tried to pull away from him Dexter held her closer, his lips trailing exquisite kisses across her brow and down the line of her cheek. She had to end this right now, while she still had sufficient willpower. Somehow freeing one arm, she drew it back and bunched her fist, punching with all the force she could muster against the solid wall of his chest. Clearly, she hurt herself more than she hurt Dexter, but the blow startled him enough to make him pause.

"What did you do that for?" he asked, seeming genuinely puzzled.

"I told you not to kiss me," Nina rasped.

He still held her. "And I told you to follow the dictates of your body. You want me, so why pretend otherwise?"

It was useless to deny it. Nina knew suddenly that the only way to get through to Dexter was to admit the truth. "Yes, I do want you," she agreed. "If you were to persist, I've no doubt that you could seduce me right here and now. And afterward, when I recovered my senses, I'd hate you for it. Is that what you want, Dexter?"

He hesitated, and she could feel the thudding of his heart against her own. Then slowly he released her. "You're talking nonsense," he growled. "You had no reservations before."

"I always had reservations," Nina told him candidly. "I smothered them, that's all. But I can't do that any longer. I don't *want* to."

"What have I done to deserve this?" he asked wonderingly.

Nina sighed, quickly pulling her zipper closed. "You

wouldn't understand, Dexter, not a man with your philosophy of life. Can't you just let go, while we still have a few good memories of each other?"

His tawny eyes were afire as he surveyed her. "Let's get this straight. You want me to walk out of here and never again make contact with you? Is that right?"

She nodded slowly. "Yes, it is."

"I see. And might I ask what I'm to tell Mandy? You made that child idolize you, Nina, and now you're abandoning her. It's heartless."

"Don't tell me what's heartless, Dexter," she blazed in fury. "I'm very fond of Mandy, but . . . it's quite impossible for me to keep up any sort of relationship with her now. How you explain that to her is entirely up to you. I've told you before, it's not fair to use your daughter as a weapon against me."

Dexter bowed his head in acknowledgment. "You're right, Nina, that was unfair. I admit it. But I've been fair enough in other ways, you must grant that. I haven't just expected you to have an affair with me. I offered you marriage."

"Oh, how noble!" she said ironically. "How self-sacrificing! You might as well know, Dexter Rolfe, that I despise your idea of marriage, just as I despise you. Why don't you go away and make some other woman miserable?"

He hesitated, and there was a strange look in his eyes that she couldn't interpret. "I can't just go, Nina," he said quietly. "I feel a certain responsibility for you."

"Then I absolve you from it," she snapped. "There, like a fairy queen I wave my magic wand and set you free. Now get out."

As the result of long, sleepless hours of agonizing, Nina was heavily asleep early next morning when the phone pierced her consciousness. She lay listening to it in a daze, convinced that it must be Dexter attempting to pressure her.

The ringing went on and on. Unable to bear it, she at last rose from bed and walked through to the phone in the living room.

"Nina, I thought you were never going to answer." The voice was Cheryl's, muffled and indistinct. "I had to talk to you. It's Jeremy . . ."

Nina was suddenly alert, the tone of her friend's voice sending shivers down her back. "What is it, Cheryl? What's wrong?"

"He's dreadfully ill. Some kind of crisis. Oh, Nina, they say he might not pull through."

Filled with horror and dread, Nina tried to think clearly. "Are you at the hospital now?"

"Yes, I've been here all night, ever since . . ."

"And your parents . . . are they with you?"

"Yes, Mum and Dad are both here. They're in almost as bad a state as I am. It's been such a shock."

Nina said with sudden decision, "Cheryl, listen . . . I'm coming right away. I'll get there just as soon as I can. The very first train. Try not to be too upset. You know all my thoughts are with you."

Ringing off, Nina quickly called British Rail and checked the train times. Luckily there was one she could just make if she hurried. She rang for a taxi, and hastily bundled together a few clothes and toilet items, throwing them into a suitcase. The journey to Nottingham seemed interminable and the view of rain-swept countryside through the train window only added to her unhappy mood. By noon her taxi from the station had drawn up outside the hospital. As she hurried through the corridors, Nina was praying that Jeremy was still alive, that he would somehow pull through.

Fate surely couldn't be so cruel as to snatch Cheryl's small son away from her at such a tender age?

She found Cheryl and her parents in a small side room, slumped in their chairs. Their faces were drawn and haggard.

"What's the news?" she asked them anxiously.

"He's no better," Cheryl said in a choked voice. "The consultant is with him now. Oh, Nina, it's terrible!"

She stood up shakily and they clung together in a sorrowful embrace.

It was a dreadful day. Most of the time Cheryl sat at her son's bedside, holding his hand, and Nina shared some of the anxious vigil with her. It was heartbreaking to see the little boy, whom she remembered as always bounding with energy, lying still and pale in the hospital bed. He was barely conscious now, not really aware of his mother's presence, and they didn't need the doctor's sympathetic warning that his slender grasp on life was slipping away. By two-thirty A.M. it was all over.

During the next few days, Cheryl's grief and agony were terrible to see. She couldn't shake off a sense of guilt, blaming herself bitterly for having failed to spend more of her time with Jeremy.

"How could you have done otherwise?" Nina asked gently. "You left him in the best possible hands, with your parents, and you had your living to earn—to support him as well as yourself."

"I could have earned my living at something that didn't take me away from home," Cheryl reproached herself. "I feel I hate my career in ballet now, Nina. I don't ever want to dance again. I'm quitting."

"But you can't," Nina protested, shocked. "You have enormous talent, Cheryl, and it would be a

225

dreadful waste to give up now. You've got a terrific future ahead of you. Throwing everything away like that . . . it would be unfair to the ballet-loving audiences as well as yourself."

Cheryl shook her head dispiritedly. "Fate has handed us both a raw deal, hasn't it? How ironic! *You'd* like nothing better than to continue dancing and reach the very heights. While *me* . . . I just couldn't care less. So what's the use of carrying on?" she finished, with a despairing sigh.

"Cheryl, listen to me," Nina said urgently. "You're in no state at the moment to make important decisions. Promise me you won't do anything hasty, like quitting the company right now. Wait until you can get things into better perspective."

"But I won't change my mind . . . ever."

"All the same, promise me. Right?"

Cheryl shrugged indifferently. "Okay, if it will make you happy." She gave a wan smile. "Those letters that came this morning . . . Sir Hugo and everyone have been so kind. The one from Alan was very sweet. It was nice of him, considering that we haven't partnered each other nearly so much lately since Boyd put me dancing with Robin."

"What did Alan have to say?" Nina asked interestedly. True to her promise, she had dropped Alan a line to tell him the sad news.

"Oh, you know . . . how very sorry he was, and if there was anything at all he could do I only had to say."

An idea began to form in Nina's mind. That afternoon when Cheryl and her mother were in the garden she phoned the rehearsal studios at Elephant and Castle and asked to speak to Alan Bryce.

"Cheryl was very touched by your letter," she told him, when he came on the line.

"How is she?" There was deep concern in Alan's voice. "It must be simply terrible for her."

"Yes, she's taking it very badly, I'm afraid. She can't seem to think straight, and she's talking wildly of quitting ballet."

"Oh no! She mustn't do that. It would be a criminal waste."

"So I keep telling her." Nina took a deep breath and went on, "Alan, somehow I've got a hunch that she might just listen to you. I wonder . . . is there any chance of you getting time off and coming up to Nottingham to try and talk her out of it? Would you be willing to?"

"Like a shot," he said at once. "I half-wondered about coming up for the little boy's funeral, but . . . I didn't know whether Cheryl would like it. Listen, I'll fix things with Sir Hugo, somehow or other, and be with you tomorrow morning. Will you tell Cheryl I'm coming?"

Nina considered a moment, then said, "No, best not. She'd probably try to stop you."

Alan arrived next morning while Nina, Cheryl and her mother were sitting in the garden drinking a cup of coffee.

"Alan!" Cheryl exclaimed in astonishment, when Mrs. Wyatt returned with him from answering the doorbell.

"I thought I'd come and see if there's anything I can do to help," he said. "I hope that's okay with you, Cheryl."

"Yes, of course. But I don't understand why."

"I *wanted* to come," he said firmly.

Alan was made welcome by Cheryl's mother, who had met him a couple of times before when they'd traveled to London with Jeremy to see his mother dance. But Cheryl herself remained very reserved with him, and Nina feared that her little ruse had been a dismal failure. She felt guilty for having dragged Alan up to Nottingham and subjected him to such a chilly reception.

"Cheryl, why don't you give Alan a break?" she demanded, when the two of them were in the kitchen getting dinner that evening. "You're treating him so coldly, when he's only trying to offer you a little comfort."

"Does he imagine he can worm his way into my good books by pitying me?" Cheryl demanded, tears glinting in her eyes. "I don't need Alan's pity."

"Perhaps," Nina said thoughtfully, "Alan needs to be able to show his pity, though. Have you considered that?"

"I don't know what you're getting at."

"No? Alan loves you! He's been in love with you for ages, you know that. Seeing you like this, heartbroken about Jeremy, is tearing him apart. You could help him, Cheryl, if only you would."

"Me help *him?"*

"That's what I said. The kindest thing, sometimes, is to accept what's generously offered by someone who loves you, rather than to be fiercely independent and reject it. Think about it!"

Cheryl shrugged, making no reply. But later, Nina was relieved to find that her attitude toward Alan had softened. At her parents' insistence he stayed overnight rather than go to a hotel, and the next day he stood beside Cheryl at the simple funeral service for Jeremy. To Nina it seemed somehow right and natural to see him at Cheryl's side at such a time.

Before Alan set out for the station that evening, he and Nina managed a few private words together. "I think Cheryl's going to see reason about staying in ballet," he said. "I can't thank you enough for telling me to come, Nina. I'd never have had the nerve to turn up of my own accord, but I think she was glad to have me here. I've got a feeling now that there may be a chance for me with her, if I keep on trying."

"I'm glad," Nina smiled. "You're two of my favorite people, and you deserve each other."

Alan gave her a friendly peck on the cheek. "You deserve the very best, too, Nina. I hope that things work out well for you."

Going to bed that night in the bedroom she and Nina were sharing, Cheryl hesitated, then burst out, "Thanks about Alan."

"What am I supposed to have done?"

"Do you really think I haven't guessed you had a hand in his surprise visit?" After a moment's silence, Cheryl went on thoughtfully, "It was a big help having him here. I'd never have imagined that someone who'd only met Jeremy a couple of times could be so upset about his death."

"That's because he cares so much about you," Nina said. "He's a really nice chap, Cheryl."

She nodded. "Yes, I'm just beginning to realize that. It's strange, isn't it, that I used to think Alan was such a bore because he'd never take no for an answer. But now . . . well, it's good to think that he'll be around when I get back."

Two days later Nina returned to London. Cheryl was to follow after the weekend.

Chapter Twelve

On the doormat, when Nina got back to the Battersea flat, was a letter addressed to her in Boyd's handwriting. Puzzled, she slit it open.

He was writing, the letter began, to tell her some news that hadn't yet been made public, but would be announced in the next few days. He had decided to accept the offer of a job as Senior Artistic Director with an Australian ballet company, and would be taking it up in a month's time.

Boyd wrote:

> To be frank, I jumped at the chance, because I don't see the same future anymore with Regency. In my opinion the company's heading downhill, without enough up and coming talent or the right dynamic drive. 'Down Under,' I'll have an altogether freer hand, and the money they're offering is fantastic. Considering the disappointing way things have worked out lately, I

shan't have any regrets about leaving. I'm looking forward to making an entirely fresh start. I wish you the best there is, Nina, and don't let them push you around. Hold out for a job of some kind with Regency that carries a decent salary. Our sponsor can afford it, and he owes it to you. Boyd added as a postscript, *I'll be seeing you around before I go, of course, but I thought I'd better let you know how things are beforehand. I'll be so up to my eyes with things this next month that we'll hardly get a chance to talk.*

Nina folded the letter and stuffed it into a drawer. It was strange, she thought wryly . . . she and Boyd had once been very close, but now she felt almost indifferent to him. There was just the lingering resentment at having been used. When she saw Boyd tomorrow at class, and murmured a few formal words of good wishes, she would be able to face him with complete equanimity. But this was something she'd never be able to say regarding Dexter Rolfe, the other man who had used her selfishly. She would never be able to feel indifference toward Dexter. Whether she were to meet him tomorrow, next month, or in ten years' time, the intense magnetic pull would still be there.

She spent a dreary Saturday, wishing that she had a few friends who were outside the small, enclosed world of ballet. Sunday was a bright autumnal day, the air wine-clear, with small white clouds chasing across the sky. Nina was standing at the front window after finishing her lunch when she saw a familiar blue Bentley draw up outside. Dexter again! She'd pretend to be out, she thought, and not answer his ring. But it was too late for that. Slamming the car door he glanced up at the window, and saw her standing there.

"What do you want now?" she demanded ungraciously as she opened the door to him.

Dexter gave her a friendly smile and held up both hands, palms forward, as if to demonstrate the innocence of his intentions. "I was very sorry to hear about Cheryl's son," he said. "I've written her a note of condolence."

"That was kind of you," Nina muttered, surprised that he had bothered. Then, fighting against the feelings of love and longing that were pulsing through her veins, she flung at him defiantly, "You needn't think that I'm going to ask you in, because I'm not."

"That's okay by me," he returned equably. "I called around to persuade you to come for a drive with me."

"You *what?* I thought I'd made it abundantly clear that I'm not having anything more to do with you."

"There's something I want to show you, Nina. Something that I want your professional opinion about, and which I believe will greatly interest you."

"What is it?" she asked coldly.

"I'd rather not say at the moment." He must have seen the suspicion in her eyes, and went on, "I give you my word, Nina, that I'm not up to any tricks. If it will make you happier, I promise not so much as to lay a finger on you the whole time you're with me."

"But I don't understand," she said uneasily. "Where is it you want to take me?"

"To Haslemere Hall."

"Haslemere Hall," she gasped. "But I can't possibly agree to . . ."

"Before you say anything more," he cut in, "I'm not trying to involve you with Mandy. She won't be there, nor will Phyllida. Only the staff."

"I wish you'd explain," Nina said, still very wary. She hardly dared glance at him, because he looked so achingly handsome. It was all she could do not to throw her arms around his neck and lean against his hard, masculine frame.

"Just trust me, please." Dexter gave a faint, rather grim little smile. "It might sound an odd thing to say, Nina, but I think you must admit that I've never given you any cause to doubt that I'm a man of my word."

She nodded, unwillingly. "I suppose that's true."

"Well, then . . .?"

"If I agree to come," Nina temporized, "will you promise that you'll bring me straight back here the moment I say so? And that you'll then leave at once and not trouble me again?"

"Very well," he said. "If that's what you want."

"Okay, then. Give me a few minutes to change. Er . . . you'd better come in and wait for me."

She refused to put on anything more glamorous than just a flared skirt and white blouse, worn with her black velvet blazer. She drew her hair back in a high bun and pinned it up with fingers that trembled. She was being a fool, she told herself, walking slap into another encounter with Dexter. Yet he had somehow seemed sincere in his plea for her opinion. And if he *was* being sincere, then it was beyond her power to refuse what he asked of her.

In the car, Nina kept well to her side of the front seat, with her hands clenched tightly together, every nerve in her body tinglingly aware of him. Most of the time she stared ahead through the windshield, but every now and again she risked a glance at Dexter, her eyes drinking in the clean, etched lines of his profile, and his strong hands on the steering wheel. Angrily, she thrust from her mind the memory of those hands caressing her, sliding over her flesh and rousing her to delirious heights of ecstasy.

"How is Cheryl bearing up?" he asked, sympathy in his voice.

"Well, she's still dreadfully shocked, of course," Nina told him. "At first she was talking wildly about leaving ballet and doing something quite different. I suppose it was a natural reaction. But, thank goodness, she's beginning to see sense now."

"You managed to persuade her?"

"It wasn't really my doing," she said. "Alan Bryce came to Nottingham for Jeremy's funeral, and he talked her around. Alan and Cheryl have partnered each other a lot on stage, and he's always been very fond of her." Nina found herself smiling. "It's too soon to say, in view of what's happened, but I think there's a real chance that they'll get together now."

"That would please you?"

"Very much. Cheryl is such a warmhearted sort of person. And she'd be wasted going through life on her own."

"Doesn't that same thing apply equally to you?" Dexter raised a pacific hand to check her swift response. "Sorry! Forget I said it." After a reflective pause, he went on, "Have you heard about Boyd Maxwell?"

"You mean about him going to Australia? Yes, there was a letter from him when I got back from Cheryl's. It was quite a surprise. I wonder who'll be taking over from him as Assistant Director."

"As a matter of fact, I can tell you that," Dexter said. "Warren Purdy."

Nina's eyes widened in astonishment. "Warren Purdy? However did Sir Hugo manage to entice him away from New York?"

"I gather that Sonia Lamartine had a hand in it. Apparently Warren Purdy had mentioned to her that he would welcome the chance to work in England. And when Sir Hugo told her on the phone about Boyd, she suggested offering Purdy the job. The whole thing was sewn up in just a couple of days."

"That's really wonderful," Nina said enthusiastically. "He'll do great things for Regency Ballet."

Dexter flickered her a sideways glance. "You don't seem particularly upset about Boyd Maxwell quitting," he said.

Nina shrugged. "Whatever there might once have been between Boyd and me was over and done with some time ago."

Half an hour later they turned off the motorway onto narrow country lanes. Within a few minutes they were driving through the parkland that surrounded Haslemere Hall, the magnificent beech and cedar trees spreading their branches to the wide blue sky. As a manservant opened the front door for them, the yellow labrador came bounding out and raced down the front steps in eager greeting.

"Hello, Bojo," Nina said, patting him on the head as she got out of the car. She swallowed a lump in her throat, reminded painfully of when she had seen the beautiful dog before, when she'd first met Dexter and Mandy while strolling in the grounds before the charity gala. Haslemere Hall had been thronged with people that day, their voices and laughter ringing through the stately rooms. The cheerful, bustling atmosphere somehow seemed appropriate for this gracious mansion, which, for all its grandeur, had a friendly quality. Now, as she and Dexter crossed the great hall there was an uneasy silence between them, and their footsteps on the marble floor made a hollow, empty sound.

"Where is Mandy, by the way?" she burst out, in an effort to cover her nervousness.

"Spending the weekend with a school friend. I'm to collect her in the morning."

"I see. Does she . . . does she know that you intended bringing me here?"

"No, I didn't say, or she'd have wanted to be here herself. And Phyllida," he added smoothly, "has seized the opportunity for a few days in Paris. So we shall be left in peace."

"Left in peace for what?" Nina challenged, as Dexter threw open the double doors to the Painted Gallery where the gala performance had been held, and ushered her through. "Why have you brought me here, Dexter? What is it you want to show me?"

"I'll explain," he said, with an easy smile. "When I started to think about things, Nina, I realized that this house would very conveniently split into two. On the other side of the entrance hall there's the green drawing room and the dining salon, plus several smaller rooms, while upstairs are the main bedrooms. On this side there's this huge room which would be the hub of it all, and lots of other accommodations suitable for everything from offices to dormitories." He looked at her expectantly. "You get the general idea?"

"I haven't the vaguest notion what you're talking about," Nina said, bewildered but intrigued.

"What is it that the Regency company lacks, if it's to hold its position in the forefront of the ballet world?" he demanded rhetorically. "Proper training facilities—right? Instead of relying on an input of young dancers from outside sources, it needs to be bringing on its own youngsters, trained from an early age in the Regency's own style. That has long been Sir Hugo Quest's dream, hasn't it?"

Still in a daze, Nina said slowly, "Do you mean . . . are you suggesting using part of Haslemere Hall as a ballet school?"

"Exactly! This seems ideal in every way. There's plenty of space, and it's the right sort of distance from London so there could be an easy interchange between pupils and members of the company. There'd be no real problem converting the place to make suitable classrooms for both ballet and academic studies, plus bedrooms and other facilities for the staff . . . you name it, it's all available here."

"But this is your home, Dexter," she protested foolishly.

"And what a huge barn of a place it is for one man and his small daughter."

"Plus Phyllida," she pointed out, before she could stop herself.

Dexter met her glance. "There'd still be plenty of room in just half the house for three people, Nina."

"But . . . but think of the noise all those children would make, the invasion of your privacy."

"I haven't overlooked that aspect," he assured her, smiling. "Not so long ago the idea would probably have appalled me. But when the company came to give that charity gala here, the house seemed to come alive. And at the Villa Mimosa, which is similar in size, there was a feeling of emptiness when the dancers had all gone. That didn't really matter to you and me, of course, but generally speaking, you have to agree that any large house needs to be adequately populated to give it life and meaning. To justify its very existence in this crowded modern world. So what do you think of my idea, Nina?"

By now she was recovering from the first shock. The professional dancer in her took over as she considered the pros and cons, and it only needed a few moments to see that it was a brilliant concept.

"With a school like this," she said eagerly, "we'd have facilities to rival the Royal Ballet itself. Over the years it would give a tremendous boost to Regency, putting it squarely among the top few companies in the international league."

"I felt sure you'd like the idea," he said with a confident nod, "so we'll do it."

Something about that "we" made Nina frown. "Why are you asking *my* opinion, Dexter?"

"Because I value it."

"But I'm not qualified to judge a thing like this. I mean, no more than any other dancer."

"I think you're uniquely qualified. In fact, without you, Nina, I wouldn't be considering starting a school here."

"Without *me?*"

Dexter nodded. "I want you to be the school's principal."

She stared at him in amazement. "This is crazy. You can't mean it."

"I do mean it, Nina. Most sincerely I mean it. You have all the qualities required for the job."

"Such as what?" she asked, with a flash of bitterness. "I can't even dance properly now."

"Your ankle injury has no affect on the vital issue—which is that you have a wonderful flair for enthusing young people. Seeing you teaching Mandy was what showed me that . . . what first gave me the idea of setting up a school here. Not that you yourself would need to spend much time actually teaching, of course, no more than you felt inclined to. But you have exactly the right mixture of sympathetic understanding and the ability to be firm—as when you told Mandy that she must on no account try standing on her points. Sir Hugo is in total agreement with me," he finished.

Nina gasped. "You've talked to Sir Hugo about it?"

"Of course. It was necessary to have his prior agreement, before putting the suggestion to you."

"You had no right to . . . to humiliate me like that," she flung at him furiously. "Why won't you stay out of

238

my life, Dexter, and let me get on with it in my own way?"

"Because I'm already part of your life," he said quietly. "If we never saw one another again, Nina, we'd neither of us ever be able to forget what we shared between us."

"And that's what this is all about, isn't it? I'm a blot on your conscience that you want to rub out. First you offer me marriage, and when I refuse that you come up with a fancy job—a sinecure with a fat salary."

"What you're being offered is no sinecure," Dexter growled. "Running a ballet school would be darned hard work, calling for stamina and dedication."

"Which plenty of other people could supply. So why must it be Nina Selby? How d'you think I'd feel in years to come, knowing that the only reason I got the job was from pity . . . to enable you to buy yourself out of the need to feel obligated to me?"

"Damn you, Nina . . ."

"Yes, you're very good at damning me, aren't you?" she stormed on. "If only you could utter the right magic incantation and banish me from your mind, from your conscience. The great Dexter Rolfe can't bear to accept the fact that he's permanently in someone else's debt. According to your philosophy, money and power and influence should be able to buy you out of every troublesome or embarrassing situation. Well, this is one time they can't!"

Dexter caught his breath, and his face was twisted with pain. "Have you no compassion in your heart, Nina? No compassion for me?"

"Compassion?" she echoed, taken aback. "I don't know what you mean."

"I have emotional needs too," he said in a low voice, "which you continue to deny me. I'm expected to stand aside helplessly, not allowed to do the least thing to make amends, when I know that your brilliant future as a ballerina has been snatched away from you because of what you did to save my daughter. You're asking too much of me, Nina; it's more than any decent man could stand. Yes, I pity you. I pity you with everything that's in me. I grieve for your lost career as much as if it were my own. I feel pain, remorse and guilt, and all kinds of other emotions concerning you mixed up together. Can't you understand that? Are you so inflexible, so heartless, that you won't let yourself give a single inch?"

A vision flashed through Nina's mind of herself telling Cheryl forcefully that Alan *needed* to express his pity for her. But the circumstances were different; Alan was in love with Cheryl. All the same, she faltered when she began to speak.

"I'm sorry, Dexter, I don't mean to seem heartless. There was something very special between us, but now it's all over and we must be prepared to let it die. I'm flattered—immensely flattered—that you even consider me capable of doing the job you've outlined, and I beg you not to drop the idea of a ballet school. It would be a wonderful thing, not only for the Regency company, but for ballet altogether. If it's any help to you, then think of the ballet school here as your way of expressing your indebtedness to me. I can accept that—but I can't take any leading part in the scheme."

"So once again you shut me out," he said bitterly, his voice deep with reproach. "I want you, Nina, and you want me. I know that, I can *feel* it. Yet you refuse to marry me. And now you refuse to take this on. It makes no sense. What more can I do, for heaven's sake?"

"Nothing. Just leave me alone. Leave me in peace."

"How can I, Nina?" he flared, his eyes glowing with molten intensity. "I need to have you in my life."

"So you imagine," she said scathingly, "that by creating a ballet school in your home and establishing me as its principal, we could pick up our affair where we left off?"

"If you won't marry me, what's wrong with that?" he demanded. "But I'd infinitely rather that you married me, Nina."

"Sexual attraction isn't a sufficient basis for marriage, Dexter. Nor is a sense of obligation."

"I was hoping," he said huskily, "that you would come to love me, Nina."

Startled, she found herself meeting his steady, penetrating gaze. She swallowed against a constriction in her throat, and whispered, "That would suit you very nicely, I suppose, to know that you had me well and truly hooked?"

"Yes, it would. I want you hooked on me, Nina, just as I'm hooked on you."

"You're back to talking about sex again . . ."

"I'm talking about *love,*" he interrupted. "I love you, Nina . . . not just desire you, but love you in every other possible way. I respect you, I admire you, I know that I could find peace and contentment with you—lifelong happiness. My heart burns with the need for you, the need to be able to do things for you . . . to please you. All that surely adds up to love?"

Nina felt her body engulfed by waves of hot and cold, felt her mind seesawing between incredulous joy and deepest suspicion. Her voice came out as a strangled murmur. "But . . . you never said anything before . . ."

"Because I didn't *know* before," Dexter told her earnestly. "I've been a blind fool, Nina, knowing that I wanted you quite desperately, yet rejecting the plain and obvious fact that I felt quite differently about you than any other woman I've dated since Judith died. Even when I first asked you to marry me, I still wasn't facing up to the truth. But I do love you, my darling, you must believe that. I beseech you, let me share with you everything that I have."

"I don't want your riches, Dexter," she said on a thin thread of voice. "Just you."

"You mean . . .?"

Nina nodded, lowering her gaze. "I love you, too."

She heard him gasp in joyful surprise, and he reached out to take her in his arms. But something held her back from responding, tiny needles of fear that pricked at her newfound happiness.

"I . . . I don't think that I can marry you, Dexter," she said sorrowfully.

"But why ever not, darling, if you love me?"

"Because I just don't think that I could bear it if you were unfaithful to me, the way you were to Judith."

There was a long pause, then Dexter said in a low, strained voice, "I was never unfaithful to Judith, except—God forgive me—in my mind."

Nina's heart clenched. It was too cruel that he should lie to her now.

"You seem to forget that you've already admitted it's true, Dexter. When I accused you . . ."

"Did you expect me to rush in and deny it?" he said, with a note of reproach. "How do you imagine I felt having such a charge flung at my head, based on nothing more than some vicious rumor you'd over-heard?"

"It wasn't a rumor," she demurred. "Phyllida spelled it out to me, chapter and verse. Judith's own sister."

"Phyllida told you?" Dexter's face went tight and she saw him clench his two fists in fury. Then his eyes softened, and he said beseechingly, "She was lying, Nina, you've got to believe that. I was never, ever, physically unfaithful to my wife . . . how could I have been, when I loved her? I swear that's the truth."

Nine felt a wonderful sense of thankfulness surge through her. Then Dexter went on, "Let me explain how it was between Judith and me."

"You don't have to," she said quickly.

"I need to." He gave her a faint, anxious smile. "I need to, darling, for my own peace of mind."

There was something in his voice that made her want to take his head in her hands and soothe away his obvious pain. But it would be the wrong move. Dexter's need was to talk, to unburden himself in words.

"Tell me," she said softly.

"We were very young when we married . . . too young, perhaps, without sufficient maturity to cope with the inevitable problems. But we did love each other—only fate didn't give us very long together before Judith's health began to fail. I think that bearing Mandy took a lot out of her, but she longed for a child so much that it would have been cruel to deny her. After Mandy was born, though, we had no intimate life, no physical relationship. I still loved Judith and I wanted above everything to make her happy and continue to be a devoted, faithful husband. And yet, despite that, I sometimes felt shamefully tempted to go astray. There were occasions, when the raw physical need to seek release became almost unbearable, that I found myself actually resenting poor Judith . . . almost hating her, as if she were deliberately cheating me out of what was my natural right. Then I'd be tortured with remorse and feel a bitter contempt for myself."

Nina looked at him with compassion. "You *still* blame yourself, don't you?" she said gently. "But you shouldn't, Dexter. You can't be condemned for having a normal man's instincts and desires. You fought back against temptation, that's what counts . . . you fought back and won."

There was an expression of gratitude in his tawny eyes. "After Judith died, I went wild," he continued. "I plunged into a whole string of affairs, none of them lasting more than a brief time. I was always careful to remain emotionally uninvolved and I never allowed any of the women I dated to touch my heart—until I met you, Nina. Since that day, the day I was entranced by a vision of loveliness on the daffodil slope here at Haslemere Hall, there's been no one else, darling. I swear it. At first I didn't appreciate that it was you preventing me from behaving in my usual carefree way with women, then I began to realize how totally obsessed I was with you; I could think of nothing else. So then I got busy convincing myself that it was a purely sexual thing—just like all the others had been, only much more intense. Don't you see, I had to believe that, because in a strange sort of way I was still proving to myself that I was being faithful to Judith in my own peculiar fashion . . . letting no other woman come to mean anything serious to me."

"When . . . when did you first know that you loved me?" Nina asked tremulously.

"You should rather ask the question—when did I allow the knowledge to break through my defenses? It was like battering at a fortress, hammering down the steel and concrete doors that I'd erected to close my mind to the truth. The reason I pursued you the way I did was because I loved you. The reason I asked you to marry me was because I loved you."

"If only you could have told me that," she breathed.

"If only I could have told myself, Nina."

They fell silent, and the hush of a peaceful autumn afternoon was all around them, with mellow golden sunlight flooding through the tall windows. Then Nina said falteringly, "You won't feel guilty anymore . . . about Judith?"

Dexter shook his head slowly. "I've come to realize that I honor her memory more by falling in love with someone as beautiful and intelligent and genuine as you, than I ever did by indulging in a string of shallow, totally meaningless relationships. Don't worry, my darling, Judith will no longer be a shadow across my life. She will be a memory of past happiness, and she'll live on in the daughter she bore me. But you will be my present and future. You will be my happiness for all the time that's ahead."

For a long, breathless moment they remained looking at one another, then they came together in a quick uprush of joy. Cradled in Dexter's arms, her cheek pressed close against his chest, Nina could feel the rapidly pounding beat of his heart. She heard him draw a long, deep breath that was ragged with relief. His kiss contained more tenderness than passion, as if reassuring her that she was infinitely precious to him.

"Darling Nina," he said softly, drawing back to look at her again. "So will you marry me after all? Very, very soon."

She bit down on her soft lower lip, but couldn't hold back the question, "What about Phyllida?"

"She'll have to find herself a new home," he said matter-of-factly. "I daresay that she'll decide to live in Paris. She doesn't deserve much consideration from me after the monstrous way she lied to you, though naturally I shall see that she's all right financially."

"But how will you tell her about us?" Nina persisted unhappily. "It's going to be very difficult, isn't it?"

"I don't see any real problem. I hardly imagine that Phyllida will expect to go on living here after we've married—or even wish to. The arrangement suited us both reasonably well at the start, but it was never intended as a permanent solution. At the time Judith died, Phyllida had just split up from her husband and was getting a divorce. She was hard-pressed for cash and needed somewhere to live; and I needed someone to take care of Mandy. But it never really worked out very satisfactorily. Phyllida has little patience with children, she doesn't really care for them, and Mandy could sense that. Now, however, Phyllida can feel free to devote herself to the career she's always talking about. As I said, I'll make sure she is financially independent—for Judith's sake. I'm rather afraid that Phyllida isn't as talented at painting as she'd have everyone believe."

"She had hopes of marrying you herself," Nina pointed out in a low, shaky voice. "She told me that you and she had a sort of arrangement."

Dexter's eyes flared and his mouth went tight. "It seems," he said, "that Phyllida has been very busy trying to spoil things between you and me. But it's no more the truth than what she told you about my being unfaithful to Judith. We had no such arrangement, I swear it, darling. My attitude toward her has always been strictly that of a brother-in-law, and I've never given her the slightest reason to think that my view would ever change."

Nina felt a great wave of relief and thankfulness flood through her. Phyllida had caused her so much pain and heartache in the past, but there was nothing Dexter's sister-in-law could do to hurt her anymore. She wound her arms around his neck and clung to him joyously, trembling with the need to express how deeply she loved him.

"Am I expecting too much of you, darling?" he asked smilingly, one hand sliding around to caress her nape. "I shall be a very demanding husband, let me tell you. And on top of that you will have to contend with the devotion of my young daughter, too."

"I can't imagine anything more wonderful," she said huskily.

"But that's only part of it, Nina. Setting up and running the ballet school is going to give you a very busy life."

She glanced at him in surprise. "Would you still want me to take that on, Dexter?"

"Of course I would, because you're the ideal person for the job. There's no question about it. And it would be a terrible waste of your talent if you didn't continue to do something in the world of ballet. You will, darling, won't you?"

Nina nodded emphatically. "It will be exciting. A real challenge that I shall enjoy."

"Good. We must get down to making plans. But not now. There's something far more urgent on my mind. Would you think it out of order if I suggest that we anticipate the wedding? There *are* limits to my endurance."

Nina laughed throatily. "You seem to be forgetting that we've already anticipated the wedding by several weeks."

"I'm forgetting nothing," he murmured softly, and kissed the tip of her nose. "Those nights at the Villa Mimosa are blazed forever on my memory. Come."

Arms around each other, they turned and walked out to the entrance hall, then began to mount the grand staircase, with its gilt balusters. But Nina had no eyes for the elegantly gracious surroundings, aware only of the man beside her, the warmth of his strong, lean body pressed against hers. Dexter led her to his bedroom, a splendid apartment with tall windows that overlooked the rolling acres of parkland, with a curve of the River Thames glinting in the distance.

As the door closed behind them he took her in his arms and kissed her long and passionately, his lips devouring hers with a flaring hunger that left Nina breathless and light-headed, the blood surging through her veins.

"I love you," he whispered, his voice so deep in his throat that it was almost lost.

"And I love you, Dexter," she breathed. "I love you so much."

Smiling, he pulled the pins from her hair so that it fell in a dark curtain around her shoulders. Then very slowly, with a reverence in every movement, he began to undress her. As he exposed her satin-smooth flesh, inch by inch, his fingertips caressed her sensuously, and the warm touch of his lips further quickened her excitement to a sweet, almost unbearable tension. The last flimsy garment shivered to the carpet and Nina stood naked, smiling provocatively before his hungry gaze. She was eager to see him naked, too, and boldly began unbuttoning his shirt. Taking the hint, Dexter stripped off his clothes and cast them aside. When he too stood totally nude, she thrilled at the sight of his finely molded body, the muscled smoothness of his limbs.

"You're magnificent," she whispered in awe.

"And you, my darling, are exquisitely beautiful." Swiftly he gathered her into his arms and bore her weightless to the bed, laying her down on the cream-colored quilt. "My wonderful, wonderful Nina. What incredible delight you've given me . . . and what agony! It will bring me endless pleasure to feast my eyes on your lovely body. And when I see you in a roomful of people, I shall gloat disgracefully to think that you're mine, all mine. I shall count off the minutes before we're alone again, and I can make love to you till we're both weak from the joy of it."

"Perhaps you'll soon grow tired of me," she teased.

"Never! As long as we live, my desire for you will only grow stronger. I know this in my very soul. I want no other woman, and never will again. Having you makes my life complete, Nina . . . complete and more brimming with joy than I ever believed possible."

His lean length stretched beside her on the bed, he traced loving patterns on her skin with a delicate touch of his fingertips, weaving a web of delirious pleasure around her slender, quivering body. With the pointed tip of his tongue he circled her lips, coaxing her mouth to open like a flower before the morning sun, to let him thrust in and plunder the inner nectar. Nina moaned with joy and arched herself against him, made shameless by the urgent desire Dexter had aroused in her. He rained kisses upon her everywhere, his mouth savoring the soft roundness of her breasts, capturing the tingling nipples between his lips until she could almost have cried out with the tormenting ecstasy. She raked taut fingers down his back, clenching into the hard muscle to strain him closer, crying out his name.

"I want you so desperately, my darling," he said thickly.

"Yes . . . oh yes," she sobbed.

Nina felt a momentary wonderment and gratitude that he could so exactly pace his demanding male passion to match her own crescendoing need for fulfillment. And then she lost all awareness of everything but their two bodies locked together in a feverish spiral of desire that ascended to the sunlit heavens and finally exploded into a million golden fragments.

Some time later Dexter stirred and looked deep into

her eyes with love, and kissed her very tenderly. A handful of autumn leaves, caught up by a swirl of breeze, were tossed against the windowpanes.

"Summer is over," he murmured, a smile of happiness in his voice. "But it will always be summertime for us, won't it, darling?"

"Yes," she whispered back against his lips. "A lifetime of glorious summers."

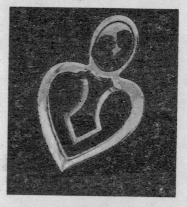

MORE ROMANCE FOR
A SPECIAL WAY TO RELAX

$1.95 each

MORE ROMANCE FOR
A SPECIAL WAY TO RELAX

55 ☐ SUN LOVER Stanford

56 ☐ SILVER FIRE Wallace

57 ☐ PRIDE'S RECKONING Thornton

58 ☐ KNIGHTLY LOVE Douglass

59 ☐ THE HEART'S VICTORY Roberts

60 ☐ ONCE AND FOREVER Thorne

61 ☐ TENDER DECEPTION Beckman

62 ☐ DEEP WATERS Bright

63 ☐ LOVE WITH A PERFECT STRANGER Wallace

64 ☐ MIST OF BLOSSOMS Converse

65 ☐ HANDFUL OF SKY Cates

66 ☐ A SPORTING AFFAIR Mikels

67 ☐ AFTER THE RAIN Shaw

68 ☐ CASTLES IN THE AIR Sinclair

69 ☐ SORREL SUNSET Dalton

70 ☐ TRACES OF DREAMS Clare

71 ☐ MOONSTRUCK Skillern

72 ☐ NIGHT MUSIC Belmont

73 ☐ SEASON OF SEDUCTION Taylor

74 ☐ UNSPOKEN PAST Wisdom

75 ☐ SUMMER RHAPSODY John

76 ☐ TOMORROW'S MEMORY Ripy

77 ☐ PRELUDE TO PASSION Bergen

78 ☐ FORTUNE'S PLAY Gladstone

LOOK FOR *ENCHANTED SURRENDER* BY PATTI BECKMAN AVAILABLE IN APRIL AND *LOVE'S GENTLE CHAINS* BY SONDRA STANFORD IN MAY.

SILHOUETTE SPECIAL EDITION, Department SE/2
1230 Avenue of the Americas
New York, NY 10020

Please send me the books I have checked above. I am enclosing $_____
(please add 50¢ to cover postage and handling. NYS and NYC residents
please add appropriate sales tax). Send check or money order—no cash or
C.O.D.'s please. Allow six weeks for delivery.

NAME _____

ADDRESS _____

CITY _____ STATE/ZIP _____

Silhouette Special Edition

Coming Next Month

An Act Of Love by Brooke Hastings

The act of mistaken anger that led Luke Griffin to "kidnap" Randy Dunne soon gave way to a passion from which there was no turning back.

Fast Courting by Billie Douglass

Journalist Nia Phillips' assignment: interview basketball coach Daniel Strahan—one of five most eligible bachelors on the East Coast. Soon Daniel was involved with the most important game he'd ever play.

Looking Glass Love by Carolyn Thornton

Winning Isaac Fielding's heart seemed hopeless, especially when his past was as unhappy as Chrissa's own. But Chrissa fought to convince him that their love was special, and would endure.

Captive Of Fate by Lindsay McKenna

Alanna went to Costa Rica to expose Matt Breckenridge but in the end she exposed only her own heart by falling in love with the arrogant colonel.

Brand Of Diamonds by Ann Major

Lannie no longer wanted Brandon for what he was worth . . . but for what he was. She wanted the man beneath the glitter and this time, she wanted him forever.

The Splendored Sky by Jeanne Stephens

Justin Kane never forgave Amber Rowland for leaving him to pursue a modeling career. Now she returned to Montana to run the family ranch and to convince Justin she was back for good.

Silhouette ❀ *Romance*

15-Day Free Trial Offer
6 Silhouette Romances

6 Silhouette Romances, free for 15 days! We'll send you 6 new Silhouette Romances to keep for 15 days, absolutely free! If you decide not to keep them, send them back to us. You pay nothing.

Free Home Delivery. But if you enjoy them as much as we think you will, keep them by paying the invoice enclosed with your free trial shipment. We'll pay all shipping and handling charges. You get the convenience of Home Delivery and we pay the postage and handling charge each month.

Don't miss a copy. The Silhouette Book Club is the way to make sure you'll be able to receive every new romance we publish before they're sold out. There is no minimum number of books to buy and you can cancel at any time.

READERS' COMMENTS ON SILHOUETTE SPECIAL EDITIONS:

"I just finished reading the first six Silhouette Special Edition Books and I had to take the opportunity to write you and tell you how much I enjoyed them. I enjoyed all the authors in this series. Best wishes on your Silhouette Special Editions line and many thanks."

—B.H.*, Jackson, OH

"The Special Editions are really special and I enjoyed them very much! I am looking forward to next month's books."

—R.M.W.*, Melbourne, FL

"I've just finished reading four of your first six Special Editions and I enjoyed them very much. I like the more sensual detail and longer stories. I will look forward each month to your new Special Editions."

—L.S.*, Visalia, CA

"Silhouette Special Editions are — 1.) Superb! 2.) Great! 3.) Delicious! 4.) Fantastic! . . . Did I leave anything out? These are books that an adult woman can read . . . I love them!"

—H.C.*, Monterey Park, CA

*names available on request